BRIAN

THE CASE OF EL

BRIAN FLYNN was born in 1885 in Leyton, Essex.
He won a scholarship to the City Of London School,
and from there went into the civil service. In World
War I he served as Special Constable on the Home
Front, also teaching "Accountancy, Languages, Maths
and Elocution to men, women, boys and girls" in the
evenings, and acting in his spare time.

It was a seaside family holiday that inspired Brian
Flynn to turn his hand to writing in the mid-twenties.
Finding most mystery novels of the time "mediocre in
the extreme", he decided to compose his own. Edith,
the author's wife, encouraged its completion, and
after a protracted period finding a publisher, it was
eventually released in 1927 by John Hamilton in the
UK and Macrae Smith in the U.S. as *The Billiard-
Room Mystery*.

The author died in 1958. In all, he wrote and published
57 mysteries, the vast majority featuring the super-
sleuth Antony Bathurst.

BRIAN FLYNN

THE CASE OF ELYMAS THE SORCERER

With an introduction by
Steve Barge

DEAN STREET PRESS

INTRODUCTION

"I let my books write themselves. That is to say, having once constructed my own plot, I sit down to write and permit the puppets to do their own dancing."

DURING the war, Brian Flynn was trying some experiments with his crime writing. His earlier books are all traditional mystery novels, all with a strong whodunit element to them, but starting with *Black Edged* in 1939, Brian seemed to want to branch out in his writing style. *Black Edged* (1939) tells the tale of the pursuit of a known killer from both sides of the chase. While there is a twist in the tale, this is far from a traditional mystery, and Brian returned to the inverted format once again with *Such Bright Disguises* (1941). There was also an increasing darkness in some of his villains – the plot of *They Never Came Back* (1940), the story of disappearing boxers, has a sadistic antagonist and *The Grim Maiden* (1942) was a straight thriller with a similarly twisted adversary. However, following this, perhaps due in part to a family tragedy during the Second World War, there was a notable change in Brian's writing style. The style of the books from *The Sharp Quillet* (1947) onwards switched back to a far more traditional whodunnit format, while he also adopted a pseudonym in attempt to try something new.

The three Charles Wogan books – *The Hangman's Hands* (1947), *The Horror At Warden Hall* (1948) and *Cyanide For The Chorister* (1950) – are an interesting diversion for Brian, as while they feature a new sleuth, they aren't particularly different structurally to the Anthony Bathurst books. You could make a case that they were an attempt to go back to a sleuth who mirrored Sherlock Holmes, as Bathurst at this point seems to have moved away from the Great Detective, notably through the lack of a Watson character. The early Bathurst books mostly had the sleuth with a sidekick, a different character in most books, often narrating the books, but as the series progresses, we see Bathurst operating more and more by himself, with his thoughts being the focus of the text. The Charles Wogans, on the other hand, are all narrated by Piers Deverson, relating his adventures with Sebastian Stole who was, as per the cover of *The*

Hangman's Hands (1947), *"A Detective Who Might Have Been A King"* – he was the Crown Prince of Calorania who had to flee the palace during an uprising.

While the short Wogan series is distinct from the Bathurst mysteries, they have a lot in common. Both were published by John Long for the library market, both have a sleuth who takes on his first case because it seems like something interesting to do and both have a potentially odd speaking habit. While Bathurst is willing to pepper his speech with classical idioms and obscure quotations, Stole, being the ex-Prince of the European country of Calorania, has a habit of mangling the English language. To give an example, when a character refers to his forbears, Stole replies that *"I have heard of them, and also of Goldilocks."* I leave it to the reader to decide whether this is funny or painful, but be warned, should you decide to try and track these books down, this is only one example and some of them are even worse.

Stole has some differences from Bathurst, notably that he seems to have unlimited wealth despite fleeing Calorania in the middle of the night – he inveigles himself into his first investigation by buying the house where the murder was committed! By the third book, however, it seems as if Brian realised that there were only surface differences between Stole and Bathurst and returned to writing books exclusively about his original sleuth. This didn't however stop a literary agent, when interviewed by Bathurst in *Men For Pieces* (1949), praising the new author Charles Wogan . . .

At this stage in his investigative career, Bathurst is clearly significantly older than when he first appeared in *The Billiard Room Mystery* (1927). There, he was a Bright Young Thing, displaying his sporting prowess and diving headfirst into a murder investigation simply because he thought it would be entertaining. At the start of *The Case of Elymas the Sorcerer* (1945), we see him recovering from "muscular rheumatism", taking the sea-air at the village of St Mead (not St Mary Mead), before the local constabulary drag him into the investigation of a local murder.

The book itself is very typical of Brian's work. First, the initial mystery has a strange element about it, namely that someone has stripped the body, left it in a field and, for some reason, shaved the body's moustache off. Soon a second body is found, along with a mentally-challenged young man whispering about "gold". In common with a number of Brian's books, such as *The Mystery of The Peacock's Eye* (1928) and *The Running Nun* (1952), the reason for the title only becomes apparent very late in the day – this is not a story about magicians and wizards. One other title, which I won't name for obvious reasons, is actually a clue to what is going on in that book.

Following this, we come to *Conspiracy at Angel* (1947), a book that may well have been responsible for delaying the rediscovery of Brian's work. When Jacques Barzun and Wendell Hertig Taylor wrote *A Catalogue Of Crime* (1971), a reference book intended to cover as many crime writers as possible, they included Brian Flynn – they omitted E. & M.A. Radford, Ianthe Jerrold and Molly Thynne to name but a few great "lost" crime writers – but their opinion of Brian's work was based entirely on this one atypical novel. That opinion was *"Straight tripe and savorless. It is doubtful, on the evidence, if any of the thirty-two others by this author would be different."* This proves, at least, that Barzun and Taylor didn't look beyond the "Also By The Author" page when researching Flynn, and, more seriously, were guilty of making sweeping judgments based on little evidence. To be fair to them, they did have a lot of books to read . . .

It is likely that, post-war, Brian was looking for source material for a book and dug out a play script that he wrote for the Trevalyan Dramatic Club. *Blue Murder* was staged in East Ham Town Hall on 23rd February 1937, with Brian, his daughter and his future son-in-law all taking part. It was perhaps an odd choice, as while it is a crime story, it was also a farce. A lot of the plot of the criminal conspiracy is lifted directly into the novel, but whereas in the play, things go wrong due to the incompetence of a "silly young ass" who gets involved, it is the intervention of Anthony Bathurst in this case that puts paid to the criminal scheme. A fair amount of the farce structure is maintained, in particular in the opening section, and as such, this is a fairly unusual outing for Bathurst. There's also a fascinating snapshot of history when the criminal scheme is revealed. I won't go into details for obvious reasons, but I doubt many readers' knowledge of some specific 1940's technology will be enough to guess what the villains are up to.

Following *Conspiracy at Angel* – and possibly because of it – Brian's work comes full circle with the next few books, returning to the more traditional whodunit of the early Bathurst outings. *The Sharp Quillet* (1947) brings in a classic mystery staple, namely curare, as someone is murdered by a poisoned dart. This is no blow-pipe murder, but an actual dartboard dart – and the victim was taking part in a horse race at the time. The reader may think that the horse race, an annual event for members of the Inns of Court to take place in, is an invention of Brian's, but it did exist. Indeed, it still does, run by The Pegasus Club. This is the only one of Brian's novels to mention the Second World War overtly, with the prologue of the book, set ten years previously, involving an air-raid.

Exit Sir John (1947) – not to be confused with Clemence Dane and Helen Simpson's *Enter Sir John* (1928) – concerns the death of Sir John Wynward at Christmas. All signs point to natural causes, but it is far from the perfect murder (if indeed it is murder) due to the deaths of his chauffeur and his solicitor. For reasons that I cannot fathom, *The Sharp Quillet* and *Exit Sir John* of all of Brian's work, are the most obtainable in their original form. I have seen a number of copies for sale, complete with dustjacket, whereas for most of his other books, there have been, on average, less than one copy for sale over the past five years. I have no explanation for this, but they are both good examples of Brian's work, as is the following title *The Swinging Death* (1949).

A much more elusive title, *The Swinging Death* has a very typical Brian Flynn set-up, along with the third naked body in five books. Rather than being left in a field like the two in *The Case of Elymas the Sorcerer*, this one is hanging from a church porch. Why Dr Julian Field got off his train at the wrong stop, and how he went from there to being murdered in the church, falls to Bathurst to explain, along with why half of Field's clothes are in the church font – and the other half are in the font of a different church?

Brian's books are always full of his love for sport, but *The Swinging Death* shows where Brian's specific interests lie. While rugby has always been Bathurst's winter sport, there is a delightful scene in this book where Chief Inspector MacMorran vehemently champions football (or soccer if you really must) as being the superior sport. One can almost hear Brian's own voice finally being able to talk about a sport that Anthony Bathurst would not give much consideration to.

Brian was pleased with *The Swinging Death*, writing in *Crime Book Magazine* in 1949 that "I hope that I am not being unduly optimistic if I place *The Swinging Death* certainly among the best of my humbler contributions to mystery fiction. I hope that those who come to read it will find themselves in agreement with me in this assessment." It is certainly a sign that over halfway through his writing career, Brian was still going strong and I too hope that you agree with him on this.

Steve Barge

CHAPTER I

I

THE seaside village of St. Mead prides itself on its exclusive character. And also on the difference that exists between it and its neighbour on the coast, Kersbrook-on-Sea. The population of St. Mead is under two thousand, that of Kersbrook tops thirty thousand. St. Mead is situated at the mouth of the charming little stream, the River Ede, which trickles into the sea shyly and almost humbly, over a pebbly beach. Great hills rise on each side of St. Mead and they end in deep red sandstone cliffs which, on their part, attain an eminence of five hundred feet.

St. Mead was one of the earliest seaside health resorts to spring up in Fernshire, and the characteristic white-faced villas of the early nineteenth century are still amongst the outstanding features of the place. The old church of Ambrosius, with its lofty tower, is its chief landmark. Ambrosius was a British king of the sixth century who had established a monastery near St. Mead and about five miles from Kersbrook. St. Mead boasts three hôtels. Literally, one hôtel and two "pubs". The hôtel is the "Royal Lion" and the two "pubs" are distinguished by the somewhat unusual signs of the "Camel's Eye" and the "Green Goose".

For many years little happened in St. Mead to excite it. Until a certain morning in early October. On that particular morning something happened in St. Mead which brought to it notoriety and a frequent position in the headlines of the more sensational daily papers. Two children, a boy and a girl, by name Lily Wells and Stephen Brannock, who were seeking mushrooms for their parents' breakfast, found the body of a man in Ebford's field. The body was naked. The two children ran home to their respective cottages, about a quarter of a mile away, badly frightened and screaming their news. The father of Lily Wells went back with them to investigate. From Ebford's field, he went straight to the police station. He was a man of quick decision and not given to the wasting of time.

II

In less than an hour later, the nude body of the dead man lay in the outhouse which did duty at St. Mead as the official mortuary. The news of its finding blazed through the village and St. Mead seethed with the sensation of excitement. Stephen Brannock and Lily Wells tasted the heady delights of fame—even though that fame tended to be ephemeral. Police-Constable Glover, to whom the father of Lily Wells had gone with his story, had also acted promptly and he now awaited, with a certain undercurrent of impatience, the arrival of the Divisional-Surgeon from Kersbrook, Dr. Pleydell.

"Bit of a teaser," Glover kept saying to himself. "Bit of a teaser! Not a stitch on him, poor fellow. Very upsetting. What about clues? Never heard of such a thing in the whole of my official career."

More than once he walked to the door of the improvised mortuary to see that no unholy body-snatching agency had deprived him of his prize. For, it must be admitted, this was exactly how Glover had come to regard it. In addition to walking to the door of the mortuary, Glover repeatedly consulted the clock and attempted to calculate how long it would take Dr. Pleydell to arrive there from Kersbrook. His phrase, "bit of a teaser", gave place to "taken his time and no mistake". It will be seen that Glover's excitement was now joined by the quality of criticism. Lily Wells and Stephen Brannock had discovered the body at ten minutes to seven. Dr. Pleydell walked into the station at St. Mead at precisely half-past nine.

III

The following is a description of the man who was dead. He was a small man. His height would have been no more than five feet five inches. He was undersized from whichever angle you looked at him. The colour of his hair was indefinite. Most people would have said vaguely, "brown". His eyes were light blue and his face was creased and puckered like a monkey's. His complexion bordered on the livid. His frame was undeveloped, his legs were thin and scrawny, and on his left foot he was the possessor of a hammer-toe. His hands were rough, hard and stained and indicated generally that he was a man who had been accustomed to manual work.

When Dr. Pleydell entered the mortuary he looked surprised when he saw the body. Suddenly he bent down and sniffed round the mouth and lips. Glover regarded him approvingly. Pleydell looked up and straightened himself.

"Sour," he commented. "Man's been poisoned. An alkaloid poison of some kind, I should say. Been dead some hours. Who is he, Constable? Any idea?"

Glover shook his head and related the full circumstances of the finding of the body.

"Couple of kids found him, eh? Just as he is? Peculiar, that! Ah well, I must run over him properly at a P.M. When I get back, I'll send the ambulance over from Kersbrook. Tell your Sergeant that when he comes in, will you, Constable?"

Glover nodded his understanding of the instruction. As Dr. Pleydell drove off in his car to return to Kersbrook, Sergeant Clancy entered the police-station and naturally demanded of Glover the fullest details as to the morning's incident. Constable Glover supplied them with appropriate gusto and perhaps more than once was guilty, here and there, of a tendency towards certain exaggerations. Clancy, according to his habit when puzzled, scratched the tip of his left ear.

"A naked stiff," he ejaculated when he entered the mortuary; "that's a new one on me. And found in a field by a couple of kids out mushroom-gathering. Some mushroom!"

Glover was delighted at the impression his story had made upon the imagination of his superior officer. Such opportunities did not often come his way. On the contrary, they were few and far between.

"You know what it means, Sergeant," he said, "don't you?"

"What?" demanded Clancy.

"Why—that Inspector Kershaw'll be over from Kersbrook. I wonder he didn't come along with the Divisional-Surgeon. To tell you the truth I expected him."

Clancy pursed his lips into a whistle. A moment later he burst into song. It was the only song he knew and he employed it to mask his feelings on every proper and improper occasion. "I dream of the day I met you-ou, I dream of the night divine . . ."

His colleagues, both superior and subordinate, had come to hate venomously the very sound of it. But Clancy was oblivious of this and, blissfully ignorant, he went his way carolling. Glover returned to the precincts of the police-station. He was sorely afraid that in a short time from now the case of the nude body would be taken out of his hands. This fear turned out to be authentic.

IV

As it happened, and of course Police-Constable Glover was entirely unaware of the fact, no less a person than Anthony Lotherington Bathurst was staying a mile or so from Kersbrook and very near to St. Mead. Anthony had endured a rather unpleasant bout of muscular rheumatism and was convalescing at the charming house of Neville Kemble, Esq., who was by way of being the brother of Sir Austin Kemble, Commissioner of Police, New Scotland Yard. Neville was seven years or so younger than his brother and the close friend, also, of Colonel Buxton, K.C.B., D.S.O., retired, and now Chief Constable of the County of Fernshire. .

The news of the body that had been found by the Brannock boy and the Wells girl reached Anthony via Sir Austin Kemble via Colonel Buxton via Neville Kemble via Inspector Kershaw of Kersbrook. The Chief Constable drove over to "Palings", Neville Kemble's house, full of his story, and the time was not long before Sir Austin, to whom appeal had been made, roped in Anthony.

"Don't bother yourself unduly, boy," said the Commissioner when he telephoned, "especially if you aren't feeling up to the mark exactly, but 'Pusher' Buxton says he'd like you to have a nose round on it and I've given him the O.K. If you want MacMorran to work with I'll have him sent down there to you."

"Well, sir," Anthony had replied, "I had hoped to be quiet for a week or so, but it seems that the hope isn't to be fulfilled. I won't promise anything, and in any case the affair may be nothing and fizzle out completely. Anyhow, I'll have a look round and let you know."

Anthony had replaced the receiver and within a few moments he found himself shaking hands with Colonel Buxton, the Chief Constable. This gentleman was by no means typical of the usual ex-Army officer. He was tall, thin and hatchet-faced. His legs were spindly. But his shoulders were good and well-formed. So much so that, in general, he created a strange impression. A man with the shoulders of a man but with the waist of an eel and the legs of a spider.

"I'm delighted to meet you, Bathurst," he said in a somewhat high-pitched voice, "and I've already informed Sir Austin Kemble I'd like you to take a hand in this extraordinary case that seems to have fallen to our lot. Maybe Fate took a hand in the game and sent you down here. I do hope that you'll accept what I insist is a most cordial invitation."

"Well, sir," replied Anthony, "that's exceedingly nice of you. I had intended to take a rest, but Fate, as you say, appears to have decided otherwise. My footsteps seem to be dogged by crime. All right, sir, you can count on me. I'll try not to let you down."

Colonel Buxton rubbed his hands. "Good! That's excellent! I feel that we've got off to a flying start, at any rate. Now where would you like to start? I take it you've heard the bare outlines of the case?"

"Yes, sir," returned Anthony. "I had them from my host, Mr. Neville Kemble. I should like to see the body of the dead man and also make a visit to the field where I understand the body was found."

Colonel Buxton nodded. "That's just what I expected you to say. I've given instructions to Inspector Kershaw to put a couple of uniformed men on duty at the gate of this field. It belongs to a small farmer and takes its name from him. Locally it's known as 'Ebford's Field'. The body's in the mortuary at Kersbrook. Been removed from St. Mead. The Divisional-Surgeon, Dr. Pleydell, is at work on it now."

"Well, sir," said Anthony smilingly, "I think a visit to the Kersbrook mortuary is definitely indicated. From there, we can go on to Ebford's field. Does the itinerary as suggested suit you, sir?"

"Down to the ground. Come along with me now and we'll keep the first appointment inside a quarter of an hour."

V

Inspector Kershaw met them at Kersbrook and, after being introduced to Anthony, conducted them to the mortuary. Pleydell, as the Chief Constable had indicated, was already at work on his autopsy. He looked up as the three men entered.

"Good afternoon, Pleydell," announced the Colonel; "we seem to have arrived at a most opportune moment."

"Good afternoon, sir," returned the Divisional-Surgeon. He looked enquiringly in Anthony's direction.

"You know Inspector Kershaw," went on the Chief Constable. "This other gentleman is Anthony Bathurst." Buxton made the necessary introduction. "Dr. Pleydell, our Divisional-Surgeon—Anthony Bathurst."

The two men shook hands. "I see you're in the throes," remarked Anthony. "Anything to tell us yet?"

"Well," said Pleydell a trifle diffidently, "this chap was poisoned all right. As far as I can tell it's a vegetable poison like monkshood or deadly nightshade. If you prefer it, either Aconite napellus or Atropa belladonna. The chap himself wasn't in good condition. Undernourished, stunted altogether. Age round about the fifties, I should say, from what I've seen of him."

Inspector Kershaw came in with a question. "How long had he been dead when the body was found?"

Dr. Pleydell cocked his head to one side in consideration of the question. "How long dead?" he repeated. "Well, that's always a rather awkward question to answer with any degree of accuracy. But in this case, I'd put it at about twelve hours. Perhaps, say, a little longer."

Kershaw noted the opinion in a book which he had produced for the occasion.

Anthony said, "May we see the body, Dr. Pleydell?"

"Certainly. Come over here."

Within a few seconds Anthony Bathurst found himself looking down at the face of the dead man. The wizened, puckered, simian-like appearance was now even more accentuated than it had been previously.

"And this, I understand, is how he was found?"

"That's so," answered Kershaw.

Anthony bent down and then suddenly straightened himself again. "Has the body been photographed yet, Inspector?"

Kershaw nodded. "Yes. Not long after it was brought over here. Why?"

"I'll tell you why I asked. Can you let me have a small hand-towel, Dr. Pleydell?"

Pleydell, after a moment's rummaging, handed over the article in question.

"Thank you, Doctor."

Anthony bent down. His three companions watched him with interest. They saw him screw up the towel to a point and gently insert it in the dead man's right nostril. After a second or so, he raised himself from his stooping posture and showed them the towel-point, "Dried soap, gentlemen, in the right nostril of the dead man."

"Indicating," said Kershaw, "that he occasionally washed himself." His tone held the implication of dry sarcasm.

"I take leave to differ," replied Anthony; "indicating rather, I think, that he had recently been shaved as to the upper lip."

The others were silent as the point Anthony had made sank into their minds. Colonel Buxton broke it.

"Shaved, you mean, I take it, Bathurst, by the murderer?"

"That is my meaning, sir, entirely."

"To delay possible identification?"

Anthony nodded in confirmation of the Chief Constable's suggestion. "I wouldn't contradict you, sir," he said. "It's astonishing the difference it makes to a face, losing a moustache suddenly that it's carried with it for years." He beckoned to the Divisional-Surgeon. "If you look carefully at the skin of the upper lip, you can tell that it's been shaved. And very recently at that."

Pleydell bent down to look.

"Agree, Doctor?" queried Anthony.

"Yes," came the answer, "I most certainly do."

"Good. I'm glad of that. It simplifies matters for me to know that you're in agreement." Anthony walked over to Colonel Buxton. "And now, sir, if it's all the same to you, I'd like to take a glance at Ebford's field."

"We'll go there straight away," returned Colonel Buxton.

VI

The journey in the car to the field at St. Mead took but a matter of ten minutes. The field was accessible from the main road. At the cross-barred gate stood a uniformed constable. He saluted Kershaw appropriately as the latter advanced towards him. Kershaw spoke a few words to him and the man stood to one side as the Chief Constable and Anthony walked into the field.

"'A corner of an English field,'" quoted Anthony, almost under his breath, "'not even a foreign one.'"

"There's a sack pegged down," announced Kershaw, "exactly where and how the body was found. At least, that's according to what the two kids who found it say."

"Good," said Anthony. "Take us over to it, will you, Inspector?" Kershaw led the way to where the body had lain. Anthony looked at the place, and then comprehensively round the field. He saw nothing whatever to excite either his interest or his curiosity. The surface of the field was flat. There were no ditches or hollows of any kind. The grass was coarse in texture, the earth entirely uncultivated and abounding in weed-growths. Anthony smiled whimsically at the Chief Constable and the Inspector.

"As full of clues," he remarked drily, "as an egg is of bananas." Kershaw grunted. Colonel Buxton looked round vaguely.

"The body," went on Anthony, "was presumably brought here and deposited in this field. We don't know where it came from, whose body it is, and as far as I can see, there's precious little here to tell us anything. The ground is bone dry. There isn't the vestige of a footprint. There isn't a finger-print. Unless and until we get the body identified—" Anthony broke off and shrugged his shoulders.

Colonel Buxton echoed his opinion. "Pretty hopeless—what?"

"Certainly not hopeless, sir. But, at the moment, scarcely encouraging. Where are the dead man's clothes, for example?"

"Burned," answered Kershaw decisively. "This job has been well carried out, if you ask me. Burned! I'd lay any money you like on it."

"I'm afraid you're right, Inspector," remarked Anthony. "And if that's the case, it's a hundred to one that the body was actually brought here in its nude state. The car would stand outside in the road there, by the entrance gate. In a few minutes the whole job could be done and the body transferred from the car to the field. What's more, seeing the size and stature of the dead man, one able-bodied person could have done the job with the utmost ease."

Kershaw nodded. "I'm not going to quarrel with you, Mr. Bathurst."

Anthony became contemplative. "I suppose we can accept it as highly probable that the body was brought here during the night or early hours immediately preceding the children's discovery? Yes—Inspector?"

"I suppose so," replied Kershaw guardedly.

Colonel Buxton corroborated emphatically. "Oh—undoubtedly! I think we can take that as a—er—*sine qua non*. It could never have lain there for anything like a whole day without somebody spotting it. Yes, yes, Bathurst, I'm positive that you can take that for granted. But why exactly, what's the point?"

Anthony was still thinking. "That would be, then, from Wednesday evening to Thursday morning. Is that right, Inspector?"

Kershaw nodded. "Yes. That would be it."

"What sort of weather did we have that Wednesday night? I think I know, but I'm asking for confirmation."

Kershaw made no reply, but the Chief Constable was able to answer immediately.

"There was a high wind. It was quite dry—but there was pretty well half a gale blowing. I know because I walked half a mile in it. Had it full in my teeth."

"That's right," added the Inspector. "I remember now."

"South-west, wasn't it?" demanded Anthony. "That's what I put it down at."

"Definitely," said Buxton with a quick movement of the head. "Definitely sou'-west."

"I'm looking at things in this way," continued Anthony. "I'm forced to look round, as it were, in all directions, in the bare chance of hitting on something. In this respect, the weather must always be considered as a possible ally. Now we've established that the prevailing weather on the night that we presume the body was brought here was wind. A car standing out there in the road by the gate would get a sou'-wester broadside on. And while this was going on, the car itself *might* have been left unattended." He looked curiously at the Chief Constable. "Do you see what I'm after?"

"I think so, Bathurst. You mean that something might have been blown out of the car."

"I was thinking that, sir. I'm afraid it's by way of being a forlorn hope. Still, you never know. What do you say, Inspector?"

Kershaw shook his head. "I'm afraid—like you. Don't think there's much chance of finding anything in here. Still—as you say—you never know."

Anthony went on again. "If my judgment's anything like sound, anything blown about would be most likely found in that corner. Taking the direction and the severity of the wind as a guide."

He waved his hand towards a corner of the field round which there ran a thick hedge. The three men walked over to where Anthony had indicated. In this corner, bounded by the hedge, there was nothing at all. There was no ditch or depression where fragments might have been blown by a frolic wind. The grass had a slight, even slope down to the hedge.

"Not so good," said Anthony as they surveyed the empty expanse. "I'm going to walk round, though, before I chuck up the sponge. No good doing things by halves."

"We may as well come with you," said Colonel Buxton.

Anthony led the way round the field, keeping closely to the edges. His two companions kept close on his heels. Anthony's eyes searched the field comprehensively. When the first circuit had been completed, he took a couple of paces from the edge of the field and started a second circuit. In this way, he considered, his eyes would eventually cover the entire expanse of the field. The task was almost completed without reward or result. When, however, they had partly completed what would have been the final circuit, Anthony caught sight of three tiny slips of paper. They were lying caught in the longer blades of a patch of extra-coarse grass. Kershaw noticed them almost simultaneously with Anthony. With inordinate curiosity Anthony stooped and picked them from their grass entanglement. They appeared to be torn fragments of a letter. Upon the fragments could be deciphered these words, or parts of words, (a) "Emma", (b) "Temple", and (c) "of Sil".

Anthony passed the fragments round. Suddenly, the Chief Constable darted off in another direction. Kershaw and Anthony watched him. They saw him bend down sharply and then come running back.

"Here's a fourth piece," he exclaimed; "it's frightfully tiny, but I spotted it from where we were standing."

Anthony smoothed it out and they read the word-part "Mai".

"Well, Kershaw," he said to the local Inspector, "what do you make of these pieces of paper?"

"Looks to me," said Kershaw very deliberately, "as though somebody's prepared a list of names. For some purpose or the other. But nothing whatever to do, I should say, with the murder. More likely for a Christmas party. Or a birthday party. Nothing to do with this job we're on."

"Names?" said Anthony. "Tell me why you think that."

"That's easy," replied Kershaw. "Emma's obvious. We haven't got to worry about that one. The others are, I suggest, Silas and Malcolm."

"What's the fourth, then?" demanded Anthony. "Shirley Temple?"

Kershaw looked annoyed. "No—I don't say it's that for a moment. I was merely chancing my arm, as it were."

"Well," returned Anthony, "you may be right. You never know in cases of this kind. Actually, I don't think I agree with you. Sometimes the solution is simple. Sometimes it turns out to be almost fantastic. But put these tiny scraps of paper into safe keeping, Inspector. They may have nothing to do with our case, as you quite properly suggest. On the other hand, they may have been dropped by the murderer, or come in some way from the dead man himself. Time alone will tell."

He looked at Colonel Buxton as he spoke. "Coming to the point," said the latter, "we may as well come to it now as later, what do you really think of the case, Bathurst?"

"Very little, sir. There's practically nothing to go on at all. That's why I can't think about it. The body was undressed somewhere, brought here by car, without a doubt, and then dumped in this field. Until we get the dead man identified we're simply groping in the dark. When the Inspector gets us the identification, things may start to move."

Kershaw nodded. "I agree with Mr. Bathurst. Photographs of the dead man will appear in all tomorrow's newspapers. That side of the business has already been seen to." Kershaw paused, to go on again immediately. "And in case they have a bearing on the crime there are these scraps of handwriting. It might be profitable to broadcast them in the Press. We may touch lucky and get the handwriting identified."

Anthony nodded cordially. "And this time, I'm happy to agree with you, Inspector."

He turned to walk along with the Chief Constable. "On the way back, sir, I'd like to drop in again at the mortuary. It's on the cards that Dr. Pleydell will be through with the P.M. by the time we arrive there."

Anthony's statement turned out to be correct. When they got to the mortuary for the second time, Dr. Pleydell was washing his hands. He looked round as they entered.

"Aconite," he said briefly. "I had an idea it was, soon after I started."

"A large dose?" enquired Anthony.

"No-o. Not so excessive. I should say there was no vomiting."

"What would have happened?" asked Kershaw.

"Oh—pulse weak. Laboured breathing. You noticed the livid hue of the face. In all probability—convulsions. After that—*finis!*" Pleydell snapped his fingers.

Anthony received the information with a strong degree of interest. The Chief Constable made certain extremely intelligent comments. Kershaw put a series of questions to the Divisional-Surgeon. Pleydell embarked on a technical explanation with regard to alkaloids, their nitrogenous substance related in composition with ammonia, their combination with acids and their alkaline reaction which turns red litmus paper blue.

The Kersbrook inspector listened to the doctor with intense attention. When he had finished this particular line of explanation Pleydell grinned at Anthony and made another announcement.

"Now I've got something else to tell you concerning our friend, the nude stiff," he remarked facetiously. "The bloke under that there sheet."

Anthony waited for it. "Yes, Doctor," he said quietly, "and what's that?"

"He was in a fairly advanced stage of diabetes. Come over here, gentlemen, and I'll show you something."

The three men followed Pleydell to the slab. "I suspected the presence of diabetes when I began to examine the skin. It's dry and . . . er . . . harsh. With a peculiar papery consistency. But look here, to clinch the opinion. This removes any doubt that I may have had." He pointed to the dead man's feet. "Look at the toes. See the condition they're in? That's moist gangrene that you see there. It's swollen, livid, and there are the 'blebs' containing fluid. If you look closely you can see the line of demarcation between the dead, and what were, the living tissues. The fluid is eventually effused from the tissues when they decay. That red ring you notice would gradually deepen and finally the gangrenous part would drop off. So you've something more which should help you towards identification. And something pretty substantial at that." Pleydell wiped his hands on a towel hanging close by.

Anthony nodded briskly. "Excellent, Doctor! To me and to Inspector Kershaw here, that statement of yours comes as a boon and a blessing. Now tell me. As a layman, I'm bound to ask you certain questions. I'm sure that you understand that. In your opinion has the man had insulin treatment?"

Pleydell nodded emphatically.—"Oh—undoubtedly. And by injections. But, in my opinion, not too recently. A fair time ago. I should say that the treatment had been discontinued for some time now."

"Not so good," replied Anthony. "I was afraid that would be the answer. That fact's going to make him more difficult to trace."

"Yes. I agree over that."

"Yes—the clue is not so good as it looked to be at first acquaintance. The treatment may have been given to him x years ago at any one of a few hundred different places. As I said, 'not so good'."

At this moment, Kershaw made a sudden exclamation.

"What's the matter, Inspector?" asked the Chief Constable.

"I've just thought of something, sir. With regard to those slips of paper we found in the field where the body was. That word 'Temple'. It may refer to the station on the District Railway in London. On the Inner Circle. I've travelled on it many a time. The dead man or the murderer may have caught a train from there. Or perhaps met somebody there. On the platform or something."

Colonel Buxton received the Inspector's idea and turned to Anthony Bathurst. "What do you think of the Inspector's suggestion, Bathurst? Feasible, do you think?"

"Oh, yes. It may be, sir. But London's rather a long way from here, I feel. Still, there may be something in the point. Any idea's worth consideration when you're questing for the truth. At the moment, speaking for myself, I'm keeping an absolutely open mind." He walked back to Dr. Pleydell. "Thank you very much for your information, Doctor. It may prove extremely valuable. If you run across anything more that you consider important, pass it on to Inspector Kershaw, will you? Then we can all have a look at it." The three men then waved good-bye to the Divisional-Surgeon and left the building. As they walked to the car, Anthony felt that, on this occasion, he was most certainly starting at scratch.

CHAPTER 2

I

KERSHAW published everything he could. Both the local press and the London dailies made it their business to broadcast as fully as possible the case of the dead man who had been found at St. Mead. His photograph and a detailed description of him were to be seen in the columns of all the newspapers. The picture papers featured the case for over a week. The clue that Pleydell had furnished in relation to the man being a diabetic was used for all it was worth. In this instance it seemed to be worth nothing, for no information was forthcoming with regard to the dead man's identity.

Intensive and exhaustive enquiries were made of all the police-stations in the county as to "missing men". All to no avail. No information was received as to who the man was, or even as to who he might be. In an attempt to assist the Inspector, Anthony suggested that a moustache should be added to the photograph that had already appeared in the Press as he was of a most positive opinion that, in life, the man had worn one. Kershaw, after a time, fell in with the proposal and the amended photograph met the gaze of millions of people in the train, in the street, on the bus and at the breakfast table. But the effort yielded no more tangible result than had attended its predecessor. And so the dead man who had been found by two children in Ebford's field remained unidentified.

Kershaw explored every avenue but not a soul came forward who had the slightest information to impart relative to the dead man's identity. Colonel Buxton, the Chief Constable, had a conference with Anthony and the Kersbrook Inspector. Anthony listened with sincere attention to what the Colonel put forward. After a time he made a suggestion himself.

"I've an idea, sir," he said. "I'll let you have it, for what it's worth. Inasmuch as we haven't got to anybody, as it were, by reason of all that's been done, suppose we try a reversal of tactics?"

"How do you mean, Bathurst?" asked the Chief Constable curiously.

"I mean in this way, sir. I'll try to explain. We are endeavouring to make Mahomet come to the mountain. Suppose we try the opposite method, the antithesis? Suppose we attempt to make the mountain come to Mahomet? Seems to me it might turn out to be profitable."

Colonel Buxton puckered his brows, as he considered the proposal. "How do you mean? I don't know that I quite follow you. I understand your inherent meaning, of course, but how is it to be applied—from a practical point of view?"

"I suggest like this, sir. It's obvious, naturally, that Inspector Kershaw is in charge of the case. He gets to that position through the natural course of events. St. Mead is in the Kersbrook jurisdiction and Kershaw automatically represents the police interest and authority operating in and from Kersbrook. But the criminal, or criminals, won't know necessarily that I'm in any way implicated with the investigation. There's nothing whatever to connect me necessarily with it. That's so, isn't it? Well, then, we'll make it known that I am. In other words we'll publicly announce the fact and associate me with the official enquiry. Get me now, sir?"

"I see your point, Bathurst." The Chief Constable spoke slowly as though he were weighing his words with scrupulous exactitude.

"What do you think of the idea, sir?"

"There may be something in it," conceded the Chief Constable, a trifle grudgingly, perhaps. "Seems to me though, you're giving something away and you aren't equally certain of any return for your gift."

Anthony turned to the local Inspector. "What do you think about it, Inspector Kershaw? I'd like to hear your views."

"Well, Mr. Bathurst, I think I feel much the same as the Chief Constable does. But let me get the idea quite clearly. If we announce that you're assisting in the investigation, what do you anticipate will happen? That's the part I'm not so sure about."

Anthony smiled. "It may be a little far-fetched, perhaps, but I was basing my opinion on the same idea as that other universally accepted one, that there's a strong tendency on the part of most murderers to return to the scene of their crime. For instance, in amplification, there have been many historic instances where the murderer has mingled with the crowd of sightseers at his victim's funeral. You would agree with the truth of that, wouldn't you, Inspector?"

Kershaw nodded. "Yes—I admit that there's something in that."

"Well then, I'm banking on a somewhat similar psychology functioning in this instance. It may not come off—it's a longish shot, I admit—but I consider that, on the whole, it's well worth chancing."

Colonel Buxton came to his decision. "All right. I'll agree. Like many a man and woman before me I'm willing to try anything once. Kershaw can see that the necessary wheels are set in motion. I'll leave that to you, Inspector."

Anthony rose from the table round which they had been sitting. "Very good, sir. In the meantime, then, I'll hang round and keep both my eyes and my ears well open. If anything turns up, or anybody that I consider in any way important or suspicious, I'll get in touch with you and Inspector Kershaw immediately."

II

The better part of a week elapsed without any development of importance. Anthony spent his time between St. Mead and Kersbrook. The dead man remained unwept, unhonoured and unsung. In addition to these three conditions, he remained unidentified. Nobody claimed connection with him and nobody appeared interested in his death to the slightest degree. But Anthony, who had learned the value and virtue of patience, in a hard and exacting school, waited optimistically for something or somebody to turn up. And it did. Or rather, they did! For on the sixth day after Anthony had had his conference with the Chief Constable and Inspector Kershaw, by a strange trick of coincidence, such as is frequently played by the long turn, there came two developments of major interest.

Inspector Kershaw came to Anthony with the first of these. The first, that is, in relation to the order of time in which they occurred.

"Mr. Bathurst," he said portentously, "I rather fancy I'm on to something. It's a bit . . . er . . . unusual and almost, perhaps unbelievable—but there you are! I've always been one who's preferred the evidence of his own eyes to anything else. And taking it all in all, I'd like to have a word with you about it."

"Good," responded Anthony heartily; "I shall be delighted to hear what you have to tell me. Is it for my private ear or do you wish Mr. Kemble to be present?"

Kershaw shook his head. "No—I think you and I'll share it for the time being. In case I should happen to be barking up the wrong tree. I don't want to jump and then find that I've jumped all wrong."

"Have it your way, then, Inspector. Now, what's the big news?" Kershaw immediately looked inordinately wise. "Something very peculiar's been happening. And it's on all fours with your idea that the murderer is apt to revisit the scene of his crime."

Anthony at once became all attention. "This is most interesting, Inspector. Very interesting. I'm all agog for your next instalment."

"Thought you would be. And you'll be even more caught up with it, I fancy, when you hear the next bit. There's been a bloke nosing round Ebford's field the last three nights in succession." As he concluded his sentence, he held his head back to see how Anthony received the item of news.

"Go on," said Anthony quietly.

"I took your tip and have had the place well watched. When the first report came to me I decided not to take any drastic action at once. To hold my hand, as you might say, and let things go on normally. The second night the man came again. And last night he made three of it."

"You had the man followed, I take it, on the first occasion?"

"What do you take me for? Followed right to the place where he hangs out."

"And where's that, Inspector?"

"To a cottage on the outskirts of Kersbrook itself. I put a tail on him each time he showed at Ebford's field. As you enter Kersbrook you go up a fairly stiff hill."

Anthony said, "I know."

"That hill's called Moonrise Hill. About half way up there's a row of little cottages. Supposed to have been built about the time of Waterloo. About half a dozen of 'em, I should think, from memory. Our man lives in the third one going from St. Mead."

"How far would that be from Ebford's field?"

Kershaw said, "About a mile I should say. Not much more."

"What's the chap's name and what's he like? Criminal type?"

Anthony thought that Kershaw looked a little uncomfortable at the question. "I wouldn't say that. Yet awhile. I haven't completed my enquiries yet. He's a fellow in the early twenties and from what I can gather, not too strong up top. You know—three ha'pence short of a shilling."

"You didn't tell me his name. I'd like to hear it."

"Fred Lord. Lives in the cottage with his old mother and an elder sister. The father's dead. I understand he had a bad time in the war and was demobbed in the early days of 1918. Picked up a spot of mustard gas. Lived the rest of his days as an invalid and died a few years after he came out of the Army."

"Have you questioned this man Lord?"

"Not yet, Mr. Bathurst. I thought I'd have these few words with you first. As I said just now. I'd like to feel my way a bit."

Anthony lit a cigarette and drew the smoke down into his lungs.

"I see. Thanks. I appreciate the action. Well, if you do ask him a few questions, I wouldn't mind being present at the interview."

"Right. Suppose you come along with me to his place right now? We can then ask him what we want to ask him. Is that O.K. with you?"

"That will suit me very nicely, Inspector." Anthony thereupon followed the Inspector out and into the waiting car.

III

They ran to Moonrise Hill in under ten minutes. The row of cottages, as Kershaw had stated, was situated about halfway up the incline. They were ramshackle and decrepit. Anthony judged them to

be about a hundred and thirty years old and to have been built somewhere about the time of Waterloo, in accordance with the statement
the Inspector had made. Kershaw walked up the untidy path of the
third cottage and called through the open front door.

"Is Mrs. Lord at home, please?"

An elderly woman with a lined face and straggling wisps of grey
hair came forward in response to his call.

"I'm Mrs. Lord. Who is it wants me, please?"

Anthony's first opinion of her was by no means unfavourable.
He put her down as a woman who for some time had been fighting a
losing battle with circumstances but who, nevertheless, had brought
courage to the contest and would continue to fight until the end.

"I'm Inspector Kershaw from Kersbrook and I wanted to have a
few words with your son, if I may, Mrs. Lord."

"What is it about, sir? I'm his mother and I'd like to know."

"I'll be perfectly frank, Mrs. Lord," answered the Inspector,
"but you'll know that there was a body found a day or two ago in
Ebford's field."

Anthony thought that the woman paled a little at the receipt of
the news.

"Yes," she said diffidently. "I've heard that—of course I've heard
it. All the village has been talking about it ever since the children
found the body there. It's created a sensation. But what's any of that
to do with my Fred?"

"We don't know, Mrs. Lord. Nothing, I hope. That's what we've
come to try to find out. But we do know this. He's interested enough
in that field to visit it three nights running. And we'd like to find out
why! You must know he's been out late several nights lately."

"Well, what if he has? He's not a child in arms, is he? Twenty-
five years old come next Boxing Day." A touch of defiance crept into
her voice.

"That may be," replied Kershaw, "but you know as well as I do
that he's not a normal person. I'm giving no secrets away when I say
that. Did *you* know he'd been down to Ebford's field?"

"No. Not for certain. But I suspected it."

"Why, Mrs. Lord, if I may ask the question?" The query came
from Anthony.

"Because of his talk. I can't help hearing what he says, living with him. It's been on his mind and on his lips as well. But my son's no murderer, gentlemen, you can take that from me. He's funny and dull-witted, but he's not that. If he was, I shouldn't speak to you as I'm speaking now."

The tears trickled down her face as she spoke. Kershaw was on to her immediately. "What do you mean exactly, Mrs. Lord, by your statement, 'on his lips as well'? Do I understand that he talks about the murder?"

Mrs. Lord set her lips. "No, I don't. Not about the murder. What I meant was that he talked about Ebford's field."

Kershaw, hearing her reply, went straight to the objective point. "Where is your son at the present time, Mrs. Lord?"

"He's upstairs. In bed. Some days he doesn't get up until very late." A dark flush mantled her cheeks again. "I told you just now that he had funny ways. He's not by any means what you'd call normal."

"Doesn't he work for his living?"

She shook her head. "No, sir. He wanders about by himself best part of the time. But there's no harm in him. Neither harm nor malice. I'll swear to that. He wouldn't do hurt to anything or anybody. I'm his mother. Nobody knows him like I do."

"I can accept that," said Kershaw. "Anyhow, ask him to come down, will you? He won't come to any injury through me, or as far as I'm concerned. All I want is to have a little talk with him. You can be present all the time it's going on."

Mrs. Lord looked doubtful for a second or so. Then she appeared to make up her mind to concede Kershaw his point. "All right," she said quietly. "You've got your duty to perform. I'll go upstairs and fetch him down."

The Inspector gave Anthony a significant look as Mrs. Lord left the little room. "Peculiar, isn't it?" he muttered.

Anthony nodded.

Kershaw said, "Rather fancy the old girl's got the wind up over something. What did you think yourself?"

"Not sure. Maybe you're right. I'd rather reserve my opinion until we've seen the chap himself."

Kershaw said, "Same here, but I can't help forming some opinions in advance."

Anthony said, "Tell you what I have been thinking. That possibly we're looking at this business from the wrong angle."

"How do you mean?"

"Why, in this way. Fred Lord visits the scene of the crime. Did he also visit it (a) before the crime was committed or (b) was he there on the night of the crime itself? I must confess, Kershaw, that I find the latter possibility definitely intriguing. It opens up a number of attractive situations."

Kershaw was about to reply when Anthony's ears caught the sound of movement upstairs. "Hang up," he said quietly, "they're coming downstairs, I fancy."

Kershaw nodded and the two men sat in the parlour of the humble cottage and waited for Miriam and Fred Lord. Steps could be heard descending the narrow staircase. Mrs. Lord led the way from upstairs into the parlour. A tall, thin, stooping figure followed in her wake. A young man whom Anthony judged to be about five-and-twenty years of age. Like his mother, he was by no means unfavourable of feature. He had rosy cheeks and large blue eyes. But the wandering look in them, the weak, loose-lipped mouth and the untidy long fair hair, tumbling over his forehead, betokened the subnormal intelligence. He shambled into the room and sat on a chair as his mother directed him. And his hands at once began to fidget over his kneecaps.

"I'll just have a few words with him first, sir, if you wouldn't mind." Mrs. Lord made her plea to the Inspector.

"All right," returned Kershaw. "Go ahead then, at once."

Mrs. Lord went across the parlour and stood close to the man that she called her son. "The gentleman wants to talk to you, Fred. Wants to ask you one or two questions."

He looked at her semi-vacantly and nodded.

"You'll answer him properly, won't you, and you'll tell him the truth? Mind, Fred, you heard what I said, *you'll tell him the truth*." The tone of her voice scored the last phrase heavily.

Fred Lord nodded again and looked up at Kershaw very much as a class of Sunday-school children faces an earnestly didactic curate.

"Hello, Fred," said Kershaw, rather heavily and pompously. "You know what your mother's just told you—so there's no need for you to be scared of anything. See?"

The young man nodded again. "That's right," he said in a strange, thick speech, "'s'right. Tell the truth. Always tell the truth. If you don't—won't go to Heaven."

"Good," went on Kershaw, "that's what I like to hear and what I wanted you to say. Couldn't be better. You and I are going to get along first rate. Now tell me this, Fred"—Kershaw paused a moment before putting his question. "What do you find to interest you in Ebford's field?"

At the sound of the last two words, Fred Lord's eyes opened wide and he nodded his head repeatedly several times. "Yes, yes," he said, "in the field. In Ebford's field."

Again Anthony noticed the strange, thick, slurring speech.

"But what about it?" persisted Kershaw. "What about Ebford's field? Why do you go there, Fred? That's what I want you to tell me."

Fred Lord's face took on a look of cunning, leering wisdom.

He looked round the room furtively with all the airs of a conspirator. "Ebford's field," he said. And then he uttered one word—"Gold." When he had spoken, he continued to nod his head.

"Gold!" echoed the Inspector. "What gold?"

Fred Lord leant forward as though he were about to take Kershaw into the secret recesses of his confidence. "Gold," he repeated. "Gold—in Ebford's field."

As the full significance of the reply came home to Kershaw, Anthony saw the Inspector project himself on to it with the artistic celerity of a cat pouncing upon a mouse. Anthony could even detect the glint of triumph in Kershaw's eye. It was as though he had completely vindicated and entirely justified his approach to the humble home of the Lords.

"Gold"—the object of man's cupidity—here then was the motive for the crime that was being investigated! Kershaw repeated the key-word again. "Gold, eh? Gold in Ebford's field? Where is it, Fred?"

"In the field."

"Whose gold is it?"

Lord shook his head aimlessly. Kershaw tried again. "Who put it there, Fred? Do you know that?"

For a second or so it seemed that Lord failed to appreciate the point of the question, but suddenly his eyes opened wider again and he stabbed upwards with his finger.

Kershaw turned to Mrs. Lord for possible enlightenment. "What does he mean by that, Mrs. Lord? Any idea?"

The woman shook her head and addressed herself to her son. "Where, Fred? Where do you mean?"

Fred, in reply, made a strange semi-circular movement with his forefinger. "Colours," he muttered.

"Is that why you go to the field, Fred?" continued the mother, "for the gold?"

"Yes. Yes. Fred Lord get rich. Buy chocolates, some trains, box of paints and motor-car. Gold."

Anthony noted the order of importance of the articles of Fred's desire as he had chosen to place them. Also the nomination of a box of paints following so closely on his mention of the word "colours". Here, determined Anthony, was a man who saw things as a child sees them. Not only physically visually, but with the mentality and mental vision of a child. Mrs. Lord tried again.

"But tell me, Fred, mother doesn't understand yet. Where did the gold come from? How did it get into Ebford's field?"

To Anthony's intense surprise, and doubtless he was no exception, Fred Lord began to sing. To sing as a child sometimes will, inconsequently and with an abrupt dissociation from that which has gone immediately before. Anthony listened to what Fred Lord was singing. From the thick speech and the hints at the likeness to a tune, Anthony recognized a hymn—"We plough the fields and scatter." Fred had probably heard it sung recently at a local harvest festival. Yes—here were the familiar words. Fred Lord was singing them plainly now. "'All good gifts around us are sent from Heav'n above, Then thank the Lord, O thank the Lord, For all his Love.'"

Mrs. Lord turned away from the contemplation of her son and Anthony saw the tears in her eyes. "I don't think it's any good, sir," she said to Inspector Kershaw. "I don't think any of us will get anything sensible out of him while he's like this."

Kershaw looked at her blankly. Anthony nodded sympathetically. "I feel sure you're right, Mrs. Lord. Besides which, you know him and you know what he's always likely to do or say."

Mrs. Lord looked at him gratefully. "Yes, sir. That is so, sir. And I thank you for putting it like that."

"Let me ask him a question," put in Anthony hopefully. "Do you mind, Mrs. Lord?"

"Not a bit, sir. But I don't think you'll get much out of him, as I just said, while he's like this. He has these moods. Sort of childish excitement. And when he's in one of them, as he is now, he's apt to be very difficult. To handle, I mean."

"I won't worry him," returned Anthony. He went up to Fred Lord and placed his hand on the young man's shoulder. "Tell me, Fred," he said, "about that gold. That gold in Ebford's field. How are you going to get it? Dig for it?" Anthony made a motion with his hands as though he were digging with a spade. "Like this?" Fred Lord shook his head in violent denial of the suggestion. "No, no. It will be there. It must be. On the very spot where the colour was. I know the spot. I go to it. Many times I have been to it."

"What colour do you mean, Fred? Tell me and then perhaps we'll come and help you find the gold."

Directly he had spoken, Anthony knew that he had made a false move. Fred Lord's simplicity gave way to a condition of low cunning. He put one finger to the side of his nose and leered at him. A new being had been created in him.

"Oh no, mister. That's no way of going on. If you do that you'll take the money away from poor Fred. Poor Fred's going to find it— then it will all be his. Oh no, mister, I don't want you in the field with me. Finding's keepings, not sharings."

He shook his head for some time after he finished speaking. Anthony watched him carefully. His lips were set tight in a childish pantomime of pretence that, come hell and high water, no other word should pass them.

Anthony looked at Kershaw and then unobtrusively shook his head.

"Nothing much doing, I fancy, from now on. I'm afraid it's our job to exit as gracefully as possible—L.U.E."

Kershaw looked gloomily pessimistic. "Seems to me you're about right. Pity you said what you did."

Fred Lord was now staring mutinously at the opposite wall with his lower lip protruding. His hands were still restless. Kershaw took a searching look at him. "All right, Fred," he said, with a heavy attempt at conciliation; "if you won't help those who want to help you—well then you won't—and that's all there is to it. Still, you may change your mind and perhaps you'll find us coming to see you again one fine day."

He turned to Fred Lord's mother. "Good-bye, Mrs. Lord. Thank you for what you've tried to do. And get into the thick head of that son of yours that it's a much better proposition to help the police than to hinder them. Especially when it's concerned with an investigation of murder. Good-bye, and don't be surprised to see us here again."

Mrs. Lord twisted the corners of her apron as Kershaw beckoned to Anthony to follow him from the cottage. That the Inspector's words were ominous to her, there was little doubt.

IV

The second development took place about twenty-four hours later.

It was on the main-line platform of Kersbrook station on the following evening that Anthony first became aware for certain that he was the object of a certain amount of attention. Anthony had paced the platform two or three times as he waited for his train. As he returned from one of these journeys to the sheer end of the platform, he noticed a man seated in the angle made by the seat and the wall of the general waiting-room. The man ostensibly was reading an evening paper. Very ostensibly—for his head and face were almost completely buried in it. At first glance, Anthony paid him but scant notice and attention. He saw the vague form of the man sitting there, and he saw the comprehensive white spread of the newspaper and, when he saw these things, his brain merely registered the simple and commonplace fact of a man reading a paper—a common enough sight on a railway-station platform in all conscience. But then, when he had travelled a few yards past the man, Anthony realized that it was distinctly dark, that there was no light whatever near the man; that the man, apart from this latter consideration, was seated in perhaps the very darkest part of the platform and that—putting the entire matter in a nutshell—it was virtually *impossible* for him seated as he was to read anything at all.

This realization gave Anthony something of a shock. The camouflage was so elaborately carried out. "Now," said Anthony to himself, each pace taking him further away from the seated man, "if he's only pretending to be reading, what is he *actually* doing? That's the question. And if I'm any judge, the fellow was watching me. Right! As I said to Buxton the other day, a case of Mahomet and the mountain. This may well be the initial step of the campaign."

When he had reached a convenient distance away, Anthony turned and began to walk back again. Glancing straight ahead of him and seemingly oblivious of the man's presence, Anthony contrived, nevertheless, as he walked by, to take a quick look at the man huddled behind the newspaper. He was by, of course, within a second. But the quick look he had been able to take had been enough. Anthony had seen as much as he wanted to see. There wasn't the slightest doubt that the man behind the newspaper was watching him, was watching his every movement closely and carefully, and in all probability had followed him on to the platform and selected that particular seat for the express purpose of carrying out that particular activity. As Anthony walked on past the man, his pleasurable emotion increased. A contact with the case of the murdered man was, in his opinion, being deliberately placed in his way. Almost being thrown at him, in fact.

"All to the good," said Anthony to himself. "I can wait patiently now and let 'them' (whoever they may be) make the next move." He saw the lights of the approaching train coming round the curve just outside Kersbrook station. As it came in and slowed down, preparatory to drawing up alongside the platform, Anthony decided to wait and see what the man would do. Then, in less than a second, he reversed the decision. If the man were watching him, there was obviously no need whatever for him to watch the man. Anthony, therefore, strolled nonchalantly towards an empty compartment. He opened the door and stepped in. And then, right on his heels, the man who had been watching him stepped into the compartment immediately behind him.

Anthony took the far right-hand corner seat. The man who shadowed him took the corner seat opposite him. Anthony smiled inwardly. His journey happened to be the length of one station only. He wondered if his *vis-à-vis* were aware of this condition. Anyhow, whether he were or not, Anthony began to take careful stock of his unexpected companion.

V

He was a small man, and undernourished at that. His face was thin and peaky. His neck was meagre, skinny, and showed dry lines of ridged creases behind an ill-fitting soft collar. The tie within the collar was frayed and worn.

"Looks as though he wants a good square meal," commented Anthony to himself. The man's hair was scanty and had been dragged across the scalp by the comb, but his little eyes were sharp and inquisitively peering like a bird's. They were, Anthony noticed, never still. If he were an adversary, there was certainly nothing formidable about his appearance.

The six minutes' run to St. Mead was accomplished and the train ran into the station with the journey quite uneventful. Again, Anthony wondered what the man would do next. He was soon to know. When Anthony alighted, the man alighted also. Anthony passed through the barrier and surrendered his ticket to the collector. The man who had travelled with him was still on his heels. When Anthony began the half-mile walk to the house of Neville Kemble, Esq., he turned his head carefully after taking just a few steps to see if the fellow were still on his track. He was! But when Anthony had gone a little more than a quarter of a mile he turned again. On this occasion and, somewhat to his surprise, it must be admitted, the coast was clear. The man who had been following him had disappeared from sight. There wasn't a sign of him anywhere on the road behind.

Anthony, thinking hard over this unexpected occurrence, turned into the gravelled drive which led to Neville Kemble's house. When he arrived in the morning-room, he found it occupied by a number of people. He knew that his host had many friends in the district, but during his stay there, Anthony had seen comparatively little of any of them. But Neville Kemble, he knew, was a Justice of the Peace and sat on the Commission for the County Borough of Kers-brook. On this particular day, Neville Kemble had been to the court in that capacity and had evidently brought at least two of his fellow Justices back with him, if not three. In addition to these, there were also present Colonel Buxton and a girl whom Anthony didn't know and, at the moment, wasn't able to place.

Neville Kemble himself, naturally, was quick to effect the necessary introductions. "Oh, Bathurst," he said genially, "I'm glad you've come in. I must introduce you all round. I forgot for the moment that of the people here you knew only Colonel Buxton. I'll make the introductions easy. I'll take them in a 'round the room' order and be hanged to conventional etiquette. Alderman Wall, Mr. Kenneth Stainsby, Miss Stainsby and Mr. Gilbert Tresillian, Anthony Bathurst."

Anthony made a comprehensive bow to the circle. Neville Kemble hastened to add certain particulars to his introduction.

"The Alderman and the other two gentlemen sat on the Bench with me this morning. We dealt with three drunks and a petty larceny. And from what they all tell me—my colleagues, I mean—they've been dying to know you for quite a long time now."

Anthony shook his head. "They're all much too kind, then, sir." He took rapid stock, however, of his host's guests. Wall was a tall, thin, melancholy looking man with two tufts of reddish hair which stood up on each side of his head. His eyes looked tired and even sad. When he spoke, Anthony was amazed that his accent was one of a most pronounced Cockney.

"Pleased to meet yer, Mister Bathurst. Of course, I've 'eard of yer many times in the porst."

Apart from the accent, the voice was not altogether unpleasing and had within it a certain sympathetic quality. The Stainsbys, father and daughter, were obviously horses of a very different colour. Stainsby himself was stout and somewhat, so Anthony thought, sacerdotal. But he was a good-looking fellow, with dark wavy hair and an agreeable smile. From an age point of view Anthony judged him to be in the region of forty-eight. He spoke pleasantly and evenly with no indication whatever of cocksureness or aggression. Elizabeth Stainsby in no way resembled her father as far as Anthony was able to trace. She was much taller than he. She was fair and she was slim. Her eyes were blue whereas his were dark brown, and altogether, Anthony thought, she must be, from external tendencies, the daughter of her mother.

Gilbert Tresillian, Anthony could soon tell, was a solicitor, in practice in Kersbrook and, in addition, an exceptionally charming man. He was of medium height, moderately good-looking, but possessed in no small degree both personality and polish.

"It's a far cry, Bathurst," he said genially, "from our trivial cases on the daily Bench to a matter such as the one which has brought you in our midst. The bridge from 'drunk and disorderly' to 'wilful murder' must have an extensive span."

"On the contrary, sir," laughed Anthony, "I'm bound to correct you. The matter which brought me to St. Mead was nothing more sensational than muscular rheumatism."

"Really," said Tresillian. "I had no idea. I imagined it must be the Ebford's field affair. Don't tell me that our dear Neville has entertained his angel clandestinely for some considerable period. Because, if that's the case, I shall have to speak to him very seriously." He swung round to Neville Kemble. "Come now, Neville, what's the truth of all this?"

Neville Kemble smiled. "I'm afraid it's true. But there's an adequate explanation. Bathurst hadn't been up to the mark and came down to me for a spot of convalescence. So bearing in mind his benefit and his best interests, I must plead 'not guilty'. For the present state of affairs you must visit your wrath on Buxton here."

"Shame," said Elizabeth Stainsby. "All you're doing, Neville darling, is to 'pass the buck'. And at your age, you should know better."

Stainsby laughed at his daughter's statement. "My dear Elizabeth," he said, "at least you might have let Colonel Buxton answer for himself."

"I assure you, Kenneth, I don't mind him doing that. I simply said what I thought, that was all."

Anthony noted her use of the Christian names. Colonel Buxton at last managed to insert himself into the conversation.

"Well, after all that, I think it's up to me. If old Neville here pleads 'not guilty', I must cry 'Peccavi' and plead guilty. What Neville says is perfectly true. Our friend Bathurst is in the murder case to oblige me. His brother put me on to him. And if he's not up to his neck in it yet, I hope he will be, before he's finished with it. Because, quite frankly, no other condition will satisfy me."

Tresillian made a pretence of stroking below his chin. "Up to his neck, eh? Might almost be prophetic."

"I hope it is," returned Buxton. "I'm an old-fashioned man and I believe in old-fashioned remedies."

Anthony smiled. "I don't know that I disagree with you, sir. But at the moment, I'm afraid, the horizon looks pretty black. We certainly can't claim to have made much progress."

"We may have to wait for the criminal to come to us, as you yourself foreshadowed the other day, Bathurst. The longer I think of it the more I'm inclined to regard that idea as decidedly likely."

Anthony rubbed his hands. "And I'm with you, sir. Somehow I fancy that we shan't have long to wait. Say that I've a feeling in my bones."

Alderman Wall looked more than ordinarily interested. "I'm sort of intrigued to 'ear you say that, Mr. Bathurst. But I suppose croime-detection's pretty well loike most other things. You've got to get right dahn to it and face up to it. That's the general ticket, isn't it?"

Anthony looked a little alarmed at the contortionist picture which the Alderman had depicted. But he hastened to assure Wall that, in effect, he was right.

"Oh yes, sir, there's no doubt about that."

Stainsby and Tresillian appeared to derive some amusement from his answer. The former smiled and the latter laughed outright. "It's all O.K., Bathurst," remarked the former. "Tresillian and I gave way to the same trick of imagination at the same identical second. You mustn't be annoyed with us."

Anthony grinned back and nodded cordially in acceptance of the position, as Elizabeth Stainsby supplied the next remark.

"Don't pay any attention to Kenneth, Mr. Bathurst. That's what he wants you to do. He's provocative. Always has been! I can remember the condition since my cradle days."

As she finished speaking, there came a light tap on the door. Neville Kemble called "Come in." A girl entered whom Anthony recognized as one of the younger maids.

"If you please, sir," she said to Neville Kemble, "Mr. Bathurst's wanted on the telephone in the library."

Neville Kemble gestured to Anthony. "Telephone call for you, Bathurst. In the library."

Anthony waved gaily to the others and walked quickly to the library to take the call. He picked up the receiver and spoke. "Anthony Bathurst speaking. Who is it, please?"

The voice that greeted him was entirely unfamiliar to him. It was rough, crude, coarse and obviously had in no way whatever been cradled in the terminology of the schools. These are the words which the voice spoke. "I'm sorry to trouble yer, Guvnor—but I tell yer stright I wouldn't do so if I didn't reckon it was important. And I'm sorry I can't give yer me name. That can wait. But what I want ter say is this. I want a few minutes' chinwag with yer over the murder at St. Mead. I can tell yer quite a few things wot at the present moment you'd give yer 'ead and ears ter know. Now listen to me, sir, and get this stright. I'll pop over termorrer mornin' and 'ave a little chat with yer. If you'll be so good as ter name the place, to say nothink of the time."

Anthony was ready and willing to play. This seemed to be the news for which he had been waiting. "Right," he said. "Eleven-thirty on the pier at Kersbrook. The first seat on the right as you enter the solarium. When you arrive, stroll towards me casually and ask for a light. I presume that you'll recognize me when you see me."

The voice at the other end chuckled. "Suits me, Guvnor. I'm usually short of matches, amongst other things. Solarium, eh? And I reckon that one's by 'Solario'. What a beauty! A 'orse and a 'alf! Personally, I never let his 'get' run loose. Like old 'Son-in-Law'. They don't breed 'em like that nowadays."

But Anthony was disinclined at that moment to enter into a discussion as to relative equine merit. He hung on to the receiver in the hope that his friend at the other end of the line would add to the conversation. His hopes, however, were destined to be disappointed. Nothing more came through. The man evidently had rung off. Anthony felt certain that it had been his travelling companion of the train. He hung up the receiver and made certain mental calculations. His principal problem was, should he communicate the news of the telephone call and of the projected assignation on the pier at Kersbrook to Inspector Kershaw? Or should he, on the contrary, and for the time being, play a lone hand with regard to it. After a few minutes' intensive thought, he decided on the latter plan of campaign and sauntered back to rejoin his genial host and the remainder of the company.

VI

Punctually at 11.20 on the following morning, Anthony passed through the turnstile at the entrance to the pier at Kersbrook and proceeded to walk down the pier towards the extension which had been added to it during the spring of the year 1929. The "solarium" formed part of this extension and was reached by ascending a small flight of steps which led to an admirably equipped area under a large glass dome. It took Anthony the better part of a quarter of an hour to reach the objective he had nominated in the terms of his telephone conversation. As he approached the first seat on the right-hand side his pulses quickened a little. He saw that his intuition of the previous day had been accurate. For, already seated in the specially selected seat, was the undersized man who had travelled in the train with him from Kersbrook to St. Mead.

The little man rose as Anthony came to within a few feet of him. His face twisted into what was undoubtedly meant to be a grin of greeting. He jerked up his chin and spoke.

"Could you oblige me with a light, Guvnor? Blessed if I ain't come out to take the autumnal air without any matches."

Anthony handed him a box of matches. "Thanks, pal." He struck a match and applied it to the end of a badly made cigarette which had been dangling from the left-hand corner of his mouth.

"My name is Bathurst," said Anthony. "Do you mind if I sit down?"

"Bin keeping a place warm for you, Guvnor. And there's nothin' I like doin' better. Always 'elpin' somebody I am. It's me unselfish natcher. Brought up religious I was. Me mother was a Plymouth Brother. Sounds a bit mixed that, don't it, but I reckon you know very well what I mean."

Anthony nodded. He was endeavouring to size the man up. He was obviously and audibly a Londoner and Anthony's mind was reverting to Inspector Kershaw's suggestion with regard to the "Temple" Underground station. Perhaps there had been something in it, after all.

"First of all," he said, "and before we enter upon any discussion I must remind you that I haven't yet the pleasure of knowing your name, whereas you appear to be in possession of mine."

The man rubbed the tip of his nose with the back of his forefinger. "Does that matter, Guvnor? To tell you the truth, I 'ad 'oped to remain anonymous."

Anthony made no reply to this statement. The little man continued.

"Yes," he said, "I'm not desirous at the moment, as you might say, of givin' away me 'monicker'. There's a sayin' among the parts where I come from, 'no names—no pack-drill', and there's a lot of 'orse-sense about that, Guvnor, say what you like about it."

He cocked his head to one side and looked up at Anthony in an attempt, obviously, to determine the effect his words had produced upon him. Anthony debated the point within himself. If he refused to do any more business with the fellow he might miss the garnering of certain valuable information. Which he couldn't afford to do. It all depended, he came to the conclusion, on the strength of the man's position and on how much the little man wanted to know. Concerning which Anthony himself hadn't the slightest idea. To a certain extent, therefore, the little man had him on one leg. He felt that his best plan would be to ignore the settlement of the main issue, for the time being, and allow the fellow to go on talking. To that end, therefore, he would endeavour to draw the man out. Anthony spoke thus.

"That suggestion, it seems to me, may reasonably be regarded as a little one-sided. But we'll let it pass for the moment. In the meantime, what do you want of me this morning? However, I warn you that I may be compelled to return to the matter of your name later on in the interview."

It was nearly mid-day by this time and the seats in the solarium were beginning to be filled up. After Anthony had spoken, his companion nodded and lowered his voice.

"Fair's fair," he said, "and that proposition don't sound too bad to me." He looked round furtively to see if anybody else were in earshot. "I don't believe, Guvnor, in beatin' about the bush. Never did. 'Tain't part of my make-up. I always say, 'When you've got anything to say, out with it and damn the consequences.' That's me, Guvnor." He shrugged his shoulders. "Now I believe I'm right in assumin' that you're in with the 'busies' on the St. Mead murder. The stiff wot was found in Ebford's field in his birthday suit." He looked up at Anthony and cocked his head to one side again. "Well, Mr. 'Olmes—am I right or am I dahn and out and underneath the old Cain and Abel?"

Anthony smiled. He had met men of this type before. He decided to use frankness in his answer and put at least one card on the table. "You may take it that you are right."

The promptitude and directness of the reply seemed to take the little man somewhat by surprise. As though he had expected Anthony to finesse and had not been completely prepared for anything other than an evasive answer. After a second or so's hesitation, however, he collected himself and got back to his original line of inquiry. "Good! Glad to know I'm barkin' up the right tree. Now it strikes me like this. Number one, you and your old chinas, the cops, don't even know yet 'oo the stiff is. In fact to put it into a nutshell, you 'aven't the foggiest notion. Well, 'ow do I go as regards that, Guvnor? Are yer man enough to admit the truth of what I've said?"

Anthony thought that his best plan again was to be straightforward. "I won't contradict you," he said. "But don't forget this, my friend. What we don't know today, we may very well know tomorrow. At any minute now, the information we're waiting for may come in to us."

"Nuts," said the little man contemptuously. "That's simply a sample of what the cat washes itself with. You don't know 'oo the corpse is and wot's more you never will know. Them wot's murdered 'im 'ave taken good care of that." He leant forward and touched Anthony on the sleeve. "And that's where I come in, Guvnor. I can't do the corpse any good, 'e's 'ad it. But I've more than a mind to set the wheels of Justice rolling. I rather fancy that talk in the old Book about eyes and teeth. It appeals to me more than I can say."

"That's O.K. by me," returned Anthony; "nothing; in fact, would please me better. Who was the dead man? You must want to tell me, or at least tell me something, otherwise you wouldn't have telephoned and fixed up this appointment with me. I don't think you're a man who would give himself neediest trouble."

The little man leant back in his seat and rubbed his unshaven chin reflectively. "No. You're right there, of course. I spent the money on that 'phone call when I 'adn't got a lot in me 'sky'. But," he paused, "I dunno! While I've been sittin' 'ere I've been thinkin' things over. They ain't so efear to me as wot I thought they was. I got to be care- ful, Guvnor. Blasted careful!"

He relapsed into a contemplative silence. Anthony let him have it straight.

"Why have you come to me? Let's get that clear for a start. For reward or revenge?"

A strange look came over the little man's face. Some seconds elapsed before he replied to Anthony's question.

"To tell the truth, I don't find that easy to answer, Guvnor. I think it would be nearest to the truth if I was to say 'a bit of both'. So leave it at that, will yer?"

"As far as you're concerned, I'm quite prepared to."

There was a silence. Eventually, after an ineffective period of waiting, Anthony returned to the attack. "Well, I'm still minus that information. Who was the dead man? Are you parting up or not?"

The little man leant forward from his seat, his legs apart, his hands clasped and his eyes on the ground. Anthony could see from his attitude that his problem was far from easy of solution. His wrinkled face worked with anxiety. "This is a strange case," thought Anthony to himself; "it may well prove the strangest of my career." He watched the little man as he weighed the "pros and cons" of his personal problem. Suddenly his companion straightened himself.

"I'll tell you what, Guvnor. I've been thinkin' things over, as I said to yer just now. Let me sleep on it. Give me twenty-four hours. I'm in a quandary. On the 'orns of a dilemma." He rioted from the serious to the mock-humorous. He put his right hand on his left breast and raised the other hand with dramatic emphasis. "Blimey. Can't yer see me? 'Put back thy Universe, O Gawd, give me but Yesterday.' All, they were the days, Guvnor! Days wot won't come again. Good old Wilson Barrett in the old *Silver King*. They don't make 'em like 'im these days. Lot o' mumblin' cissies. Can't hear 'em past the front row of the stalls. But look 'ere. Let's get down to brass tacks. I'll meet you 'ere, Guvnor, termorrer mornin', same spot, same time, and I'll spill the beans. All of 'em, not the first half dozen. The whole ruddy lot! That suit yer, Guvnor?"

Anthony deliberated. As far as he could see, there was nothing to be gained by a refusal on his part to co-operate. The little man might stick his heels into the ground so firmly that nothing Anthony could do would shift him. He decided to accept the offer as it had been outlined to him.

"All right," he said, with the deliberate air of one who is making a concession. "I'll accept that suggestion of yours. And I'll meet you here tomorrow morning at the same time as we met today. But there's one thing I'd like you to understand before we part company today. I don't intend to be put off again. And if you don't come clean tomorrow, I must reserve the right to take any action I think fit. I don't want you to have any illusion with regard to that. Is that thoroughly understood between us?"

The little man ran his forefinger along his upper lip. "That's fair dos, Guvnor, and I can't find fault with what you say." He rose from his seat and buttoned his coat tightly across his chest. "Bit nippy for October. I'm one for the summer, myself. Well, good mornin', sir, and thank you for the trouble you've taken. It's not everybody wot would 'ave been as considerate as you've been. See yer termorrer."

Putting two fingers to the peak of his shabby cap, he sauntered off, out of the solarium and down the broad-planked pier. Anthony remained seated. He rubbed his chin and reflected. Very strange, all of it—but very shortly to become even more strange, as he was soon to discover.

CHAPTER III

I

ANTHONY kept his assignation on the pier on the following morning, on the very stroke of time. When he ascended the flight of steps and entered the solarium, the area was almost empty. It contained but three people in addition to himself. There was no talkative little man on the seat as there had been yesterday. Anthony looked at his wrist-watch. The time showed, as he had expected, at exactly half-past eleven. There was neither need nor reason for impatience or disappointment yet awhile. The wind was chilly off the pier at the

entrance to the solarium, so Anthony decided to walk round for a
while rather than to sit down.

He walked round twice, and the effort ate into the better part of
ten minutes. There was still no little man to be seen. At eleven-forty,
Anthony knew that he wasn't coming. He felt as certain of this as he
knew his own name to be Anthony Lotherington Bathurst. "All the
same," he said to himself, "I'll give him until twelve o'clock. That's half
an hour's grace. And it's quite a reasonable assumption, I suppose,
that he may have been delayed."

Anthony made several more turns round the solarium, musing
thus. The hands of the clocks and watches, however, crept inexor-
ably round to the twelfth hour of the day. There came no little man
to the rendezvous. Anthony looked at his watch for the last time in
that particular connection. It was just on noon. As the thought registered, he heard some of the clocks in the town of Kersbrook striking
the twelve strokes. Well, he had given the little fellow the half hour
and he wasn't inclined to concede any more. It was a glorious October morning, whose early gossamer mists had by now surrendered
unconditionally to the warm assault of the ascending sun. Anthony
decided that he would be in plenty of time for lunch if he strolled
back to Neville Kemble's house and, in addition to the time factor,
that he would enjoy the walk. He commenced to put the decision
into effect. He had covered the length of the pier and travelled about
a quarter of a mile down Kersbrook High Street when he heard the
grinding sound of brakes being suddenly applied to a fast-moving
car just behind him. Turning quickly, he saw that a car had pulled up
sharply near the kerb at his side and that Colonel Buxton's head was
being pushed out of the window towards him. Anthony bent down
to catch what the gallant Colonel was saying, and as he inclined his
head he saw that Inspector Kershaw was sitting in the car behind the
driving-seat. The latter looked both worried and anxious.

"Get in, Bathurst," said the Chief Constable. "I've been chasing
you for the last hour. Called at 'Palings' for you and Neville Kemble
told me I should probably find you in the town somewhere, said he
thought you'd strolled out for a constitutional. Get in, man, for the
love of Mike!"

Anthony noted the edge of nervous irritation in Buxton's voice as he inserted his long length into the car and took the seat in the front on Buxton's left. "Why have you been chasing me, Colonel Buxton? Am I to understand from that statement that there have been developments?"

Buxton's face was grave as he peered ahead through the driving-screen. "Developments, you say'," he remarked quietly. "You've undoubtedly hit on the right word. Do you know where I'm driving you to? Because I'm prepared to lay a thousand to one you don't."

Anthony considered the question. After some seconds' intensive thought he replied to Colonel Buxton's question.

"I've always been attracted by the long shot, Colonel. And this occasion is no exception to the rule. I'll take your offer, in pennies."

The Chief Constable looked at him curiously and Kershaw leant forward from the back seat in unconcealed excitement at the exchange of words he had just heard.

"Where, then?" demanded Buxton.

"Ebford's field," answered Anthony. "And I'll go the limit and hazard another long shot in connection with it. A second body has been found in Ebford's field this morning. The body of a small man. His body, like that of his predecessor in death, lay there entirely unclothed. I can, even, I think, describe his features and general appearance—"

"Hold hard!" cut in Colonel Buxton, almost roughly. "I don't get any of this! Where in hell have you got your information from? We didn't get it ourselves till close on eleven o'clock this morning."

"I'll explain that point later," responded Anthony. "In the meantime, drive me as fast as you can to Ebford's field and on the way I'll describe the dead man to you. I only started to do it just now and I dislike only half doing any job."

The Chief Constable's jaws set, but he put his foot hard down on the accelerator. At the moment he felt, not entirely without cause, that he was in Anthony's hands. As the car swept onward, Kershaw leant forward again from his seat at the back. He began to speak quickly and unevenly.

"There's something else, Mr. Bathurst," he said, "something that Colonel Buxton hasn't told you. Who do you think was found in Ebford's field with this second naked corpse?"

For once, Anthony was found wanting. "I've no idea," he replied. "Fred Lord," replied Kershaw laconically. And this time he sank back into his seat with some degree of satisfaction.

<h2 style="text-align:center">II</h2>

Anthony repeated the name after Kershaw. "Fred Lord, eh? Yes . . . of course . . . I should have known." He turned back in Kershaw's direction and craned his head. "Where was Lord exactly, Kershaw, and what was he doing?"

The Inspector rolled the words of his reply round his tongue. "He was lying full length near the head of the corpse. He'd been digging with his hands and finger-nails in the earth near the corpse. The nails were broken and his hands were all earth-stained. All he could say when we went there was 'gold—the gold'. Much the same dope, if you remember, as he gave to us when we called upon him at his mother's house."

Colonel Buxton swung the car adroitly round a corner. "Here we are," he said—"Ebford's field of unenviable reputation. I should think that from now on people would give it a wide berth for all time."

Two uniformed constables barred the way to the field but gave way, of course, at the sight of the Chief Constable and Inspector Kershaw. Anthony walked quickly into the field, a few paces ahead of his two companions.

"Thanks for not having had the body moved, Colonel Buxton," he said unemotionally. "It may prove of inestimable benefit to me."

Anthony walked quickly to the body. Yes . . . he had been right! Here was the reason why the little man hadn't kept his rendezvous in the solarium at the end of Kersbrook pier. He had kept the rendez-vous with a grimmer master!

"Has he been vetted?" asked Anthony.

"Yes," replied Buxton. "Pleydell came along at once. Same as before, so he says. Poison. In fact, my dear Bathurst, it's exactly identical with the previous murder. Technique, venue and general conditions—just a repetition *in toto*."

"Anything to pick up this time?" Anthony's eyes were eloquent. The Chief Constable quickly took his meaning.

"Not a scrap, Bathurst. That's the one difference. I had every inch of the place searched and patrolled within a few minutes of my getting here. Not one of us was able to pick up anything."

Anthony nodded. "Thanks, Colonel Buxton. I'll take that particular point for granted then." He dropped on one knee and looked at the body. "At least, sir," he said, "there are two more dissimilar features. You noticed that, Inspector, of course?"

"What are they, Mr. Bathurst?" asked Kershaw.

"The absence of any evidence of diabetes and no barber's work has been performed on the features." He shrugged his shoulders. "I agree—they mean nothing. And, of course, because of that, they get us nowhere. It's an entirely negative condition. I merely mentioned them because they break up the pattern of the two murders." Colonel Buxton cut in. "Yes . . . I take your point, Bathurst, and I suppose from your own personal angle, it was well worth making. As you say, though, it gets us nowhere."

Anthony turned to Kershaw. "I presume you've picked up nothing from the photographs that were published in the daily Press? In relation to the first murder?"

Kershaw shook his head. "Nothing at all, Mr. Bathurst. Not the suspicion of a 'squeak' from anywhere."

"You'll follow the same procedure, of course, with regard to the second murder?"

"I shall, Mr. Bathurst. I've already made arrangements about the photographs."

"Good." Anthony looked at the ground near the body. "Not a footprint. Not a mark of any kind. Who would be a detective?" Kershaw nodded ruefully. "I agree. As I told Colonel Buxton just before we caught up with you, we don't start from scratch in this case, we start from well behind it."

"What did you do with Lord?" inquired Bathurst.

"Sent him home. It was worse than useless trying to interrogate him. Every question I put to him I got the same answer. 'Gold! The gold.' I tried him for just on a quarter of an hour and eventually I got fed up with the job. So, for the time being, I gave it a miss."

Anthony rubbed the ridge of his jaw. Kershaw noticed the expression on his face. "Do you think I did wrong, Mr. Bathurst?"

"Eh? Oh no. We can always pick him up later if we want to."

"Good. I'm glad you agree. I thought that you seemed—"

"No. That's all right, Inspector. I was thinking of something else, that's all." Anthony turned to the Chief Constable. "I certainly owe you an explanation, sir. You, too, Inspector. Perhaps now's the best time to give it to you. It's not of unduly long origin. In fact it dates back as far as yesterday. So you'll realize that I can't be accused of having kept you in the dark for any undue length of time. The facts are these."

Anthony proceeded to relate the incidents of the train journey and of his encounter with the little man on the pier at Kersbrook.

"It's obvious what has happened," said Inspector Kershaw, when Anthony had finished, "the murderers moved first. To prevent him meeting you again. That's as plain as a pikestaff."

The Chief Constable nodded. "Yes, there's little doubt about that. If only we were as sure of the other parts of the case. Then we might reckon on getting somewhere." He looked in Anthony's direction. "Don't you agree with me, Bathurst?"

Anthony was slow to reply. When his answer did come, it rather surprised both the Chief Constable and Inspector Kershaw. "I don't know that I do, sir."

Buxton was quick for argument. "Why not, Bathurst? Surely it's as plain as the nose on your face?"

"I'm not so sure, sir. Sometimes noses are as awkward as pikestaffs. And I think that if I can get you to look at things as I'm looking at them you'll probably agree with me."

"How do you mean?"

"Well, I look at it this way, sir. Seems to me it's the only reasonable way you can look at it. If they wanted to stop this fellow making contact with me, why didn't they? Originally. Don't forget that I'd already had one fairly long interview with him. What was to prevent him from providing me with all the dope on the occasion of our first meeting? Moreover, carrying the same idea to its logical conclusion, how do they know even now how much he *has* told me?"

"He may have informed them, Bathurst," put in Colonel Buxton. Anthony shook his head. "Again, sir, I disagree with you. That would imply, to a certain extent at least, that he was acting in collusion with them, whereas I feel perfectly certain in my own mind that he wasn't."

"On what do you judge that opinion?" asked Kershaw.

"On several things. That were said to me by him. I may be wrong, of course, but I don't think I am. I'm placing faith in my own judgment. I'm prepared to. Confidently. I had the opportunity of talking to him, of watching his face when he was talking to me, of noticing his reactions when I was speaking to him, and I'm positive that in no way whatever was he hand in glove with the person or persons who've perpetrated these two crimes."

"Having heard you, Bathurst," contributed the Chief Constable, "I'm quite prepared to accept your opinion and to take your word."

"There's another thing," said Kershaw. "I've had the road outside examined most thoroughly. For car tracks. But there wasn't an earthly. Far too dry a surface. So that, on the whole, it seems pretty hopeless, doesn't it?"

Anthony nodded. "I certainly can't contradict you, Inspector. Wish I could." He turned away with the air of a man who had come to a decision. "Well, gentlemen, I don't think I need to see any more for the moment. You can have the body removed to the mortuary, Inspector, for the Divisional-Surgeon to complete his job. He'd probably like to give it a 'twice-over'."

Kershaw made his way towards one of the uniformed men, and Anthony, with the Chief Constable, walked back to the car and waited for him. The Inspector joined them within a matter of five minutes.

"Drop me at 'Palings' will you, Colonel Buxton, please?" asked Anthony. "I'm beginning to realize most acutely that I've got a job of work to do. Unless I get to grips with this problem very quickly, the vital clues—and they *must* be there somewhere—will become too blurred for me to see and understand their significance. I simply must strike while the iron's comparatively hot. Once let the scent become too cold, well, you can whistle then for the clues that count."

"I'm in your hands to a great extent," said "Pusher" Buxton. "That is to say, I'm relying on you. Although, as things are, I must confess that I'm pretty pessimistic."

"You're in the same boat with Kershaw and me," responded Anthony. "All the same, I'm not surrendering the position yet awhile. As I've often been compelled to remind certain of my colleagues in the past, 'tomorrow is also a day'."

The car drew up outside "Palings".

III

After lunch Anthony borrowed Kershaw's personal notes on the case and retired to the seclusion of a private room. Neville Kemble, his host, had been good enough to place one at his disposal and he had been glad to avail himself of the offer. He had made up his mind, as he had indicated to the Chief Constable and the Inspector, that he must assemble his data, logically and methodically, and endeavour to see, from an intelligent survey of them, whether he could arrive at anything resembling a definite conclusion.

He obtained a sheet of note-paper to this end, and made the following notes. Crime Number One. (a) The victim. Nude body of man found in Ebford's field. According to autopsy by Dr. Pleydell, death by belladonna or another vegetable poison something akin to it. Subsequently found to be aconite. Man pronounced by Divisional-Surgeon to be in fairly advanced stage of diabetes. Certain evidences unmistakable. Also, undoubted evidence that upper lip had been recently shaved to remove fairly heavy moustache. (b) The venue. Ebford's field, as stated above. Body found by two children. Almost certainly conveyed there by car some time during the evening before and equally, almost certainly, man murdered during that same evening. No trace of any marks in the field itself. No trace of tyre impressions on road or anywhere in the vicinity. (Here Anthony referred to Kershaw's notes as a check-up on his own memory.) But certain scraps of torn paper found within the field which may or may not have a connection with the crime. Upon these scraps were found written words or fragments of written words. To wit (1) "Emma", (2) "Temple", (3) "of Sil" and (4) "Mai", (c) Summing up. Middle-aged man of lower-class type—possibly, even, with criminal antecedents—query, probably poisoned and body dumped in field, (d) Motive? Robbery? Revenge? Expediency?

Crime Number Two. (a) The victim. Nude body of man found in Ebford's field. Herein complete similarity of condition to first crime. Death again caused by poison. In all probability by the same poison that had been used to kill the first victim. Evidence of that will be shortly forthcoming. No physical peculiarities or abnormalities. (b) The venue. Same as before. Query, who found the body? Anthony castigated himself here. Why hadn't he inquired of the Chief Constable and Kershaw when he had been with them? But body, as on previous occasion, almost certainly taken to the field by car some time during the previous evening. No footprints, no tyre impressions, no findings of any character whatever, (c) Summing-up. In the main and as regards the principal features, on all fours with Case Number One. (d) Motive? Robbery? Revenge? Expediency?

Anthony pushed away the sheet of paper and leant back in his chair. As he considered what he had written down, he made a wry face of disapproval. "Progress," he said to himself caustically, "nil." He concentrated for a few moments on the question of "motive". If he were able to establish something merely moderately convincing in this particular direction, it might well prove to be of great assistance to him. He considered the question of robbery. Was it at all likely that either of the two dead men, the two *murdered* men, had possessed anything of such paramount value that he had died on account of that fact of possession? "Not likely," deliberated Anthony, "but possible." Each of the dead men, or even both of them, might have stolen an object or objects of great intrinsic value. And then subsequently been relieved of it or them by another person who desired it or them to a degree which didn't stop at murder.

Anthony next considered revenge as a possible motive. On the whole, taking all the circumstances into account, as he knew them, he was strongly inclined to discard "revenge" as a likely motive. He was chiefly urged to this opinion by his personal assessment of the calibre of the two dead men. One of whom he had met and with whom he had conversed. Taking the second man as a fair example of the first (and Anthony considered that he was justified to do this), neither of them seemed likely to have had much personal connection with the majority of the inhabitants of St. Mead and Kersbrook. And Anthony had always felt that the desire for revenge almost invariably arises out of personal contacts and relationship. This brought him to the possible motive of "expediency". „

After but a few seconds' intensive thought, Anthony came to the conclusion that herein lay the most likely motive of them all. That it had eminently suited somebody's book to poison these two men and deposit their nude bodies in Ebford's field. As he registered this thought, it seemed to him that he had made his first real step towards a possible solution of the problem. That he had established, as it were, a definite starting point which he could first of all employ in direct relevance to his encounter on the pier at Kersbrook with the man destined to become the second victim. From this thought, a second point emerged quite clearly, and almost immediately. A matter which he considered with meticulous care and attention before he brought his mind to the state of definite acceptance. That the murderer or murderers of these two men were to be found either in the district of St. Mead or Kersbrook, or to have some connection with it. Anthony reached that conclusion via the following mental route. Victim Number Two had deliberately come to St. Mead in connection with the death of his predecessor. That fact was a positive one. Anthony knew that beyond the shadow of a doubt out of the interview that the man had arranged and subsequently held with him. Now there were two reasons that might have brought the man into that part of the world. The first, the more direct one, that victim Number One had been murdered there, and the second, that not only had that happened, but that victim Number Two *knew* that, not only had his forerunner met his death there, but also that the killer lived in, or was connected with, that particular district.

The more Anthony thought over this, the more certain he became that he was treading on sound ground. The little man had promised to meet him for the second time, within a time-period of twenty-four hours. This fact clinched the argument. As Anthony saw things, the man had made contact with the murderer in some way during the intervening period and had died for his pains. Unless—Anthony thought again. Unless the murderer had stepped in quickly, as it were, fearing the result of a second interview and had removed the victim from what, in effect, would have been an ambushed position. At this juncture Anthony shook his head. He much preferred his original conclusion, that contact had been made, in all probability at the murderer's house or headquarters. Herein was more progress.

He turned again to Inspector's Kershaw's personal notes on the first case, being particularly desirous of finding out whether any result had been achieved from the diabetes angle. Evidently, from what Anthony was able to read of Kershaw's annotations, no hospital had so far identified itself with treatment of this unknown man whose photographs in the Press were its only means of identification. Anthony had been afraid of this from the start. He knew from experience that no murder problem is more difficult to solve than the crime which produces an unidentified corpse. He then realized that there was yet one angle to both deaths which he had not included within the scope of his recent effort of analysis. The entanglement of the moronic Fred Lord.

On the occasion of the first murder, Lord had been observed to visit Ebford's field after the body had been found and deported. On the occasion of the second crime; he had actually been discovered *in* the field when the body was there, and close to the dead man. And attached to Lord were his repeated babblings concerning "gold" and the presence of gold in Ebford's field. What treasure could there possibly be in an obscure field in an equally obscure place such as St. Mead undoubtedly was? Anthony was unable to make rhyme or reason of it. But having thought matters over for some time, he decided to tackle Colonel Buxton, with the idea of securing co-operation from the "Yard" in the person of Chief-Inspector Andrew MacMorran. The more he thought over this last decision, the more attractive it became to him. Anthony knew full well that there were no resources of the type needed, equal to those possessed by the "Yard" and no powers equal to the powers which the "Yard" wielded. He would speak to the Chief Constable and 'phone to MacMorran that same afternoon.

IV

Anthony put his intention into effect soon afterwards. He was fortunate enough to find MacMorran in and less engaged, possibly, than usual. The professional listened carefully and attentively to what Anthony Bathurst had to tell him. After a time he made his initial contribution.

"I've seen the photograph of the first chap, and your point has been thoroughly well looked into up here. And even allowing for the addition of a moustache, the idea of which, so I'm told, emanated from you, I can tell you for certain that the man isn't a known old 'lag'. That covers your first point, Mr. Bathurst."

"That may be," answered Anthony, "and as far as I'm concerned, I'll admit it's a disappointment, but at the same time it doesn't dispose of my idea entirely. Let us take the burglary angle, for a minute or two. Which is a theory I've been coquetting with for some little time now. Have there been any sensational burglaries in town or in the Home Counties say, lately, which haven't been cleared up satisfactorily, and in which stolen goods haven't been traced or recovered?"

MacMorran smiled his dry smile. He was aware that Anthony couldn't see it. "That's a tall order. It'ud be difficult to hit on any time when that condition didn't exist to a certain extent."

"I get you, Andrew. Cautious as ever. Still, even allowing for that, what have you got to tell me in answer to my inquiry?"

"Come off it, Mr. Bathurst. It's not yourself to be jumping at conclusions. You've never done that in the past and I'm pretty sure you're not going to start doing it now. I could give you quite half a dozen cases of the sort you mentioned just now. More than that, if I set my mind to it. More like a round dozen."

"Well, then, do it, Andrew. Let me have 'em. Better still, come down here to me at St. Mead and bring the dope with you. Then perhaps we can get down to something tangible. Two heads are proverbially better than one, even though one of 'em's mine, Andrew!"

The Inspector considered the possibilities of the invitation. He had no doubt that the Commissioner would agree to it readily enough, if it were put to him. And there was nothing he liked better than working in double harness with Anthony Bathurst. As he held the telephone-receiver in his left hand, he fingered his chin with his right.

"Well?" came Anthony's voice from the other end. "What about it? I don't suppose, if the truth's known, that you've anything else to do,"

"That statement's worthy of a politician," countered MacMorran. "Not only is it flagrantly untrue, it's irresponsible and absurd."

"Andrew," returned Anthony, "I do believe that I've got under your pachydermatous hide at last! Still, all that's by the way. When shall I meet you and where? St. Mead station some time tomorrow?"

"What's a good train?"

"There aren't any. Good trains disappeared years ago. But some aren't quite as bad as the others. Get away early tomorrow morning and catch the nine-twenty-two. That gets in here, by timetable, just after twelve o'clock. It's fast, almost all the way. By repute, that is. I'll meet you on the platform at St. Mead. O.K.?" The Inspector sent a grumbled assent down the telephone. "All right. I can see it's no good my refusing. You will have your own way, won't you? I'll be there."

"Good man. And don't forget the data, Andrew, with regard to those dozen cases of robbery you mentioned just now. Although a dozen's rather a lot. I'd like to put those under the microscope for a quarter of an hour or so. I've a hunch that that's where this case here is leading. In fact, I'm more than usually confident about it. Are they all cases that have come to the 'Yard'?"

"They are, Mr. Bathurst, every one of 'em."

"Righto, Andrew, and don't forget, there's a good chap. I'm relying on you more than I can say."

"I'll endeavour not to," replied MacMorran, with a shake of the head which denoted complete surrender.

V

Anthony met MacMorran at St. Mead station as he had arranged. As the Inspector alighted from a train which was just on half an hour late, Anthony was pleased to note that the attaché case MacMorran carried gave an indication that to a certain extent, at least, he had complied with his request.

"You're coming straight to 'Palings', Andrew," he announced. "I've made all the arrangements for that with my host, Mr. Neville Kemble. I didn't let you into that fact beforehand, in case you made a confidant of Sir Austin."

MacMorran saw that Anthony's eyes were twinkling as he spoke. The Inspector found a handkerchief and wiped his forehead.

"For a moment," he said, "I thought you were serious. You sent cold shivers down my back."

"Don't worry, Andrew. What Sir Austin's eye doesn't see; Sir Austin's mind won't think of. You'll be in perfectly safe hands."

The two men entered the car that was waiting for them in the station yard. Anthony inclined his head towards the Inspector's attaché case. "Glad to see you've brought me something, Andrew. I expected you to. Because I felt certain you wouldn't let me down."

MacMorran nodded. "I've got details of eleven cases in this file of mine. But I don't share your optimism, by any means. I'll get that opinion off my chest to start with. Still," he shrugged his broad shoulders, "you can play about with these to your heart's content."

Anthony grinned. "When we've had a spot of lunch, Andrew, I will. But I never believe in flogging my brain on an empty stomach." MacMorran fidgeted in his seat. "Who'll be at lunch with us? You know I'm far from keen on meeting anything like a crowd."

"We, Andrew, and that's you and I, are due to lunch with Mr. Neville Kemble and none other. So you can allay your fears on that particular score."

"Is he like his brother?"

"No-o. Not so's that you'd notice it. 'An improvement on' I should say. Seven years younger. A keener intelligence and considerably less effort in all he does or even attempts to do."

"I'm pleased to hear all that," replied the Inspector; "you've reassured me."

Anthony's vaticination proved to be entirely accurate. MacMorran soon settled down to the luncheon meal with their host, Neville Kemble, and after a comparatively brief period the Inspector became almost talkative. But, in accordance with Anthony's expressed request, Kemble was careful to shepherd the conversation away from the two crimes which had occasioned MacMorran's visit. After lunch, and at Neville's suggestion, Anthony took MacMorran into the privacy of the library in order that they could get down to business.

"The time has come, Andrew," said Anthony, "when I want to play, as you call it. Let's have a look at that dope you brought down here with you."

MacMorran opened his attaché case and took out his file of papers. "Here you are," he said, "there are the full details of eleven cases, all in this one file."

"Sort 'em out, Andrew, and then we'll take 'em in some sort of order."

MacMorran promptly did some sorting. "I'll tell you what, Andrew," said Anthony when the Inspector had achieved an order of sorts, "let's take them in alphabetical order of locality. By locality I mean the districts or whatever they are where the robberies took place. That will help to impress the different details on my mind."

"I should say so," retorted MacMorran; "your mind as a rule requires a lot of help of that kind, I don't think!"

Anthony grinned. "All right, Andrew. Have it your way." MacMorran got to work on the lines indicated. "Number one," he stated, "took place at Beckenham in the county of Kent. On the 21st of September last, Lady Sophia Isaacs, wife of Sir Leopold Isaacs, a previous Lord Mayor of London, lost an extremely valuable emerald necklace. Stolen when the family were at dinner, at about seven o'clock in the evening. All the likely men who might have pulled off the job have been given the once-over by the police, but nothing could be pinned satisfactorily on any one of them."

"Thanks, Andrew." Anthony made suitable notes. "Go on, will you?" he said.

MacMorran cleared his throat. "Number two," he announced. "Scene of the theft, Godalming in Surrey. Know the place?"

"Very well, Andrew. I could murmur feelingly, 'Come along, Charterhouse.' But I digress. Proceed, Andrew, please."

"Mrs. Chase-Bannerman, wife of F. G. Chase-Bannerman, Member of Parliament for the Paddock Division of Great Lanning, had the misfortune to lose a ruby collar which had been in the possession of her husband's family for many generations. Again, the police are completely baffled."

"When was this robbery, Andrew?"

"July last. July the ninth to be exact. Why the hell people can't take the necessary precautions to see that their jewels are properly safeguarded, I've never been able to find out."

Anthony jotted down the salient features of MacMorran's latest statement. "Carry on, Andrew," he said eventually, "I'm ready for Number three."

"Number three," continued the Inspector, "comes from Great Baddow in Essex. That's a little place near Chelmsford. A Mrs. Hugh Dixon had a valuable assortment of silver plate stolen. Date, August the fourteenth. No clues left behind and all subsequent investigations by the police have proved fruitless. In this instance, the lady is a widow. The husband died some years previously. He was a highly successful butcher in Chelmsford and district."

"Go on," said Anthony laconically after making certain notes. MacMorran laid a number of papers face downward on the table.

"Right. Number four now. At Great Nelmes. Also in Essex. Nothing like so much involved in this affair. From the £ s. d. point of view, I mean. A Mrs. Courtenay concerned. Had her personal jewellery stolen one afternoon when she had left her house. The value of the loss here wouldn't run to much more than a few hundreds."

"Date, Andrew, please," queried Anthony.

MacMorran searched for the required information among his details. "September twenty-fourth," he replied.

"Thank you. Number five, Andrew?" Anthony waited for the Inspector.

"Well, here's one I was a trifle doubtful about including."

"Why?"

"Well, it's away from the beaten track. Most distinctly so."

"In what way, Andrew?"

"Oh, come to that, in almost every way. That's why I hesitated with regard to its inclusion in your list. The articles that were stolen are most unusual. The robbery took place a fortnight ago."

Anthony looked at MacMorran. "From what you've already told me, Andrew, I like the sound of it. I'm definitely looking for something of the sort that you've just described. Tell me all you know about it."

MacMorran smiled at Anthony's eager interest. "The stolen articles were a number of designs for tapestries. I understand that they were the work of—let me look at this name again, it's a foreigner—of Rafaelle."

MacMorran spelt the name over in emphasis. "I don't pretend to know their intrinsic value, but I presume that they would be of great worth to a collector of such things and similar *objets d'art*. They were stolen during the night of September the twenty-ninth from a private museum at Hampton Court. They are reported to have been purchased in the original instance by no less a person than Charles the First of England. Still interested?"

"I should say so. More than ever, my dear Andrew. What did they represent? Can you tell me that?"

"I can. I brought all the relevant particulars down here with me." The Inspector went to his papers again. "The subject interest in every one of the tapestries is of Biblical—er—origin. There are eight of them in all. These are the titles. 'The Widow's Son at Nain', 'The Raising of Jairus's Daughter', 'Simon the Cyrenian carries Christ's Cross', 'On the Road to Emmaus', 'Peter Strikes off the Ear of Malchus', 'The Miraculous Draught of Fishes', 'Christ Scourges the Money-changers in the Temple' and 'The Pool of Siloam'. That's the lot, Mr. Bathurst."

Anthony, when he heard MacMorran's remark, pulled at his top lip. "That's your fifth case, Andrew. Out of the eleven you brought down here with you. Leaving a round half dozen to come. Now tell me this. In those remaining six, is there one, or are there more than one, of an unusual nature similar to the tapestry robbery? Or are they all connected with the usual commonplace jewel thefts? If so, I'm inclined to disregard them for the time being?"

MacMorran had recourse to his papers again. "Er—yes—I suppose that they would be. But there is another unusual one. As a matter of fact it has unique features. When I turned it out I realized it. The robbery actually took place as long ago as May last. From a riverside house near Bray. The person robbed is a Miss Drusilla Ives. She started on a stage career some years ago, but an uncle in Warwickshire died and left her much more than comfortably off, so she abandoned any ambitions she might have possessed of becoming a star and accepted the new position in which she found herself. Bought this place up the river and settled down to a life of comparative luxury."

"What was she robbed of, Andrew? I presume that's the particular direction of the 'unique features' angle you spoke of just now?"

MacMorran smiled and nodded in assent. "Your presumption is correct. Miss Ives was robbed of a large number of extremely valuable first editions which her uncle, who was a keen collector, had managed to obtain, of a collection of fine old English porcelain figures, of a set of cottage pastille burners, of several beautiful Satsuma vases, and also of a number of original cartoons by famous cartoonists, chiefly the widely known 'Spy' and the late Sir John Tenniel."

Anthony rubbed his chin. "I see. I admit the conditions here are definitely unusual. And the robbery took place as long ago as last May, you say?"

"May twenty-seventh to be exact. But I haven't finished yet." MacMorran paused. The pause had both subtlety and intention. Anthony responded to it.

"Oh, you haven't, eh, well spring the worst on me."

"I thought you'd come up for more. This to my mind is the most interesting—and what I called 'unique' feature. It *is* unique, too, from the point of view of the particular pair of glasses through which we're looking. Miss Drusilla Ives has a house in St. Mead. In addition to her riverside residence at Bray."

Anthony whistled. "By Jove, Andrew! Now I'll admit that *is* interesting. Far from here do you know?"

"The address is 'The Dancers', Kersbrook Road."

"I must ask Mr. Neville Kemble for more details. He will be able to help us in that direction. If the lady's been resident here for any length of time, he must be acquainted with her, I should imagine."

"I agree. Ten to one on it. It shouldn't present any difficulty." MacMorran, having delivered himself of this opinion, proceeded to fold up his papers and put them away in his case. He looked towards Anthony for spoken confirmation of the action.

"From what you said just now, Mr. Bathurst, I take it that you have no desire, at the moment, to hear any more?"

Anthony toyed with his fountain-pen. "On the whole, Andrew, I don't think I do. For the reason that I've been lucky. Lucky, that is, in a way."

"How do you mean? I don't know that I altogether—"

Anthony smiled. "Look at it for yourself, Andrew. In the words of the immortal Holmes, 'you know my methods. Apply them."

MacMorran shook his head. "I'm afraid, in this instance, that's beyond me."

Anthony did what the Inspector had done before him. He shook his head. "Consider the normal motives for murder, Andrew. Revenge, gain, hatred, to keep somebody quiet. Dead men tell no tales, etc.

Then take a good look at the two men whom we have in this case as murdered. To my mind, they both fall into the last class, without the shadow of a doubt. Why? Because, in my opinion, they had knowledge dangerous to somebody, which concerned theft or illicit gain of some kind. Nothing could be gained from *them*, probably, but they *might* have come into the *possession* of something highly valuable, down the avenue of robbery. That, very roughly, is as I saw and still see things."

MacMorran rubbed his chin. "I get your drift, Mr. Bathurst. And maybe you're right Time will tell us, no doubt. But I don't—"

Anthony raised a deprecating hand. "As a matter of fact, Andrew, I've found the Ives robbery case extremely interesting. A lady who actually has a place of residence in St. Mead. In addition to this, we have the robbery from the Hampton Court museum almost sitting up and begging for our special consideration. Between the two, my dear Andrew, who knows?"

MacMorran embarked on the severely practical. "Hadn't we better have a word with your Mr. Kemble re Miss Ives? As we agreed to do just now?"

"Perhaps we had, Andrew. And the sooner the better. I expect we shall find him in the library."

Neville Kemble's eyes flashed back immediate interest the moment that Anthony mentioned the name of Drusilla Ives. Actually, Anthony thought that they reflected something more than mere interest.

"Do I know Drusilla Ives? My dear Bathurst, my dear boy, you might just as well ask me do I like oysters, asparagus or Russian caviare."

"Your answer then is obvious," returned Anthony. "And as for the gallery in which you so instinctively place the lady, am I to understand that the choice is beyond argument?"

Neville Kemble's eyes ceased to flash. On the contrary they took unto themselves an undoubtedly genuine twinkle. "Yes. You are to. Drusilla is—er—altogether delightful. There is but one Drusilla. Which, perhaps, is just as well for our peace of mind."

"That's as well to know. You probably kept her from me owing to my condition of convalescence. Which, no doubt, was as well for *my* peace of mind."

Neville Kemble raised his eyebrows. "On the contrary, my dear boy, I did not keep her from you. The matter of your meeting was never in my hands. Drusilla hasn't been in residence during the time that you've been staying down here with me. She's been in the Maidenhead district. Her latest appearance in these parts was somewhere about the middle of August."

Anthony smiled. "In that case, sir, you're forgiven. I spoke without having given the matter proper thought. But I expect you're wondering at what lies behind my original question. You must saddle the blame for that on to Chief-Inspector MacMorran here. He's routed out certain facts for me with regard to a burglary with which Miss Ives was visited about five months ago. At her riverside place at Bray."

MacMorran looked incredibly indignant. He fell to protest.

"At your request, Mr. Bathurst. I mean about the routing out. I think you owe it to me to make that much clear to Mr. Kemble. I don't care for sailing under false pretences." The Inspector's voice was stiff with the justice of explanation.

Neville Kemble laughed. "And for myself, I'd like you to know that I don't much care for any sort of sailing. The sea and I are coldly hostile to each other. Put your mind at rest. I am aware of the robbery. Drusilla has told me all about it. For the life of me, though, I can't see what it's doing in our present bout of conversation. Do I understand that Bathurst has dug it up for some ulterior motive of his own which is unrevealed to simple folk like you and me, MacMorran?"

Neville Kemble looked towards Anthony for clarification. MacMorran moved his feet awkwardly. Subtleties and oblique references invariably caused him uneasiness. Anthony deliberately side-stepped Kemble's invitation to explanation.

"Tell me, please," he said to him with gentle persuasion, "of the robbery at Bray."

Neville Kemble looked at him with cold, hard curiosity. "Are you hinting, Bathurst, that these recent deaths in Ebford's field, St. Mead, have anything to do with the robbery at Drusilla Ives's house in the spring?"

Anthony's eyes met his. "Suppose I am?"

Kemble shrugged his shoulders. "Well, you know your own business best, of course, but to me the idea's rather fantastic. I don't see how you can link up the two affairs in any way whatever. They haven't the slightest thing in common."

"Neither do I. But that isn't to say that I shan't be able to at some future date—if the effort becomes really necessary."

"I see." Kemble spoke slowly. "Well, I'm in your hands. You know best. You and MacMorran had better sit down while I tell you the yarn as Drusilla told it to me when she was down here in August. I'll sketch in the background for you to commence with . It should help you."

Anthony nodded his approval. "That's just what I'm wanting you to do."

Kemble's normal geniality returned. "Good. Glad I'm getting in right at the beginning. Nothing like it. I always say that a bad start takes a rare lot of wiping out, even though it may result in a good ending. There's usually a long journey to encompass in between. Drusilla's money—and her stuff generally—came to her from her uncle, Sir Herbert Ludford, who had a very charming home just outside Leamington, in Warwickshire. It was about fifteen years ago when he died. At the time of his death, Drusilla was on the boards. Musical comedy. She was a highly talented dancer. Right at the top in her own particular line. When the Ludford fortune fell into her lap she had the good sense to think twice about the stage as a permanent career. Ultimately she decided to give it best and settled down to enjoy the good things her uncle had left her, without having to work for them. I can't say that I can blame her. She spends most of her time at this house of hers at Bray, near Maidenhead. Outside an occasional fortnight here round about August, she usually spends November to February with us in this district, knocking off in the middle of her stay to spend Christmas in town. She always says St. Mead's far too slow to spend Christmas in. Now I'd better tell you about the robbery. It happened towards the end of May. She lost a good deal of stuff which Sir Herbert Ludford had got together in his time—books, vases, porcelain and his famous collection of original cartoons. Drusilla was extremely annoyed, let me tell you. But chiefly for sentimental reasons. She wasn't concerned too much as to the loss in value, but because she knew only too well how old Sir Herbert had valued them. There you are, now you know about Drusilla and also about Drusilla's robbery."

Neville Kemble smiled genially as he concluded his story. Then, as neither Anthony nor MacMorran showed any immediate reaction to it, he came in again.

"And as I said before, I'll say again while you're doing your pondering, I can't see what possible connection there can be between that robbery and the two dead bodies in Ebford's field."

He waited for Anthony's response. When it came, Kemble considered it as being particularly lame.

"Anything," said Anthony, "is *possible*. Question to be answered is, 'Is it probable?'"

"In this connection," replied Kemble, "it doesn't seem to me that there's a powerful lot of difference between the two adjectives. Despite the way you're looking at them."

Anthony went off on a new tack. "Miss Ives," he said quietly, "who are her especial friends in this neighbourhood? I presume that she has some."

"Naturally," smiled Kemble, "she moves more or less in my own circle. The Buxtons, the Tresillians, the Stainsbys and some people you haven't yet encountered—the Vicar of St. Mead and his wife, the Rev. Miles Sherwood and Mrs. Beatrice Sherwood. She has other acquaintances, of course, but those I have mentioned are the closest cronies Drusilla has in this district."

"Things might be worse, Andrew," said Anthony with another smile. "Having heard our host, you must admit the truth of that. We should have no difficulty in making certain valuable contacts with Miss Ives when the time comes, or even directly we feel called upon to do so." He turned to Neville Kemble. "None of Miss Ives's stolen articles was recovered, I believe, sir."

Kemble shook his head. "I never heard of any returning to the roost. But, doubtless, Inspector MacMorran can tell you more about that than I can."

The Inspector hid the fact that he had already given Anthony Bathurst this information. "As far as I can say, Mr. Kemble, when I left the 'Yard' to join Mr. Bathurst on this jaunt, none of the missing articles had been recovered. And so much time has elapsed since the robbery that I very much doubt if any of them will be. I think that's a fair statement, sir."

"Pity," said Anthony, as though musing to himself, "that the lady Drusilla is not in residence at St. Mead at the moment."

"Why?" demanded Neville Kemble.

"Why?" repeated Anthony, with an air of mock innocence. "Why, so that I could have had the pleasure of a few words with her. I adore oysters."

"Well, if that's the time of day," said Neville Kemble, "I don't know that certain reaches of the Thames are such an impossible distance. My memory tells me that the district is well served from Paddington."

Anthony smiled. "And my memory tells me, sir, that your memory is perfectly sound on that point."

VI

The autumn day turned into sunshine during the afternoon, and Anthony walked and talked in the garden of "Palings" with Andrew MacMorran.

"Andrew," he said, "you can pat me on the back for having followed my 'hunch' and turned up lucky."

The Inspector saw that Anthony was rubbing his hands, a sign of satisfaction which he knew and recognized of old.

"Look where we are today," continued Anthony, "compared with our position yesterday. We have made a definite advance. The significances we've run up against are enormous! Assuming that the kernel of these crimes lies in the proceeds of robbery—and I assure you I'm convinced on the point—my initial investigation brings me the highly portentous fact that a lady connected with the very district has recently been robbed of the most unusual possessions. 'Unusual', that is to say, from the point of view of their figuring as the main proceeds of a robbery. Surely you will agree, Andrew, that the point cannot be ignored?"

"I suppose it can't," conceded the Inspector. "Although—"

MacMorran broke off what he had been on the point of saying. But Anthony pressed him.

"Although what, Andrew?"

"Well, I don't know that I'm prepared to go as far as you are. The whole thing may be nothing more than a coincidence."

"The odds are against it, Andrew. At least, to my way of thinking."

"But it seems so—so—I'll use the word that Mr. Kemble used just now—'fantastic'."

Anthony asked a question with extreme coolness. "Why? I can't see your reasons for making such a definite statement. Honestly I can't."

MacMorran attempted to justify himself. "Well, take the people that you've run across down here. If you like—I'll concede this point— the people that our host described as Miss Ives's closest cronies. I'm giving you the lady, you'll notice, as the queen-pin of the affair, just to please you. Would you seriously connect any one of them with such a thing as burglary? And, more particularly, with burglaries such as those we've been discussing? I ask you, Mr. Bathurst! Now seriously, would you?"

Anthony argued. "I wouldn't choose 'em for it under normal circumstances. I'll grant you that, Andrew. But you never know! As an old friend of mine used to wisecrack, 'you never can tell and you never can B. Shaw'."

"You must admit my point. You're simply stalling."

"No, I am not, Andrew. I assert deliberately that the history of crime has known many 'gentleman crooks'—and you know the truth of that just as well as I do."

MacMorran shrugged his shoulders. "Yes, I know. But these people down here at St. Mead—to me the idea doesn't hold water for a moment. Still, I'm only one. What do you propose to do next?" Anthony scratched his cheek. "I'm considering paying a visit to the fair and delectable Drusilla. I don't think I can wait until her fancy drives her down here again. Maybe months, Andrew!"

As he spoke, Anthony heard his name called. Turning quickly, he saw Inspector Kershaw approaching down the path. He seemed to be labouring under some form of excitement, for his features were less under control than was usual with him. He came up alongside them and spoke at once. Before, indeed, he gave greeting to the "Yard" Inspector.

"Mr. Bathurst," he said, "I had to come to see you at once. I've some news at last. The body's been identified!"

"Which body?" asked Anthony, curiously and critically.

"Of course! Stupid of me. I spoke thoughtlessly. I should have made it clear to you. The second dead man."

"Good," returned Anthony, "that's certainly excellent news. Which spells more progression. And who is he?"

"His name's Steel. Christian name Peter. And he comes from Bromley-by-Bow. Near Poplar that is, so I'm told."

Anthony nodded his approbation. "Good again. And I presume that, professionally, you've found him difficult to place. Am I right, Inspector Kershaw?"

Anthony's confidence, however, was to receive a severe shock. Kershaw replied with a quiet but studied firmness.

"No, Mr. Bathurst. I had no difficulty about that whatever. According to what I've heard today, Steel worked in an oil-cake factory near where he used to live. You know what I mean—linseed stuff for cattle feeding."

Anthony looked disappointed. "Who identified him? His wife?" Kershaw shook his head. "No. It's not quite so satisfactory as that. As it happens, he turns out to be a single man. No, one of his mates from the factory has turned up and identified him. Gives him an excellent character, too."

Kershaw watched the effect that his words had produced on Anthony's face. The Inspector saw at once that surprise had now been added to the disappointment which his face had already shown.

"Tell me, Inspector," said Anthony quietly, "is the man still here? The man who has come down from Bromley?"

"Yes, he is. I left him with the station-sergeant at Kersbrook. He's returning to town by a fast train this evening. But why do you ask?"

"Simply this. I expect Chief-Inspector MacMorran here would like a word with him, and I know that I should. Frankly, Inspector Kershaw, what you've just told me puzzles me considerably. It doesn't fit in at all with the pattern of things as I'd traced it. And traced it to my satisfaction, too."

The local Inspector nodded. "I guessed it hadn't from the look on your face just now."

"Sorry if I wear my heart on my sleeve." Anthony turned to MacMorran. "You'd like to give this chap the once-over wouldn't you, Chief? If I know you at all, that is."

MacMorran accepted his cue. "I most certainly would, Mr. Bathurst. And if he's returning to town this evening as Inspector Kershaw ıas just told us he is, I suggest that we get down to the Kersbrook station as soon as possible. Got your car here, Inspector?"

"Yes. I ran up in it. I didn't want to waste any time."

"I can quite understand that. What do you say, then? Will you run Mr. Bathurst and me down to Kersbrook?"

"Only too delighted, Chief. Come along and we'll make it at once. That should reduce to a minimum the chance of the identifier of Mr. Peter Steel having already left."

The three men entered Kershaw's car and they were at the police-station at Kersbrook in a matter of a few minutes. "Steel," muttered MacMorran, "Peter Steel. Don't know that it conveys anything to me."

"Thou shalt not steal," murmured Anthony reflectively.

The man who had journeyed to identify the body of Peter Steel was still with the station-sergeant when Anthony walked in with his two companions. Kershaw spoke at once to his subordinate.

"Very good, Inspector," replied the latter, "I've just finished with Mr. Stacey here. I'll see to that other business for you and leave Mr. Stacey in your hands."

The station-sergeant pushed a pen behind his ear, closed a long book that had been open on his desk, and made his departure.

"Mr. Stacey," said Kershaw, "I've brought two gentlemen along here with me who would like to have a few minutes' chat with you. Chief-Inspector MacMorran from the 'Yard' and Mr. Anthony Bathurst."

Anthony thought that Stacey looked tired and troubled. "You lead, Mr. Bathurst," said MacMorran imperturbably, "and if I should want to, I'll come in at the death. But I may not want to."

"Mr. Stacey?" said Anthony interrogatively.

"That's me," answered the man. "Tom Stacey, my name. And as you're aware, I'm here on an unpleasant errand."

Anthony put him down as cordial and comradely. He was fair and plump with a good deal of healthy colour in his face. "Yes. So I understand from Inspector Kershaw," he said. "A bad business for you no matter which way you choose to look at it. You've identified the body, I hear, as that of a colleague of yours?"

"That's right, sir," replied Stacey, "the dead man's Peter Steel. He's worked under me for the last eleven years at Charles Smart's oil-cake factory, Aberfeldy Row, Bromley-by-Bow. And a right good fellow was Peter. I can honestly say I've never met a better. Wouldn't have hurt a fly. You can take that from me, sir, as gospel."

Anthony looked towards the local Inspector. The latter nodded. "Sergeant McCarthy has taken all the necessary particulars, Mr. Bathurst."

"Good. Now what would have brought your Mr. Peter Steel down here, Mr. Stacey? Can you give us any idea of that?"

"Search me," exclaimed Stacey emphatically. "I haven't an idea in the world." He looked over to Kershaw. "I've told your sergeant that, Inspector Kershaw, several times while you were out. Steel had no interests here, so far as I know, no relations down in these parts, and to me why he should have ever come here's a fair corker. Never breathed a word to me he didn't! Which, although I says it myself, is a bit surprisin'. Because he confided in me a lot did Peter Steel. I don't mean we was 'buddies', but he'd usually ask my advice on most things that came his way and I flatter myself he sort of respected my judgment. And I don't think I ever let him down. But on this last occasion when he must have come down to St. Mead, I knew no more about it than a fly in the air."

"Had he seemed troubled at all lately?" asked Anthony.

Stacey passed his hand round his cheeks. "Well, now you come to mention that, I'm inclined to say yes, he had. He hasn't been himself just lately. Nothing much. Nothing I could put my finger on. You couldn't make a song and dance about it, but there it was, he seemed extra quiet over most things. Like as though he didn't want to talk to you much. Kept himself to himself. I'm pretty sure now, knowing what I do, that he must have had something on his mind. But as to what it was—well, as I said—'search me'." Stacey shrugged his shoulders rather dramatically.

"He was a single man, wasn't he?"

"Yes, sir. As far as I know again, Peter Steel had no living relatives. Certainly I've never heard him talk of any."

"Where did he live?"

"He lodged in Ullin Street, Poplar. Had a couple of rooms there. Along of a Mrs. Rogerson. Widow woman. Had been there ever since he started working for Charles Smart's."

"How did he spend his spare time?"

Stacey grinned. "Just ordinary-like. Old Peter had no vices if that's what you're probing for. Glass o' beer now and again, game at darts, hand at cards, no more than that. No, you're barking up the wrong tree, sir—not a drunkard, not a gambler. Except that he followed the gee-gees and liked a bob each way now and then. And a bit too old in the tooth for the other game that a good many men burn their fingers over."

Anthony smiled. "How was he placed with regard to money?" Stacey shrugged his shoulders. "Well, there you are. That's an awkward question. He never had any too much, people of our class don't roll in it, as you might say. We've never got much to spare. You don't want me to tell you that. But he picked up fairish wages when he put in a full week's work."

"How much?" inquired Anthony. "That is to say, on an average?" Stacey pursed his lips. "Round about three quid a week. Never much less than that and sometimes a bit more, when he'd put in a spell of overtime. But that didn't come too often."

"So bearing in mind what you've said, Mr. Stacey, Steel never had any particular spare cash to speak of, but on the other hand was never altogether without any and 'up against it'. Would they be fair statements to make?"

Stacey nodded his agreement with the two positions. "They would, sir. That's putting it just about as it should be."

"Thank you, Mr. Stacey." Anthony turned and spoke to Inspector Kershaw. "Do something for me will you, please, Inspector? Bring in here a photograph of the first dead man. One of each of those that were taken, if you don't mind. One clean-shaven, as he was in death, and the other showing him with the moustache."

"Certainly, Mr. Bathurst." Kershaw went out to get the two photographs.

MacMorran said, "That was going to be my suggestion. But I guessed it would occur to you."

Kershaw was quickly back. "Here you are, gentlemen. Here are the two photographs you asked for."

"Put them in front of Mr. Stacey, will you, please?"

Kershaw did as he had been requested. "Now, Mr. Stacey," said Anthony, "you see those two photographs. Do you know that man?" Stacey looked long and hard at the two photographs. After a time he shook his head. "No, I don't. I don't recognize the man at all."

"Not at all, eh? Does he remind you of anybody that you know, or even that you may have met? Think carefully before you answer." Stacey put his hand over the lower part of the faces and then repeated the action with regard to the upper part. Only to shake his head again.

"The answer's still no," he said. "I don't recognize this chap and to the best of my knowledge I've never seen him in my life."

"Quite sure of that?"

"Positive, sir."

MacMorran leant forward and made his second contribution. "Those photographs at which you're looking, Mr. Stacey, appeared in most editions of the daily Press. And very recently at that. Did you happen to see them there by any chance?"

Again Stacey replied in the negative. "No, Inspector. I didn't." But MacMorran didn't appear to be entirely satisfied. "How do you account for that? You saw the other man, the one of your friend, Peter Steel."

Anthony watched carefully to see Stacey's reaction to MacMorran's question. But Stacey was unruffled and unmoved.

"I can explain that very simply, sir," he replied. "I'm not much of a one for newspaper reading. I don't get the time. As a rule, I content myself by just glancing at the headlines and the main items of news. And as a matter of fact, and also of interest, I should probably not have seen Steel's photograph if somebody hadn't called my attention to it."

"Who was that?" cut in MacMorran.

"A chap in our works. A man who knew Steel as well as I do myself."

MacMorran seemed fully disposed to accept the explanation that had been offered. Anthony therefore intervened again himself.

"That photograph—or rather those photographs that you've just examined and which you say mean nothing to you—would you be surprised to hear that they meant something to your old colleague, Steel?"

"Well, it's a peculiar sort of question, you must admit, but quite candidly and truthfully I should! Did they?"

Anthony nodded his assent. "They did. They meant so much to him that he came down here because of them. And he came down here you will note, Mr. Stacey, to his death."

Stacey spread out his hands with an air of resignation. "Well, as I said and I stick to it, you do surprise me. But of course there were many years that belonged to Peter Steel's early life concerning which I know nothing. Nothing whatever. To realize that will help you to understand my position."

Anthony nodded. "Yes, I realize that, Mr. Stacey, and I accept it as an eminently fair and reasonable statement. But I must be forgiven if I find myself forced to ask you one more question. I haven't *really* asked you it before. You are quite certain that you never saw the original of these photographs in Peter Steel's company anywhere?"

Stacey stared at him. "It's a point," continued Anthony, "that you *may* not have considered when you answered our previous questions. I must ask it because to neglect to do so would be unforgivable on my part."

But there was no shifting of Stacey's position. "No, sir. To the best of my knowledge and belief, I have never seen this man anywhere with Steel."

Anthony swung round to the two Inspectors. "I'm finished with Mr. Stacey, gentlemen. So that I'll retire and leave the field to you."

Kershaw signified his thanks. "I'd like to put at least one question. Do you know, Mr. Stacey, if Steel had any particularly close friends?"

Stacey answered with promptitude. "To my knowledge again, none. I never saw him with any and I certainly never heard him talk of any."

"What part of the country did he hail from? This end at all?"

Stacey laughed at the idea. "Not on your life, Inspector Kershaw. He was a Londoner, born and bred. Proper little Cockney, and no mistake."

Anthony smiled. "And I can subscribe to that, Inspector. I have no doubt whatever in my mind with regard to it."

This time Kershaw shrugged his shoulders. "Nothing seems to get us anywhere, does it?"

"I'm sorry about that," said Stacey, "if I could help you, I would."

"What was that address you mentioned?" interposed MacMorran. "Where Steel lodged. In Poplar somewhere."

"Number 3, Ullin Street."

"Thank you. I'll make a note of that." MacMorran did the necessary.

"And the landlady name is Mrs. Rogerson."

"Yes. I remember that," said MacMorran. He looked up at the others. "Like Mr. Bathurst, I'm through," he added.

"Right you are then, Mr. Stacey," said Kershaw. "I don't think you'll be wanted any more this evening and many thanks for the very timely assistance you've been able to give us."

Stacey put on his hat and overcoat and bade them all good night. "You can always get in touch with me at Smart's should you want to," he said, as he made his way out.

CHAPTER IV

I

ON THE following afternoon, Anthony had a surprise. He had decided to travel into Kersbrook by train and was on the platform at St. Mead when he ran into the spare, lugubrious figure of Alderman Wall. The Alderman, catching sight of Anthony, advanced towards him with outstretched hand.

"Good afternoon, Mr. Bathurst," he said, "you're abaht the lorst person I expected to see this afternoon."

Anthony smiled at the greeting. "What do I say in reply to that, Mr. Alderman? Should I apologize?"

"Not on your life, Mr. Bathurst. Poppin' in to Kersbrook? For a seat on the old pier?"

Anthony was a trifle startled at the words. "The two answers are 'yes' and 'no' respectively."

"Don't quite know what to mike of that," said the Alderman. "We're rawther prahd of our pier, you know, and I can't allow you to poke fun at it."

"Nothing," said Anthony, "I can assure you, was farther from my thoughts. To tell the truth, I've sampled the Kersbrook ozone, as supplied on the pier, more than once."

"I wish I could this afternoon," went on Wall, "but unfortunately I'm due at a Cahncil meeting. Nothing would please me better than to have a whiff of the briny. I was tellin' our Deputy Tahn Clurk that only the other day. You should 'ave 'eard him larf when I told him."

"I've never met him," said Anthony, somewhat at a loss for an appropriate reply.

"Brilliant feller," said Wall, "it 'ud do you good to know 'im. His name's Shorp. You should see 'is qualifications. I always say 'Shorp by name and Shorp by natcher.' But 'ere comes our trine, I fancy."

Alderman Wall's fancy proved to be well-founded and Anthony and he entered an empty compartment. The Alderman took a corner seat and proceeded to make himself comfortable. "It's only a short journey," he commenced with a smile, "but that's no reason why we shouldn't mike the best of it. I've no time for railway companies— they're only vested interests whatever you think abaht them—and they don't ply fair with either their employees or with members of the travelling public. Do as you would be done by has always been my motter."

He promptly put his feet on the opposite seat. Anthony made no reply. "Not interested in politics, Mr. Bathurst?"

"More perhaps in politics than in politicians," Anthony replied. But Wall was impervious to the shaft.

"Tell yer what, Mr. Bathurst," he went on unabashed, "you might care to come to the open Cahncil this afternoon. Sit up in the gallery. It's a sort of red-letter diy for us. It might give you a different opinion of us. But pr'aps the ordinary public gallery wouldn't be up to your mark. You'd be 'appier placed in the Distinguished Stringer's Gallery." He laughed at his own witticism. "Well, what do you siy? How abaht comin' along? As my guest."

Anthony smiled and shook his head. "It's very kind of you, Mr. Alderman, but I don't know that I—"

Wall interrupted him. "But I told yer. It's by wiy of bein' a special occasion. We're the recipients, this awfternoon, of a small pleasure-ground. A pork. It's bein' donated to us by a lidy. One of our residents—she's lucky enough to 'ave plenty of dough—is givin' it to the Cahnty Burrer of Kersbrook."

"One of the—er—capitalist class, I presume," said Anthony.

Wall nodded. "That's the idear, Mr. Bathurst. You've tumbled to it. It won't 'urt 'er—the gift. She's got plenty, as I said, she won't miss it. Come and 'ear one of our speakers. He's the goods, I can tell yer. Chairman of our Porks Committee. Alderman Bumstead. An able man, Mr. Bathurst."

"The name certainly has an unusual appeal, Mr. Alderman."

Wall cocked a wary eye at him. He was beginning to feel a little less sure of his ground.

"Who's the Lady Bountiful?" inquired Anthony. Wall's reply, when it came, took him completely aback.

"A Miss Ives, Mr. Bathurst, a Miss Drusilla Ives. Spends some part of every year in her house in this district. Very charmin' lidy. But 'ere we are, 'ere's Kersbrook."

The train stopped and Anthony followed Alderman Wall on to the platform. He was still attempting to assess at its true value the stroke of good fortune that had unexpectedly come his way.

"Do you know, Mr. Alderman," he said, "I'm more than half inclined to accept your invitation."

"Good," exclaimed Wall, "I'm dahnright delighted to think you've changed your mind."

"It's a privilege that we shouldn't accord entirely to the gentler sex, Mr. Alderman. I'm sure you'll agree with me in that."

Wall laughed good-humouredly. "Yes. I won't quarrel with you over that. It isn't worth tikin' a conveyance. It's only a little wiy to the Tahn 'All. I always walk up. I don't suppose you'll mind if I suggest you do the sime?"

"Not a bit," said Anthony, "only too delighted."

They walked down the station slope and up the High Street to the rather imposing red-towered Town Hall of the County Borough of Kersbrook.

"I'll tike you up to the Cahncil Chamber," volunteered his companion, "and then you can tike yer seat in the Public Gallery. Come along with me this wiy, will yer?"

Anthony followed the genially disposed Alderman. He could see that the Council Chamber was beginning to fill up as Wall directed him to the entrance to the Public Gallery. Herein, Anthony seated himself on a singularly hard-bottomed chair in the front row of many rows and behind a brass rail. Taking stock of his position, he saw that his only companions in the gallery were two elderly ladies of more than ample proportions and a thin, scrawny youth inflamed doubtless by devotion to citizenship (whatever that may be), with untidy hair which he regularly scratched enthusiastically and an unusually dirty nose. Evidence of this last-named condition was available to his near neighbours down the avenue of two senses.

Anthony leant over the brass rail at the front of the Public Gallery and noticed that by now almost all the seats within the Council Chamber were occupied. There was a hum of expectation in the atmosphere. That hum which to the sympathetic and understanding listeners is the unmistakable harbinger of the rise of the curtain. Anthony thought this immediately. He was right. For as he looked, the door of the Council Chamber opened and a harsh, strident voice announced in curt and businesslike tones, "Ladies and Gentlemen— His Worship the Mayor." Anthony watched the entrance of a small procession. It was headed by the Mayor in his scarlet robe of office and he was followed by the Town Clerk, the Mayor's chaplain and a slim, elegantly dressed woman whose smile and general demeanour were certainly things of beauty and might be possibly joys for ever.

The Mayor took his seat. His face was kindly and Anthony was favourably impressed with him. Then Anthony saw that the Mayor had risen from his seat and was addressing a remark (completely inaudible) to the Chaplain. The members rose to their feet and the Chaplain said two short prayers (also inaudible). When they were finished, the company sat down. The Mayor, however, remained standing and proceeded to say something further (still inaudible). But Anthony's ears just caught the last words of His Worship's concluding sentence. They were "Alderman Bumstead". Anthony, remembering Wall's eulogy in the train, prepared himself for the *bonne bouche* of the afternoon. He saw a small man with red hair rise from his place in the front row of the tiers of seats which formed a horseshoe shape round the Mayoral dais. This, no doubt, was the redoubtable Alderman Bumstead. He smiled round the gathering with an air of paternal benevolence and began to speak. Anthony was surprised with the quality of his voice. It possessed excellent tone-colour and his diction, enunciation and articulation were all distinctly good. It looked to Anthony at these first few moments of hearing and listening that Wall's praise of his colleague had not been ill bestowed.

"Mr. Mayor, Aldermen and Councillors," began Alderman Bumstead, "as Chairman of your Parks and Small Holdings Committee I can confidently state that this is a unique occasion—er—as far as Kersbrook is concerned. Quite frankly, I am unable to remember one quite like it. That is to say—er—as far as our Parks are concerned. We are met here today, this afternoon, to receive the gift of a pleasure-ground for the use of our burgesses and their—er—youngsters from a lady who by so making this gift establishes herself as a benefactor—er—benefactress to Kersbrook in the sense that—er—as far as our open spaces are concerned. Quite frankly, I feel, that just as upon occasion, as far as the Freedom of the County Borough has been concerned, we have conferred it upon certain citizens of distinction, for their services, or for their abilities or for their acumen, on this occasion Miss Drusilla Ives is conferring very much the same upon us. Because—er—that, quite frankly, is what she is doing. She knows our needs. She is conversant with the fact that Kersbrook is lamentably short of open spaces. Quite frankly, some of the people who sat in this chamber in days gone by were lacking in vision." Here he looked round the gathering and his small eyes glinted in appreciation of his own wit. "We, their successors, have made up a great deal of leeway—er—er—as far as that lack of vision was concerned. I can confidently claim that. No matter what Councillor Randall, of the other side, may be thinking."

Here Alderman Bumstead smiled sarcastically at a figure seated on the opposite side of the Council Chamber. "It is not the fault of my party if—er—Councillor Randall's lack of intelligence equals—er— quite frankly, his lack of personal charm. Still"—and here Bumstead waved a pontifical hand, "that is by the way." The Alderman drew himself up to his full height (to be exact about five feet two) and his voice pulled out the tremolo stop. "Mr. Mayor, we in Kersbrook have many municipal problems. Problems that we must get right down to and face up to."

Anthony shuddered at the physical picture thus presented. Had Bumstead taken it from Wall, or vice versa? "But quite frankly, Miss Drusilla Ives, our benefactress of this afternoon, is providing the solution as far as one of them is concerned. Our particular problem of providing sufficient open spaces for the burgesses of our Borough. Quite frankly, her help is accepted by us with both hands! With all our hands! We shall remember her generosity for many years after we ourselves are forgotten."

Anthony thought that this was a rather tall order. The little red-haired Bumstead was evidently either visionary or modest. But Anthony devoted himself to listening again. The Chairman of the Parks Committee was nearing the end of his address.

"In your name, therefore, Mr. Mayor, and in the name of the burgesses of this County Borough, I accept this gift of land from Miss Drusilla Ives, and I thank her from the bottom of my heart, for her public spirit and noble disinterestedness."

Bumstead beamed fatuously at his audience, looked round in all directions for applause and approval, smiled his customary oleaginous smile and bounced backwards into his seat again. The Mayor tapped with his gavel and the applause gradually subsided.

"I will now call upon Miss Drusilla Ives." He rapped again on the sloping desk in front of him. "Miss Ives."

Anthony, turning his head, saw a figure rise on the Mayor's left. It was the slim, elegantly dressed girl who had entered the Council Chamber with His Worship and the Town Clerk. So this was Drusilla Ives, the lady of his especial interest. She began to speak. Her voice was charming, her smile delightful and her manner all that the most exacting critics could have desired. She began by thanking Mr. Alderman Bum-Bum-Bumstead—yes, that was it, Bumstead—for his most kindly references to herself. It was far too generous of him. What she was doing was very simple and there was no need whatever for anybody to make a fuss of it. She wanted the good people of Kersbrook and St. Mead, parents and children, and particularly the children, to be happy! A nice park would help them to be that. Grass and swings and cups of cold water and flowers. What better thing could she give them with that object in view? So there it was, she had bought the piece of land and she gave it to them. That was all there was to it. She hadn't done anything out of the way really, although it was extremely nice of that dear Alderman Bum-Bumpus to say that she had. Whereupon Miss Ives smiled radiantly at everybody and resumed her seat.

A similar burst of applause greeted her address as had been evinced when Alderman Bumstead had spoken. A few other speakers followed. It would perhaps be more correct to state that other members of the Council took a great deal of time to contribute nothing, very badly, and almost, without exception, completely inaudibly. Anthony had taken careful stock of Drusilla Ives and, as far as he was able, continued to do so. She was still sitting close to the Mayor. Once or twice, Anthony caught the genial eye of Alderman Wall, who nodded to him with a kind of gay irresponsibility. Anthony formed the idea that, on the whole, Wall was deriving a certain amount of enjoyment from the afternoon's proceedings. Not a bad fellow—Wall!

From the items on the agenda which quickly followed one another, upon each of which Alderman Bumstead rose to speak "quite frankly" and, "as far as each one was concerned", Anthony was able to tell that the meeting had undoubtedly been called specially to deal with the Ives Gift and would have to run its course. Within the space of about ten minutes he noticed that Alderman Wall was gesturing to him. The gesture, upon closer examination, turned out to be a beckoning, so Anthony promptly made his way from the public gallery into the vestibule. Wall met him by the main door of the Council Chamber.

"We shall be finished in abaht a couple of minutes," he whispered confidentially, almost as though he were imparting a secret upon which hung the fate of mankind. "I'll tike you to the Parlour and introjooce you to His Worship and the others."

This was what Anthony had desired, though the direct course of his desire ran contrary to the Alderman's anticipation. "To whom?" said Anthony. "Who are the others?"

"Oh, to people that count, His Worship, as I said, Alderman Bumstead, and if you like, to the 'Lady Bahntiful' of the afternoon!" This was the name that Anthony had waited to hear. "Thank you,

Mr. Alderman," he replied; "you're kindness itself. I shall be pleased to come along with you."

Wall conducted him to the Mayor's Parlour. By the time they reached there, the main stream of people was leaving the Council Chamber.

"It's particularly generous of Miss Ives to mike this gift to Kersbrook," went on Wall, "and I'll tell you why. In the earlier part of the year she 'ad a stroke of bad luck."

"What was that?" inquired Anthony.

"She 'ad a burglary at her plice near Maidenhead. You know, up the river. Lorst some pretty valuable things, so I've been told."

"Oh, that is bad luck. What was the nature of the loss, any idea?"

Wall lowered his voice to a whisper again. "Chiefly, I believe, what the French would call objects de art."

Although Anthony was compelled to doubt the veracity of the last statement, he evinced a show of keen interest. "Really! That's most interesting. What particular form did they take? Do you know?"

Wall shook his lean head. "Sorry, but I corn't give you any details. Or anything loike chapter and verse. I did 'ear a bit at the time, but I've forgotten. But 'ere we are, Mr. Bathurst. I'll introjooce you to the Mayor. Don't suppose he'll be stoppin' overlong,—'e's on late shift this evening. Picks up his bus at the Promenade Garage abaht half-past five. Won't come 'orf till well past midnight. It's surprisin' he managed to get 'ere this awfternoon. Come on, I'll tike you up to 'im."

Anthony followed Wall to the little figure in the scarlet robes. Wall performed the introduction and the Mayor of Kersbrook shook hands with Anthony.

"Pleased to meet you, Mr. Bathurst," he said cordially. "I hope you enjoyed our little ceremony this afternoon?"

"Very much, Mr. Mayor. It was an eye-opener for me, I can assure you."

The Mayor half turned to the figure on his other side. "Here's somebody you might like to meet, Mr. Bathurst—and you, too, Mr. Alderman Wall. I don't think that you've met the lady before, you turned up on the stroke of time today, didn't you?"

Wall nodded an affirmative. "Miss Ives," continued the Mayor, "our good fairy of this afternoon, Mr. Alderman Wall of Kersbrook Council—Mr. Bathurst."

The lady extended her well-shaped hand in greeting. When it was his turn, Anthony murmured a conventional phrase. Drusilla Ives smiled a smile, both bewitching and flashing.

"I'm really delighted to meet you both," she said. "And I mean that. You, Alderman Wall, seem to convey the idea that there are many things which you and I could discuss with interest—your eyes tell me that—and as for you, Mr. Bathurst, I take it I'm addressing Mr. *Anthony Bathurst*—" She uptilted her eyebrows in interrogation and paused for Anthony's reply. He returned smile for smile.

"I plead guilty, Miss Ives. So spare the indictment. Blessed are the merciful, for—but you know the rest, Miss Ives."

Wall was watching her inquisitively, and he smiled to himself as she shook her head at Anthony's last remark.

"I assure you that I don't, Mr. Bathurst. What must you think of me?"

"I find it difficult to believe you."

"I don't really, Mr. Bathurst! I swear to you I'm telling the truth. What is the rest of it? How does it go? Please tell me."

"'Blessed are the merciful, for they shall obtain mercy.'"

Drusilla Ives clapped her hands. "Oh, of course! I remember now. It's from *The Merchant of Venice*—Portia's speech. I do think Shakespeare was wonderful, don't you, Mr. Bathurst—and you, Mr. Wall?"

A surprised Anthony thought that his agreement with the thought, even in the somewhat peculiar circumstances, was entirely justified. The Alderman considered it was time he said something.

"I brought 'im along this afternoon, Miss Ives, because I told 'im there was something special on the meanyou. I meant you. But I 'ad a job to persuide 'im I can tell you. Talk abaht obstinacy." Wall wagged his head with a hint at most extraordinary confidences.

Drusilla Ives affected mock displeasure.

"Don't tell me that I'm in the same category as things to eat."

Wall cocked his head to one side. "Well," he started, and then stopped, as though at a loss for words. Anthony cut in gallantly and on the Alderman's behalf.

"Could a man ever pay you a greater compliment, Miss Ives? When you come to assess it accurately?"

Drusilla's eyes danced. She thrust out a hand impulsively. "Perhaps you're right, Mr. Bathurst. Perhaps he couldn't. And that's very nice of you."

Anthony fell to a mental description of her. These are the details thereof. "Exceptionally charming voice, tall, willowy, graceful and refined. Definitely not 'brainy'. The eyes are normally slumbrous but they *could*, upon occasion, shine with pinpoints of excited light." Her movements were quick, alert and as graceful as her body itself. Anthony was able to see at once the art of the dancer. As he was musing thus he heard Wall's voice break in upon them.

"I must introjooce you to our Tahn Clurk. I'm sure the Mayor won't mind me doin' some of the honours. Brikes the work up a bit, if somebody gives a 'and."

Wall beckoned to the bewigged figure that had just entered the Mayor's parlour. "You've already met his brother, Mr. Bathurst. Or to be more precise 'is 'arf-brother. But 'ere 'e is, Mr. Bathurst—Mr. 'Umphrey Tresillian. You and the Tahn Clurk 'ave already met, Miss Ives, so I needn't introjooce you two."

The Town Clerk and Anthony shook hands. Anthony noticed the likeness between the Town Clerk of Kersbrook and his half-brother, Gilbert, whom he had met at the house of Neville Kemble. He estimated that Humphrey was a year or two older than Gilbert.

"Pleased to meet you, Bathurst," said the Town Clerk. "This is indeed a red-letter day in the municipal annals of Kersbrook which brings both Miss Ives and you into our Council Chamber. Sort of double event, eh? We are indeed honoured." He smiled, but Anthony was of the definite opinion that the smile was forced. The eyes flashed but the mouth was cynical.

"On the contrary," returned Anthony, "it is I that am honoured. I leave the lady to speak for herself."

"And she will," cut in Drusilla. "And she'll range herself with you, Mr. Bathurst. We'll both be extra-gallant for once, and cheerfully admit that an honour has been done to us, no matter, of course, what we may really think."

Miss Ives gurgled with laughter. Humphrey Tresillian's eyes swept over her a little more boldly than convention usually permits. Then he turned and spoke at Anthony through Alderman Wall.

"Do you know, Alderman Wall, I can't help wondering what it is that brings friend Bathurst into our midst. There's usually something, you know, behind these stormy petrels of crime and their adventurings."

"Well," said Wall, "yer wouldn't 'ave to think very 'ard, would yer? Knowing what yer do know?"

The Town Clerk pursed his lips. The action gave his face a slightly more boyish appearance. Then he let go a soft whistle. "Oh-h—I see! So that's the programme, is it? Bathurst, my boy, you're a dark horse if ever there was one."

Anthony shook his head. "I'm afraid that some of you gentlemen may be putting two and two together and making it five. Whereas you know—"

Humphrey Tresillian patted him on the shoulder rather paternally. "I understand, my dear boy—in fact we *all* understand."

At that moment Drusilla Ives led from trumps. "Mr. Bathurst," she said, "the Town Clerk has given me an idea! I scarcely realized when I first shook hands with you why you are down here. Of course—I'm beginning to wake up and see the light."

Anthony rallied her. "Don't forget, Miss Ives, what I've just said to these two gentlemen."

"You're not going to get out of it as easily as that," she countered, "even if you imagine you are."

Anthony glanced round and satisfied himself that the Mayor, Alderman Wall and the Town Clerk were in close conversation. "Do me a favour, Miss Ives," he said in a slightly lowered voice, "come back to 'Palings' with me as Neville Kemble's guest. Let me act as proxy. For this evening at least. You need have no qualms as to the acceptance of the invitation. Only a day or so ago Neville Kemble was singing your praises to me so thoroughly that he made me feel life was empty until I met you."

"Why do you ask me this?"

"Because—I must speak guardedly, I suppose—I feel that we may be able to help each other. I think that perhaps you'll be able to guess at what I'm hinting."

Miss Ives looked at him with an air of serious concern. "Do you happen to be actually staying at 'Palings' with Neville?" she asked pointedly.

Anthony grinned. "In the circumstances it would be useless my denying it," he stated frankly.

"Then I'll come," she said, "and I'll leave you to make the peace with our mutual host. Despite all you've said, I have my doubts." Anthony thanked her with a pressure of the hand and, as he did so, he saw Alderman Bumstead leering and peering and edging towards the small group of which he and Drusilla Ives were members. Anthony felt that this was more than he could bear, so he whispered to Drusilla not to take her eyes off his face in order that Bumstead might be deprived of the slightest glance from her which he could interpret in any way affecting him or affording him satisfaction. Drusilla played up well and Anthony saw Bumstead waddle by with a look of annoyance active on his heavy loose-lipped features. Anthony plucked Wall by the sleeve.

"Do you mind if I buzz off now?"

Wall said, "Not a bit. I'm coming myself. I didn't intend to stiy as long as I have. I'll come along with you—if I miy."

"Miss Ives is accompanying me, so you'll have to ask her. She's making her apologies to the Mayor now."

"But there's tea for her, before she goes. It's being served in the large Committee Room. Tea and cike."

"So there may be, Mr. Alderman, but she's coming along with me I tell you. I understand she's a special appointment or something. So you can't find it in your heart to blame her. Hang it all—she's just presented you with a park. What more do you want? You don't get parks given you every day of the week, you know." Anthony waited for Drusilla to finish her round of apologies within the Mayor's Parlour. On the whole it was a triumphant round for her. When she returned to Anthony's side, Wall was waiting with him.

"My chauffeur is waiting," she announced. "We'll go where we're going by car. Where do you want me to drop you, Alderman Wall?"

"That's very nice of you," he answered; "a few yards porst St. Patrick's Church. I'll tell your 'showfuer' when he comes to it."

"Come along then, gentlemen," she said brightly, "let's get cracking. I don't know what that really means, but I believe it's the correct expression."

Drusilla and her party moved out into the grounds of the Town Hall where her chauffeur quickly appeared and did the normal necessary. Wall took one of the seats with his back to the driver—facing Miss Ives and Anthony. The Kersbrook Alderman made himself as comfortable as possible. In accordance with his democratic principles, he was strongly attracted by anything in the nature of opulence. He eyed Anthony with a suggestion of incipient criticism.

"Well—and what did you think of Sid Bumstead?"

"May I answer that," asked Drusilla Ives with some show of eagerness.

Wall eyed her with a look of paternal benevolence. "Certainly, my dear lidy. Then I can hear Mr. Bathurst's opinion awfterwards."

"My reply will be one of very few words," snapped the lady. "I think that he's a nasty piece of work. I wouldn't trust him in the kitchen with my canary."

Wall grinned. "You know your own mind, lidy, don't you? But my question to Mr. Bathurst wasn't exactly bised on those lines. He knows that I meant Sid Bumstead as a speaker."

Anthony for once was blunt. "Do you want the truth? My plain, unvarnished opinion? Or do you want criticism dictated by counsels of courtesy?"

Wall spread out his hands. Drusilla noticed that they were not too clean, especially where the nails were concerned. "Now, Mr. Bathurst, I ask yer!" said Wall. "Surely you know me better than to put a query like that to me? 'Ave I ever demanded from you anything but the truth—and general sincerity?" He made another deprecating movement with his hands and then replaced them in their former position, on his knees.

Anthony laughed. "All right, then, if you feel like that about it, I'll give you my honest-to-goodness opinion. Shorn of frills and flounces. Your friend Bumstead has a voice of excellent quality. Far above the average. He's not been trained to use it to its best advantage, but hat's his misfortune probably much more than his fault. In addition, ne's always audible. A great asset in any and every speaker."

Wall nodded. It was evident to both his companions that the nod signified both approval and apprehension. "I'm glad," he announced, "very glad to hear you siy that and to know that you agree with me. Because we're a bit prahd of old Sid in the Cahncil Chamber."

"Ah—but hang on for a moment," returned Anthony, "you haven't heard the rest yet. Because that's as far as I'm prepared to go with you. You've had the sugar, the pill is to follow."

Drusilla nodded this time—in full support of Anthony's statement. "In all other respects connected with the speaker's art," continued Anthony, "your friend Bumstead falls lamentably short."

"Of course he does," echoed Drusilla. "Please don't tell me that Alderman Wall thinks otherwise, because I have too high an opinion of his judgment to believe that. But go on, Mr. Bathurst, I interrupted you."

Anthony obeyed the lady. "Well—I haven't a great deal more to say and I'll gloss over such minor matters as mispronunciations. I need not point out, for instance, that almost every word he used of three syllables or over was mispronounced. No, I was just thinking of the all-important condition of fluency—the be-all and end-all of every aspirant to oratory. To be fluent there must be a regular supply of both ideas and words. And quite frankly," and here Anthony's eyes twinkled, "as far as your worthy Alderman is concerned, he just doesn't fill the bill. He just hasn't got it."

Wall shook his head. "You're hypercritical, Mr. Bathurst. But here's St. Patrick's Church, so I'll bid you good-bye. Thanks for the lift, Miss Ives."

"And thank you, sir," said Anthony, "for an invitation which for me has ended up so propitiously. I am in your debt much more than you can possibly imagine."

"Don't mention it," said Alderman Wall curtly, as he alighted.

II

Neville Kemble endorsed to the hilt all that Anthony had told Drusilla. "My dear Drusilla," he said, when Anthony delivered her into the lounge at 'Palings', "I assure you that I should have been excessively annoyed if you *hadn't* come! In fact, Bathurst would have remained unforgiven for all time."

"Thank you, Neville," said the lady, "and for once I believe you. Don't tell me that I've arrived just in time for tea."

"That's just what you have done, and in addition there are buttered muffins. Touched with just a soupçon of anchovy sauce. My memory tells me that they should make an instant appeal. But why on earth didn't you tell me that you were due in Kersbrook this afternoon? I regard your failure to advise me as the worst example of low cunning that has ever come my way."

Drusilla laughed high-spiritedly. "Well, I had no intention of staying and I just didn't bother to bother you. Also I didn't tell the Stainsbys. Elizabeth will be simply furious if she ever finds out."

"That's a good one," returned Neville Kemble, "one right out of the bag."

"Oh—and why's that, may I ask?"

"For the best of all reasons," replied her host; "she and her illustrious sire are due here for afternoon tea. Which, being interpreted, means they should be in our presence within the next quarter of an hour. But what I can't understand, Bathurst, is how *you* come to be on in this act. I wasn't even expecting you. I understand that you intended to—"

But Drusilla cut in without ceremony. "Never mind that. Mr. Bathurst can explain all that later. He's a man that can explain anything. What I'm concerned about is making my peace with Elizabeth and Kenneth when they come. That will exercise all my ingenuity."

"Drusilla," said Neville Kemble, "you have only yourself to blame." He spoke with mock severity.

"That's all very well," replied Drusilla, "but blaming yourself, such as you suggest, and no matter how meritorious the effort may be, won't put me right with Kenneth Stainsby. Which is what is worrying me at the moment."

She looked a little sullen, but Anthony, when he saw her expression thought that it made her even more attractive.

"Some time during tea, Miss Ives, or just afterwards," he said to her, "I'm frightfully anxious to ask you one or more questions. I do hope that you'll see your way to answer them."

"Heaven help the man!" exclaimed Drusilla. "He orders me here against my will merely to ask me questions! Did you ever hear the like? Me! Who has always simply loathed being interviewed."

Before Anthony could frame the words of a reply, there came the entrance of the Stainsbys.

"Drusilla," cried Elizabeth as she went and embraced her, "by all that's wonderful! And we never even knew that you'd be here! Just the last person in the world. I simply must hug you before Kenneth does."

Drusilla looked the girl up and down. The look was not devoid of affection. "Elizabeth," she said, "you mustn't blame me, I didn't know that I was going to be here myself."

Kenneth Stainsby advanced towards her. "This is a glorious surprise, Drusilla. I must echo what Elizabeth has said, lame though it may appear to be. I knew that you'd be in Kersbrook, but I understood from Tresillian, Humphrey Tresillian, that you weren't staying beyond the ceremony, but scurrying straight back. I presume that something caused you to change your plans. Lucky old Neville."

"Even then, Kenneth," retorted Drusilla Ives, "you *could* have come to Kersbrook to see me if you'd really wanted to. Actions, you know, my dear Kenneth, speak louder than words. Even than your words."

"My dear lady," countered Stainsby, "even the delights of seeing you would not compensate me for the horror of the Kersbrook Council Chamber. Be reasonable, Drusilla."

Neville Kemble's voice interrupted them. "Now, you people, stop verbal wranglings and apply yourselves to my best China tea and buttered muffins. You'll enjoy yourselves better, believe me."

Anthony, Drusilla and the two Stainsbys drifted over to the table. "Seriously, though," continued Kenneth, "you have changed your plans, haven't you?"

Drusilla mocked him, a buttered muffin poised daintily between her fingers. "Oh, dear, it's already got to 'seriously, though'—"

Kenneth Stainsby came again. "You must have done."

"Not necessarily," she countered lightly; "there is another possibility. They might have been changed for me. Did your great mind stop to think of that?"

Stainsby laughed. "Since when has Drusilla Ives sunk so low that she permits other people to influence her decisions? Don't tell me that she's developing an inferiority complex, because if I am told that I shall point blank refuse to believe it."

Drusilla grimaced at him. "All right then, prepare yourself for a shock. Because you've got one coming to you. My decision to come to tea with Neville this afternoon was entirely due to Mr. Anthony Bathurst. Verily—he persuaded me. I won't say *against* my will exactly. I mustn't give him too much credit. It'll mean that I'm presenting him with ideas."

She beamed at Anthony across the table. Anthony responded to her at once. There was warmth about her, and her grey eyes, wide set, looked out at him from beneath a smooth brow. Now that her outdoor clothes had been discarded, Anthony saw that she was dressed entirely in grey with a superb simplicity that merely enhanced its expensive worth.

"You're paying me a most rare compliment, Miss Ives," he stated. "I think it's the first time during the whole of my commonplace career that an attractive woman has publicly admitted that she has allowed me to influence her. I shall regard the admission as one of my greatest triumphs."

"Don't quite know how to take that," replied Drusilla; "fancy it must be double-edged somewhere. Still, it comes to this, Kenneth can shut up about it. He probed and probed and now that he's exposed the nerve of truth, he doesn't recognize it (which of course is exactly what one—knowing Kenneth—would expect) and starts flinging accusations."

The grey eyes were full of banter as she delivered the shaft, and Anthony could see that Elizabeth Stainsby positively enjoyed the conversational give-and-take which was going on between her father and Drusilla Ives. He formed the opinion that it was a usual and ordinary interchange between them. Kenneth Stainsby made a little bow to his opponent.

"All right, Drusilla," he said. "You win—as always. I concede you unconditional surrender. And there's only one more thing I feel I'd like to say." He turned to Anthony. "You'll have to give me a course of instruction, Bathurst. 'The Taming of the Dru.' Please tell me that the terms will be moderate, because I'm a comparatively poor man, you know. But of course, Drusilla wouldn't understand that."

He grinned as he spoke and his pink, round, clean-shaven face rippled into the inevitable creases. Much small-talk ensued in which Neville took a hand, and the last cup of tea had been drunk and the last muffin eaten before Anthony was able to get those few words he wanted with Drusilla Ives, in quietude. He piloted her to the library and found her a comfortable chair.

"You promised to answer one or two questions I want to ask. May I start now?"

Drusilla nodded. "Aren't you being frightfully mysterious? You're rousing in me a tremendous flame of curiosity. What are they?"

"They're to do with that burglary at your Bray residence. Back in May wasn't it?"

Drusilla nodded again. "Quite right. Five months ago. But what on earth has resurrected it? I'd almost forgotten all about it. The police have failed to catch my burglars so I'd written off the losses, shrugged my shoulders, and made up my mind to make the best of a bad job. Now you come along nearly five months afterwards and remind me of something I'd much rather forget. Do you have to—or is it that you're just nosy? Tell me the worst at once, please. Because I'm an impatient person at the best of times."

Anthony smiled at the way Drusilla had put things. "How do I look? Abashed?"

"No, you don't, but you ought to. And that fact doesn't make me feel any better, I assure you."

"I'm sorry to disappoint you. And I had so wanted to make a good impression. Still, I'm resurrecting the affair, using your own word, for an excellent reason. It's on the cards that the last word hasn't been spoken about it. But tell me, you lost some valuable articles, didn't you?"

Drusilla explained. She gave Anthony certain details of the robbery. "I wouldn't say that they were frightfully valuable," she concluded; "my association with them was rather more sentimental than anything else. Most of them had been the property of the uncle who left me all his money and, by so doing, revolutionized my little world. That was the main reason why I was sorry about my loss."

Anthony lowered his voice a little. "Don't be too alarmed at my next question. Had you ever discussed at any length with anybody here at St, Mead these valuables your house at Bray contained?"

Drusilla remonstrated. "But they weren't valuables, I tell you! Intrinsically, they wouldn't have fetched—"

Anthony stopped her. "Well then, we won't say valuables—we'll merely say articles. Had you?"

"Discussed them? With anybody in this district? Now, my dear Mr. Bathurst, do you seriously expect me to remember—"

Again Anthony cut in. "Please remember what I said. I said 'discussed at any length'."

"I see. Yes, I suppose that does make a difference." Then her thoughts seemed to strike off at a tangent and she stared at him fixedly. "Mr. Bathurst," she said, "fair's fair and sauce for the goose, etc. Let me ask you a question. I understood by implication that you were down here because of the two murders in Ebford's field. Are you?"

"I won't contradict that idea of yours, Miss Ives. Does it matter—very profoundly?"

"Does it matter?" she echoed indignantly. "Is my commonplace little theft at Bray, many miles from here, to be entangled with two horrible murders?"

"If it is we shan't be able to disentangle it, shall we, Miss Ives? Nothing that we may do will affect the main issue."

Again she stared at him. "One thing, you're direct," she said, before falling into contemplation. "I see," she added after a time and almost to herself under her breath. For a moment or so there was silence.

"Well?" prompted Anthony eventually. "Can you answer my question?"

"Discussed at length. They were the terms, I think. Well, yes—I can answer it, and I will answer it."

But Drusilla hesitated again. Some seconds elapsed before she brought herself to continue. When her answer did come, she spoke haltingly.

"I'm probably going to surprise you, Mr. Bathurst," she said, "but I'm a little handicapped. You see, I don't know altogether what's in your mind—I may guess—but if I do that, I'm only able to guess at part of it, I can't guess *all* that you're thinking or imagining. Well," she paused and then went on again, "I'm putting this very badly, I'm afraid, but the knowledge that I have doesn't leave me devoid of worry or anxiety. I do hope you see what I'm trying to say."

Anthony nodded. He intended the nod to convey sympathetic understanding.

"Well then," continued Drusilla Ives, "I'll play fair with you and tell you what you want to know. And it's by way of being a coincidence. The man who knew most about my possessions in the house at Bray—those that were left to me by my uncle—was Humphrey Tresillian, the Town Clerk—the man you met this afternoon in the Council Chamber at Kersbrook."

Drusilla looked prim and folded her hands in her lap. There would be no point in failure to record that Anthony was surprised. The name she had given to him was certainly one that he hadn't expected.

"Humphrey Tresillian, eh? The Town Clerk of Kersbrook?"

"None other, Mr. Bathurst. But you can set your mind at rest on the point. You'll never make me believe that Humphrey Tresillian is a modern 'Raffles'. Because I shall simply refuse to accept such a monstrous absurdity."

Anthony smiled reflectively. "A myth?" he quoted, "a phantom? An up-to-date Jack o' Lantern invented subconsciously by the police?" He rubbed the ridge of his jaw with his forefinger. "Knowing what I know, Miss Ives, of the dark corners of crime—and my knowledge, I assure you, is far from meagre—I don't feel that I can accept with equanimity your description 'monstrous absurdity'. What about Canon Lazenby of Melchester Cathedral, who made it a practice to steal half-crowns—and half-crowns only—from the offertory box? A kink, undoubtedly, but he did so, nevertheless."

"Yes, I remember the case well." Drusilla pursed her lips. "But he's only one. One swallow doesn't make a summer, Mr. Bathurst. You don't need me to remind you of that."

"That's very true, Miss Ives. But are we looking for a summer? Wouldn't another swallow—to maintain your allusion—be much nearer the truth?"

"Perhaps you're right. But at any rate, if we're going to—"

At that precise moment Drusilla was fated to be interrupted. The person responsible for the interruption was Elizabeth Stainsby.

"Hullo, you two," she exclaimed, as she entered. "I'm ever so sorry if I'm breaking in on a *tête-à-tête*—I had no idea you were in here—but Neville wants his ordnance map of the Lodings. He's trying to convince Kenneth that there's no finer country in the south of England. Neville says it's in the bookcase here. Do you mind if I look?"

Anthony murmured a commonplace, and Elizabeth made play with Neville Kemble's bookcase and contents. Before she could find the map for which she had been sent, Neville Kemble also appeared.

"Haven't you found that, Elizabeth? You shouldn't have any difficulty—it's right in the front there. Or should be—unless anybody's had it. That's the worst of allowing people to . . ."

Neville broke off what he had been about to say and joined Elizabeth at the bookcase. When this happened, Anthony realized that his conversation with Drusilla Ives—*à deux*—might well be regarded as over. Which was a profound pity from his point of view, because it had just begun to be highly interesting. Then Neville Kemble found the ordnance map he was seeking and publicly proclaimed the fact.

"Here we are—what did I tell you? Knew it was there all right." He turned and included Drusilla and Anthony within the range of his conversation. "You two coming in the lounge again? Or going to stay in here? Looks to me like a conspiracy of some kind." He shook his head banteringly. "Don't like conspiracies. They're anti-social." Anthony looked at Drusilla meaningly. She rose at the look and they followed Neville Kemble and Elizabeth back into the lounge. Stainsby looked up as they went in.

"I've read this, Neville," he said, and the tone of his voice was argumentative, "but you'll have to go a long way before you convince me. There are parts of Hampshire, round the New Forest—near Brockenhurst to be exact . . . Oh, hullo, Drusilla, I didn't realize you and Bathurst had come back. I was too intent on pulverizing old Neville here. When he starts comparing districts and customs and dialects as he has been, he starts the ball rolling as far as I'm concerned, and usually finishes up by getting me all hot under the collar."

Anthony seized an opportunity for which he had been waiting for some time. "I wonder if I'd be forgiven if I sidetracked you a little. It was your mention of dialects, Stainsby, that started this particular hare."

Stainsby showed interest. "Ah—yes, Bathurst. What's the particular direction of the sidetrack? I'd be pleased to hear."

Anthony smiled. "I expect you would. But my query's in relation to our mutual friend, Alderman Wall. At whose very kind invitation I attended this afternoon's ceremony in the Council Chamber at Kersbrook. I take it, from his pronounced London accent, that he's not a native of these parts. Am I correct in the assumption?"

Stainsby and the other laughed wholeheartedly. Neville Kemble took it upon himself to supply the explanation to Anthony's question.

"You are, my dear fellow. Wall's a Londoner—born and bred. Cockney to the backbone. He retired down here, as a matter of fact, about nine years ago. He's a pensioned ex-employee of one of the big City printing firms. There was a little touch of romance, by the way, concerning the manner of his retirement. He and his wife had been spending a fortnight's holiday down here. One September, when they got back, and Wall returned to his daily job, one of the firm's bosses sent for him and to his utter consternation told him that his services wouldn't be required after the end of that week. Poor old Wall, he's told me this many times over, was completely flabbergasted. He managed to stammer out, 'Why, sir?' or words to that effect—and the boss told him that his health wasn't sound enough for further employment with them. Wall, of course, had visions that weren't far removed from Public Assistance, and went all of a dither, but the boss put on a friendly grin act and told him to pull himself together, things weren't as bad as they looked and that there'd be a pension of £3 a week for him until he shuffled off this mortal coil. Poor old Wall was so taken aback that he nearly chucked a dummy then and there. Anyhow, he went home, told his wife the news, and they came straight back to St. Mead, found a small bungalow and rented it. They've been here ever since, during which time Wall—always a keen 'Labourite'—has got himself elected on the Town Council, been made an Alderman, and also snaffled a J.P.'ship. Not such bad going in about nine years."

Neville Kemble pressed out the stub of a burning cigarette. "There you are, Bathurst, that's the story of Alderman Wall since he came to sojourn in St. Mead. I hope it satisfies you."

Anthony thanked his host for the information. "Thank you very much, Mr. Kemble. Your explanation gives me far more information than I had any right to expect. I'm a bit puzzled, though, at the close attention that the worthy Alderman pays to me. I can't quite make it out. He actually seems to seek my company."

"There's no accounting for taste," cut in Drusilla drily.

"Et tu, Brute?" retorted Anthony, as the company laughed at his discomfiture.

"I don't know, Bathurst," said Neville Kemble, "old Wall's not so bad when all's said and done. For example—take his crony—Alderman Bumstead. I infinitely prefer Wall to him. Bumstead's subtle. Wall's much more direct in his methods. If Wall were your enemy, he'd come into the open about it and avow it. But I doubt very much if Bumstead would. No," and Neville Kemble shook his head, "Bumstead, in my opinion, would work against you in the dark. I wouldn't trust Bumstead one inch. There are rumours, I might tell you, that Bumstead has designs on Parliament."

There came murmurs of incredulity. Drusilla put hers into words. "Never! Well, if that's so I'm a greater supporter of good old Guido Fawkes than ever. I've always had something more than a sneaking regard for him. If that is the kind of man that's decorating Westminster—well, all I can say is—no wonder we are where we are."

Neville Kemble chuckled. "I'll tell you a little anecdote about Bumstead that may amuse you. I didn't get it second-hand—it happened with me personally—so that I can vouch for the truth of it. In February of this year I ran into Bumstead one morning. I'd gone into Kersbrook for something—forget what it was now—and I walked into Bumstead in the road which leads down to the pier. It was raining hard—coming down cats and dogs, as they say—and this was about the fourth day of its kind we'd had in succession, so I playfully remarked to Bumstead, after we'd bade each other good morning, 'I observe that Dame February is up to her time-honoured occupation of filling-dyke.' Well, what do you think Bumstead's reply was?"

Stainsby said, "No idea." The others, appealed to, shook their heads. Neville Kemble chuckled again before he satisfied them.

"Bumstead said, 'I couldn't say, I haven't seen the papers this morning.'"

There were roars of laughter, and Elizabeth very nearly doubled herself up. "Tell me," said Anthony, "what is friend Bumstead by calling, profession, trade, or occupation?"

Neville Kemble replied at once. "He's a florist. Locally. He has no less than three shops in the district and its vicinity. They're all flourishing, too! Oh, he's very comfortably breeched. Bumstead has a keen and lively sense as to how to butter his bread, believe me."

"I presume he holds the seat in the Labour interest?" asked Anthony.

"You bet he does. No other ticket would stand a dog's chance in the Shrubbery Ward which he represents."

"Has he ever actually contested an election?"

Kemble nodded. "Yes. One. About nine years ago. Just about the time Wall arrived for permanent residence. Soon after that—to use Bumstead's own grandiloquent phraseology, 'he was raised to the Aldermanic Bench'. Of course it's a travesty of terms—an 'Alderman', as the name indicates, should be a man that's 'senior', but the Kersbrook Council's a law unto itself in that respect. I've known an Aldermanic appointment going to a man or woman with less than two years' service—if it suited the book of the Party in power to promote him. I tell you, my dear people, we've a democratic Government functioning in Kersbrook."

Anthony rose to make his departure. "Well, I'm sorry I have to leave you. But I've an appointment with Inspector Kershaw, and I mustn't keep him waiting. Expect me back about half-past ten this evening." He walked over and shook hands specially with Drusilla Ives. "Good-bye, Miss Ives. To employ Alderman Wall's term, I shall always regard this afternoon as a red-letter date. Perhaps I shall have the pleasure of seeing you again one day and in the not too distant future, I hope. And who knows—I may be able to pass on some interesting information to you."

"I echo your suggestion, Mr. Bathurst," replied Drusilla, "and I've a strong idea that you're a young man who usually keeps his hand to the plough once he's put it there. And in addition to all that, I'm delighted to have met you."

Anthony waved gaily to the Stainsbys and made his way out.

III

Anthony found MacMorran in Kershaw's company. He hadn't expected to, when he set out, but he was by no means displeased with the fact. The two inspectors had been discussing the visit of Stacey. After a few moments' conversation, MacMorran turned to Anthony and made an announcement.

"I've come to one decision, Mr. Bathurst, while I've been talking things over with Inspector Kershaw here—and that's this. I'm going up to Ullin Street, Poplar, to have a look at Steel's lodgings and a little chat with his landlady, Mrs. Rogerson. I can't afford not to. I'm going up there tomorrow. Would you care to make the journey with me?"

Anthony nodded. "There's nothing I should like better, Inspector. A great deal of the difficulty which has beset us in this case has its origin in the fact that we know nothing whatever of Victim No. 1 and precious little of Steel—Victim No. 2. Any chance that comes our way of repairing this condition mustn't be neglected. It's more than feasible that there were many points about Steel which Stacey didn't know, and never would know. A visit to the place where Steel lived may give us something."

Anthony looked across at Kershaw. "Tell me, Inspector," he said almost casually, "what sort of chap is your Town Clerk, Mr. Humphrey Tresillian?"

Kershaw looked a little surprised at the question. "Mr. Tresillian?" he repeated. "Why, a very nice gentleman as far as I know. Quite a decent bloke. Got a good name wherever you go. I've never heard a whisper against him. I'd go as far as to say that he's the most popular Town Clerk that Kersbrook's ever had."

"I see. For about how long has he held his present appointment?"

The Inspector made a mental calculation. "Just on ten years, I should say, when the old Town Clerk died. He came here from a place in the Midlands. Warwickshire, I fancy—from memory."

"Was his brother here, then, before he came?"

"Mr. Gilbert Tresillian, the solicitor? Oh yes, he had quite a lucrative practice here before his brother was appointed. No doubt he had more than a finger in the appointment pie. At least, that was the general impression in the town at the time."

Anthony nodded his understanding. "Yes, and I can see the general effect the appointment would have here. It seems to me that the two brothers between them would almost control the entire legal business of the town. What didn't come before Humphrey down the avenue municipal would be presented to brother Gilbert through the channel ordinary. Quite a good stroke of business for both of them."

Kershaw grinned in appreciation. "Yes, and I should say, too, that's how it has worked out in practice. Both the Tresillians are the possessors of more than comfortable incomes."

"Interesting," replied Anthony, "very! Still, the job's done and what's done can't be undone. Or so 'tis said." He swung round to MacMorran. "What train tomorrow, Andrew?"

"Early, Mr. Bathurst. As early as we can get away in comfort. There'll be no lying in bed for you tomorrow if you're coming with me. 9.33 out of St. Mead."

"H'm," returned Anthony. "That means breakfast at half-past eight. Not a minute earlier. All right, Andrew . . . expect to see me at the breakfast table."

The two inspectors waved to him as he left them.

IV

Anthony and MacMorran made inquiries at the terminus and acting upon the information received made Bromley-by-Bow their next destination objective. From there they walked to Ullin Street. On their walk to the lodgings of the late Peter Steel they passed two lorries bearing the name and inscription of "Charles Smart's Oil-cake Factory". As they encountered the first of these, Anthony caught hold of MacMorran's sleeve and called his attention to it.

"There you are, Andrew," he said, "we're warm at least. We are in the parts that knew Peter Steel and now know him no more."

MacMorran's reply was a grunt. After a brisk walk they came to Ullin Street and knocked on the front door of No. 3 thereof. Of the little girl in the bright pink frock who answered the summons, MacMorran made inquiries for Mrs. Rogerson. The little girl looked, said nothing, hung her head, put her finger in her mouth, and then incontinently fled.

"Good start, Andrew," said Anthony laconically; "let's hope she'll be relieved by Mrs. Rogerson herself."

Anthony's hope was fruitful. For a moment later a thin, pale-faced woman with black hair and brown eyes and a troubled expression on her face came to the door, with the pink-frocked child clinging to her skirts.

"Who is it wants me?" she asked, in a colourless, high-pitched voice. When she heard the Inspector's explanation her face cleared. "Please come in," she said. "I've been expectin' you. Now mind, please, Myrtle, and do get out of my way. And don't be a silly girl. The gentlemen can't pass if you stand there like that."

Myrtle "minded", and MacMorran and Anthony followed Mrs. Rogerson into the "best room". They were invited to sit on green plush chairs. Mrs. Rogerson went on talking.

"Ever since Mr. Stacey come and told me the dreadful news about poor Mr. Steel, I guessed some of you gentlemen 'ud be comin' along to look his things over. Don't touch that fern, Myrtle."

Myrtle, however, did touch it and for her pains was pulled back unceremoniously to her mother's side.

"What we want to do," went on the Inspector in further explanation, "is to have a look over Mr. Steel's rooms. There will be no difficulty about that, will there?"

"Oh no, sir! Only too pleased, I'm sure. I'll take you up to his rooms right away, sir, if that will suit you. Mr. Steel had two rooms here, sir. And no woman could 'ave wished for a better lodger. He didn't give no trouble at all, sir. He 'ad a bedroom—my small back-bedroom and another room that he used as a living-room."

"Before we go upstairs, Mrs. Rogerson," said Anthony, "I wonder if you'd be good enough to let me have a little information. With regard to Mr. Steel's habits."

"Only too pleased, sir. Myrtle, will you let Mummie's fern alone? I shan't tell you again."

Myrtle, who had made temporary escape from her mother's skirts, looked up fearfully from the forbidden fern and returned to them. Mrs. Rogerson looked at Anthony. "What was it you wanted to ask me about, sir?"

"Your Mr. Steel—did he have any visitors here?"

"The only what you might call 'regular' was Mr. Stacey from the oil-cake factory. 'Ardly anybody else ever came. Nobody I could name, as you might say."

"Nobody at all—eh?"

Mrs. Rogerson became meditative. "Well," she answered at length, "perhaps there's one thing I might tell you. And that's this. A woman come 'ere for Mr. Steel about a month ago. But I never set eyes on 'er again. She only came that once."

Anthony glanced across at MacMorran. "About a month ago, you say? A woman? What was she like?"

"Ordinary. Stoutish. Red-faced. About Mr. Steel's own age, I should say. Not a young party by any manner of means."

"Was he in when she called?"

"Yes, sir. She called one evening. About the beginning of September, I fancy it was. Perhaps more like the end of August."

"Was he expecting her, would you say?"

Mrs. Rogerson shook her head decisively. "Oh no, sir. And I can tell you that for positive. Because as she went upstairs to his room I 'eard 'im say, 'What—you! . . . Well, this is a surprise.' Or words to that effect, sir."

"How long did she stop?"

"A couple of hours, I should think—or thereabouts. Come about seven and went between nine and ten."

"Did he go out with her when she went away?"

"No, sir. I'm pretty certain I 'eard 'er come down the stairs and go out by herself."

MacMorran came in with a question. "Was she a Londoner in your opinion, Mrs. Rogerson?"

"I couldn't say, sir. I didn't see enough of 'er to answer that."

"But didn't you hear her voice? Didn't she speak to you, or didn't you hear her speaking to Steel?"

Mrs. Rogerson shook her head. "No, sir. The only thing she said to me was to ask me if Mr. Steel was in. That was when she knocked. I answered the door, you see. And I didn't notice anything particular about her voice. It was just ordinary-like."

"And she only called on Steel that once?"

Mrs. Rogerson nodded. "That's all, sir."

"Did you ever hear him refer to the visit—in any way at all?"

"No, sir. But there's not a lot of importance in that. Because Mr. Steel was never one to talk, sir. He'd never talk much about anything. He kept himself very much to 'imself—I can tell you."

Anthony turned and smiled at MacMorran. "Well, none of that gets us very far, Inspector, does it? Despite all our efforts."

"No, Mr. Bathurst," replied MacMorran, "it certainly does not. I suggest that Mrs. Rogerson shows us round upstairs."

"I'll be very pleased to, sir," said that lady. She turned to the now passive Myrtle and issued instructions. "Now, Myrtle, you go into the kitchen and sit on your little chair while Mummie goes upstairs with these gentlemen. I shan't be very long, so you sit down quietly like a good girl, and don't touch anything. Run along now. Oh—and if the kettle boils over be sure to call out and tell me."

Myrtle made her unwilling way to the kitchen, and Mrs. Rogerson prepared to conduct her party of two to the rooms which had been Peter Steel's. She opened a door at the top of the landing.

"This was his living-room, sir," she said to the Inspector, "just as it was when he left it for the last time."

Anthony felt a wave of disappointment pass over him when he saw the room and its contents. There were a round table, one armchair and one small chair of the bentwood variety. The room had a small fireplace, one equally small fender, two pictures, a faded carpet and a black long-haired rug in front of the fireplace. Beyond these articles, it contained nothing.

"Did Steel have his meals here, Mrs. Rogerson?" inquired Anthony.

"All except his midday meal, sir," came the answer, "he used to get that at the factory canteen. I just used to lay his cloth and then bring him up a tray with everything on it. It was quick and tidy and, well, that's how he used to like things."

MacMorran shook his head at the blank prospect the room displayed. "Nothing here, Mr. Bathurst, not a glimmer. Bare and empty of everything. Let's pass on to the bedroom."

Mrs. Rogerson led the way to the other room which Peter Steel had occupied. When she opened the door, it looked to be as meagrely furnished as Steel's living-room. But Anthony's eyes detected a small box on a rickety-looking table that stood by the side of the iron bedstead. In size it was about 12 inches by 6, but the wood of its composition looked good and durable. Mrs. Rogerson saw that Anthony had noticed it.

"Yes, sir," she said, by way of explanation, "if you're thinkin' that that box was Mr. Steel's property, you're quite right. It was. But there's nothing in it of any value. I've looked. Not for myself, sir, or even out of idle curiosity. If there had been anything in it, I was going to 'and it over to Mr. Stacey. That was my idea, sir. All that's in it is an old envelope. Look for yourselves—I'd like you to—and you'll find out that what I say is right."

Mrs. Rogerson's face flushed a little as she made her last statement. MacMorran walked over to the table and opened the box. That is to say, he lifted the lid. Inside, and in verification of Mrs. Rogerson's statement, lay an envelope. Of foolscap type and bearing the discoloration of age. It was open. That is to say the flap was not sealed. It was obvious that it had never been sealed. The Inspector pulled up the flap edge and shook out the contents on to the rickety-looking table. A document, cream coloured, fluttered out. MacMorran picked it up, and Anthony looked over his shoulder to see what he had come upon. He soon saw that the Inspector was looking at a birth certificate.

"I'm not unduly surprised," said Anthony. "I had an idea it would be a birth certificate of somebody. Whose is it?"

"His own," replied MacMorran. "Born at North Mimms in Hertfordshire, 57 years ago. October the 27th. Father, George Steel, wheelwright; mother, Louisa Mary Cornell. His own name, Peter Lindsay Steel. He evidently set a high value on his birth certificate, the way he looked after it."

Anthony extended his hand. "Let me have a look at it, will you, Andrew?"

The Inspector handed over the birth certificate. Anthony looked it over carefully. Then he handed it back to the Inspector, who replaced it in the envelope. Anthony took a tour round the bedroom.

"What other possessions did Steel have, Mrs. Rogerson? Didn't he have any other clothes?"

Mrs. Rogerson nodded towards a wall-cupboard in one of the corners of the room. "In there, sir. 'Anging up. You'll find an old blue navy serge suit, some collars, a clean shirt, two ties, one black, some socks and handkerchiefs, a little underwear, much the worse for usage, and a pair of old black shoes. I think you'll find that's about the sum total of his belongings, sir. But as I said to you just now, 'ave a look for yourselves, gentlemen."

Again the white face of Mrs. Rogerson pinked a trifle. MacMorran walked to the cupboard door and pulled it open. The clothes which it disclosed were almost exactly as Mrs. Rogerson had described. The Inspector ran his hands through the pockets of the blue suit. He turned and shook his head at Anthony.

"Drawn blank again, Mr. Bathurst," he announced, "all of 'em empty. We seem to have done quite a lot of work to capture one birth certificate." MacMorran snapped his fingers with annoyance.

Anthony strolled over and looked into the cupboard. The suit was hanging on a hook. The other articles were scattered along a shelf at the top. He saw that the details of Steel's sartorial possessions, as supplied by Mrs. Rogerson, were substantially correct. Anthony examined the various articles of clothing. With one exception they had all seen their better days. This exception was the black tie. This, both to Anthony's eye and to the feel of his fingers, seemed to be comparatively new. He turned to the landlady again.

"Your Mr. Steel didn't buy many clothes, I take it?"

Mrs. Rogerson shook her head. "No, sir. He wasn't one to fling his cash about. I wouldn't say he earned a terrible lot—just enough, I suppose, to make both ends meet and put a bit by for a rainy day." Anthony held the black tie up in front of her. "This tie, Mrs. Rogerson? Have you any idea if it's a recent purchase?"

To his satisfaction, she nodded in the affirmative. "Yes, sir. It is. I can say that. Because I noticed 'im wearing it—two or three times, I suppose it would 'ave been. But he didn't keep it up."

"When would that have been? Any idea? When he wore it, I mean?" Mrs. Rogerson thought over the question. "About the end of September, I should think, sir. That wouldn't be far out."

"Thank you, Mrs. Rogerson."

"What are you thinking?" asked MacMorran. "That Steel bought the tie as mourning for somebody?"

"Yes, Andrew. Congratulations! That is exactly the idea with which I was toying. And I'd be inclined to go just a wee bit farther than you did."

MacMorran wrinkled his brows. "How do you mean?"

"Well—just this. Not mourning for just a 'somebody'. But for a close friend—and even, possibly, for a member of his own family."

"But he had no relations."

"That's only as far as we know. I wouldn't care to bank on it."

MacMorran rubbed his eyebrow. Anthony went on. "Let me develop my idea a little. I read Steel in this way. He was secretive. Kept himself to himself much more than most people. We find that trait popping up in all directions. Mrs. Rogerson, for instance, referred to it only a moment or so ago. Remember—I've met him and talked with him. Somehow, I can't see Steel putting himself to the expense of a new black tie unless it was for somebody pretty close to him. In short, I deduce a death, a funeral and the dead person, a relation of some sort. I wouldn't hazard any statement, however, on the degree of affinity."

MacMorran's answer came immediately. "And I think you're absolutely barking up the wrong tree. I'm convinced of it. *I'll* tell you who Steel bought his black tie for! And I'm surprised you haven't cottoned on to it before this. The first murdered man found in Ebford's field! To me that's very plain."

Anthony's reply was quiet. "I had thought of that possibility, Andrew. I discarded it. I *don't* think you're right. There *was* no funeral of *him*—in the normal sense that is. Personally, I should be astounded to hear that Steel attended *his* last rites and I'd lay at least a thousand to one against Steel buying a new black tie as a fragrant memory of him. Which, summing up, Andrew, means that you and I are in total disagreement."

MacMorran shrugged his shoulders. "All right. We must agree to differ, that's all."

As the Inspector was speaking, sounds of certain disturbances ascended from below. Mrs. Rogerson's face exhibited traces of anxiety. She went to the bedroom door and listened attentively.

"That's my Myrtle up to mischief," she said anxiously. "I mustn't leave her alone downstairs any longer. If you gentlemen would care to—"

The Inspector held up his hand in an attempt to allay her fears. "You pop down, Mrs. Rogerson. There's no need, as I see it, for you to trouble about us any longer. I think I can say with confidence that we've seen all there is to see. I don't know whether my friend agrees with me or not? What do you say, Mr. Bathurst? Are you desirous of staying?"

Anthony shook his head. "No, Andrew. I think I'm clear. And we'll let Mrs. Rogerson resume control over her wayward child. So lead the way downstairs, will you, Mrs. Rogerson? You lead the way and we'll follow."

V

Anthony travelled to North Mimms by bus. He got off at the terminus, glanced in the direction of the waters of the Mimram and walked towards the imposing-looking church that stood in its churchyard at but a moderate distance away. Anthony walked up the path which ascended from the street to the church itself. He had come to Peter Steel's home with a definite purpose actuating him, and all that he asked for and hoped was that a reasonable measure of good-fortune might attend his efforts.

When he came near to the church it pleased him still more. It was both noble and ancient. Optimistic always, Anthony tried the door of the church, found it open to his impetus and entered. To his disappointment the church was empty. He walked round its austerity and then decided to prospect again in the churchyard itself. He made his way out, therefore, and looked at the names carven on the older tombstones and memorials. He came across no name, however, which satisfied, or even reawakened, his curiosity or interest. He strolled round after this, to the south side of the building, and then within a few minutes there came to him his first stroke of good fortune. A tall lean figure, clad in a blue shirt and trousers of corduroy, came towards him, wheeling a barrow full of dead leaves, weeds, and uprooted grass. As this figure came abreast of him, Anthony smiled and said, "Good morning." The man addressed halted the wheel-barrow and put his finger to his cap.

"Good morning to you, sir. And a lovely morning at that." Anthony smiled again. "I wonder if you could help me," he said. The man lowered the handles of the wheelbarrow. "Depends on what help you would be requirin', sir."

Anthony proffered him his cigarette-case. "That's a very sensible answer," he said. "Have a cigarette."

The man with the barrow took a cigarette and carefully placed it behind his ear. "Thank you, sir. I'll smoke it later, if you don't mind. Vicar here doesn't care for me to be smokin' in the churchyard. Thinks it's a bit irreverent. So I never go against his inclinations."

"I understand," said Anthony smilingly, "and I suppose the good Vicar is right, I, for one, wouldn't run counter to his beliefs. No, I'll tell you about the little matter concerning which I was going to ask for your assistance. Have you been employed here for long?"

The man with the barrow straightened himself and placed his hands on his hips. "How old would you take me to be, sir? Have a good look at me before you answer the question."

Anthony took careful stock of the man. He looked at his head, the lines on his face, and at his neck. "Between forty-eight and fifty-five," he replied, after a moment or two's consideration.

The man laughed and there was a certain amount of self-satis-faction in the laugh. "I'm sixty-two come Martinmas. Reckon I've worn well—eh?"

"You have that," replied Anthony sincerely. "And that makes me about ten years out in my judgment. Well, anyhow, my congratula-tions. If you're sixty-two, you certainly don't look it."

"Thanks." The man grinned and showed a set of strong white teeth. "And I've worked here for the church nigh on forty-six years."

"Good," said Anthony, "in that case, then, there's a strong like-lihood that you can help me."

"Say the word, sir."

"The position's this. I'm anxious to trace a family by the name of Steel. In particular relation to a man named Peter Steel. Peter Steel would have been born in this parish when you were about five years old. Do you recall him at all?"

The man smiled approval and nodded his head. "You've come to the right shop. I knew Peter Steel. Bound to have in a small village like this was. I won't say I knew him well—but I certainly knew him. But you see, that five years difference in our ages made me getting on for a man, as you might say, when young Peter Steel was only a boy. And another thing he left here when he was round about sixteen. But I can't tell you where his steps led him to. His father was the village wheelwright, sir. Old George Steel—he'd been here years. He died in one of the influenza epidemics we had down here." He ran his fingers through his ruffled hair.

"That's the chap," said Anthony, "and I'm glad I've been able to trace him. But now tell me this. And this is the main point I'm needing information on, did that Peter Steel have a brother?"

The man in the blue shirt rubbed one of his eyebrows. "No, sir. He did not. You've drawn a blank there, sir. There was only one in the Steel family in addition to young Peter, and that was his young sister— Ada Steel. She was, I should say, about three years Peter's junior."

Anthony considered the possibilities of the gardener's answer. From his point of view, the balls hadn't broken too badly. He had hoped for a brother to appear, but although this hope had failed, the advent of a sister wasn't at all discouraging. A sister was certainly the next-best-thing. He therefore at once evinced interest.

"Ah," he said, "now that's most important. This sister—did you know her at all well?"

The man in the blue shirt possessed more than the average fund of intelligence. He smiled and shook his head slowly. "No. Not her. But *of* her. Quite well."

Once again Anthony felt that this was the next-best-thing. "Tell me," he said, smiling back. "Do you mind?"

"Well," said the gardener, "as I told you, young Peter Steel left the district when he was in his 'teens. But Ada, the sister, stayed on. After old George, her father, the wheelwright, came to rest in this here churchyard where you and I now stand. She stayed on with her mother, old George's widow. Until she married—and she was married, as you may well guess, in this here church." He smiled at Anthony again. "I was present at the wedding, so I ought to know. Couldn't say stronger than that, could I?"

"You couldn't! How long ago was that, now?"

The gardener rubbed his top lip with his forefinger. "About thirty-five year—near as a whistle." He paused and appeared to be engaged on an effort of recalculation. Then he nodded his head as though entirely satisfied with the result thereof. "Yes, that would be about it. Thirty-five to thirty-six year ago."

Anthony tried yet another shot. "Any idea whom Ada Steel married? Or is that testing your memory powers too highly?"

"Ada Steel married an American," came the reply. "And if I can't tell you his name, I know who can!"

"And who's that?" inquired Anthony.

"Why—my missus." The man's tone held the tinge of triumph. He proceeded to elaborate his previous statement. "My missus went to school with Ada Steel, and she's a proper walkin' encyclopaedia as to the various fellers the various girls married. She'll know. I haven't a doubt on it."

"And where can we find your admirable partner?" smiled Anthony again. "At any reasonable distance?"

"Down the hill, sir—and only a few yards from where the buses stop. But if you'll give me a matter of ten minutes or so, I'll walk down with you. I've just got these leaves to dump on the heap."

"I shall be only too delighted," replied Anthony.

The man lifted the handles of the wheelbarrow and trundled off to a distant corner of the churchyard. Anthony waited where he was for the gardener's return. Within a few minutes the man was back.

"That's all O.K., sir. I've seen to that little lot and left the barrow in the shed. And if you'll be so good as to come along with me, I'll take you down to my little place, and we'll have that word you want with my missus. This way, if you don't mind, sir."

Anthony followed the gardener out of the churchyard down the hill. As they walked, the man came at Anthony with a question.

"I haven't asked you anything yet, sir, but you've made me a bit curious. Only natural, too, I think. But I take it you've some good reason behind your visit here today and the questions you've put to me, so I'll ask you now. Has Peter Steel come into a legacy or something?"

Anthony shook his head. "A legacy of sorts, perhaps, but one that neither you nor I would run after."

His companion's eyes invited further explanation. Anthony supplied it. "He was murdered a few days ago at St. Mead and his body found in a field. Perhaps you saw some account of it in the daily Press?"

The man frowned in an effort of recollection. "I do recollect something of the kind, but I never connected it with Peter Steel of these parts. Was his name published?"

"Not yet. There hasn't been time. We've only just run it to earth. But there was a photograph of the murdered man published in all the daily papers. You may have seen it."

"I may have done. I fancy I did, now I come to think of it. But I certainly didn't recognize it as Peter Steel."

They had reached the bottom of the hill. "Here we are," announced the gardener. "Here's my little place. All on its own. Come round the back way with me."

Anthony took the hint and they went round to the back of the old-fashioned cottage which was evidently the gardener's home. A rosy-faced, broad-bosomed, comely woman stood in the scullery, her strong, sun-tanned arms deep in a wash-tub.

"Louie," said Anthony's companion, as they stopped at the door of the scullery, "here's a gentleman what's asked me a question I can't answer. But I've told him you can. So don't you let the family down, old girl—otherwise I'll stop you a week's wages."

"You'd better," replied the woman good-humouredly. "I don't know where you'd be if you did. I reckon you'd be the first to shout. But what's it all about first?"

Anthony raised his hat to her while her husband explained the circumstances of the visit.

"Well," said her husband, "it's like this—you remember the Steels, Louie? Old George Steel's family? Him that was the village wheelwright?"

"I do that. And I've got very good reason to. Two children George Steel had—Peter and his sister Ada. I knew Ada well. Went to school with her."

"I said you did. Told this gentleman so just now. Well—what he wants to know is this. Who did Ada Steel marry? I can't remember beyond he was an American, but I'm staking your reputation that you can."

The woman at the wash-tub smiled broadly. "Don't worry, Albert," she said. "I won't let you down. Ada Steel married a Yank. From New York itself. And I shall be able to think of his name in about two ticks. You just give me time."

She paused and bent over her wash-tub, her arms deep in the sud-water, to her elbows. Suddenly she straightened herself and looked up. "I've got it," she announced quietly, but decisively. "Elmer Oliver. That was his name. He'd be a year or so older than Ada herself. Oh—yes, I remember her wedding all right. I went to it and threw rice at the happy couple. Albert was there, too, but he took another girl, not me. That was in the days when he thought he was a bargain and hadn't made up his mind." She bent down and pounded the wash-board vigorously.

Albert winked at Anthony. "He made his mind up all right afterwards, though, didn't he? Still, that's neither here nor there as my old grandmother used to say, and what she didn't think of would have gone into a small ice-cream glass. You've got the information you wanted, sir, and my old dutch has been the means of passin' it on to you."

"She has," assented Anthony warmly, "and I'm more than ordinarily grateful for it. But if she doesn't mind, I'm going to ask her a few more questions, and I only hope she'll be able to answer them as readily as she answered your first one."

"I'll try, sir, I'm sure," replied the gardener's wife, genially.

"Good. Now this Elmer Oliver, bridegroom of Ada Steel, your old school friend—what was he like?"

The woman regarded him doubtfully. "It's a rare long time ago, sir. You're askin' me rather a lot, aren't you?"

Anthony nodded acceptance of her statement. "I know I am. But do your best. You won't find me exacting."

"Come on now, Louie," prompted the agricultural and admiring Albert, "don't let the old firm down."

"Give me a picture of him," said Anthony, "as you remember of what you saw of him the day he married Ada Steel."

"He was a little man. With not a lot of hair on his head, considering his age. A creased-up sort of face. Wore a lightish-grey suit with a pink flower of some kind in his buttonhole." She shook her head. "That's about all I can remember, sir."

"And not so dusty, either," exclaimed Albert with enthusiasm. "You're as good as Datas, himself, Louie, blow me if you're not." He turned to Anthony for adulation. "What do you think of that yourself, sir? The old girl's mustard, isn't she?"

"Your wife has certainly done remarkably well," responded Anthony. "And now I'd like her to take a glance at this."

He took out his pocket-book. From this he extracted a press cutting with a photograph (clean-shaven) of the man the finding of whose body had been the starting-point of the inquiry. The lady of the wash-tub dried her hands, took the piece of paper, her eyes wide-opened with the twin emotions of interest and curiosity. Anthony watched keenly to observe what her first reactions were. Eventually she gave her verdict. It was disappointing.

"I really couldn't say." She shook her head. "Really, I couldn't. You're wantin' to know, of course, is this a photograph of the man Ada Steel married? I only saw him that once, you must remember—and it's years and years ago. But I'll say this. It *might* be him! It's not *unlike*!"

Her eyes took on a far-away look as though she were endeavouring to remember something. While she was thus occupied, Anthony produced the second newspaper photo of the man he hoped was Elmer Oliver, complete with moustache.

"How about this one, then?" he asked as he handed it to her. When she saw it, and realized its difference, she smiled across at Anthony.

"I still couldn't say anything definite, but this is certainly much more like Ada Steel's husband as I remember him. I can't say *more* than that. That moustache makes a big difference and he did have a bit of a 'toothbrush' when he took Ada Steel to the altar."

She handed the newspaper-cutting back to Anthony and plunged her arms into her washing-water again.

"Thank you very much indeed," said Anthony. "I'm beginning to think you've been a great help to me. Now—don't say no—have a drink together this evening on me."

The gardener protested when he saw the note which Anthony had placed on the ledge at the rear of the sink. But Anthony would have none of his protestations, and when he left the cottage he felt that, on the whole, the time in North Minims had been well spent. For, in his opinion, it was "odds on" that the first body found in Ebford's field had been the body of Mr. Elmer Oliver.

VI

Anthony walked in on MacMorran and Kershaw that evening and remarked casually, "Oh, by the way, you chaps, I rather fancy I've identified the bloke that we've been in the habit of describing as Victim Number One."

The local Inspector looked incredulous, but MacMorran waved Anthony to a seat and accepted the statement with coolness and composure. "Who is he?" he inquired quietly.

"Elmer Oliver, once of little old New York, U.S.A., and—which is perhaps more to the point—brother-in-law of Peter Steel."

"But Steel wasn't married," burst in Kershaw.

"I know he wasn't," said Anthony; "but his sister Ada was. And I've talked to two people today who actually saw her married, which, dear comrades, can be regarded as evidence."

"North Mimms?" queried MacMorran.

Anthony nodded. "Yes, Andrew. At North Mimms I was lucky. I ran across a woman, a native, who proved to be a veritable mine of information. What I want you to do, Andrew, is to put a feeler across to the other side re Elmer Oliver, Esq., and after you've done that, to find out when Ada Oliver, née Steel, died. Which demise, I think you will find, occurred fairly recently."

"Why do you think that, Mr. Bathurst?"

Anthony shrugged his shoulders. "That's the only way in which I can account for her non-appearance."

"Non-appearance?"

"Yes. All that. Non-appearance in the cast. Scene—the home of Peter Steel. Peter Steel discovered. Enter Ada—long-lost sister. Scene Two. The home of the Olivers. Enter Peter Steel. And then, mark you, Andrew—exit Elmer Oliver, and by exit I mean that grand exit which is final. Venue Ebford's field. Followed by similar grand

and final exit of Peter Steel himself. But *no appearance,* my dear Andrew, no further appearance whatever, of Sister Ada, who surely had the best of reasons to appear at each of those exits. Or should we say 'exeunt'?"

"Seems to me," said Kershaw, "that this is going to be a long, tortuous job. And I feel far from confident about it."

For the second time that evening Anthony shrugged his shoulders. "I agree with your first opinion. But not necessarily with the second. And after all, Inspector Kershaw, what else can be expected? You've only just had your first victim identified! It's difficult to discover why 'X' may have murdered—say the Aga Khan—but much more difficult, believe me, to discover why 'X' may have murdered 'Monsieur X'. And that's the exact position we were faced with in this case."

MacMorran came to Anthony's assistance. "I agree," he said, "and I differ from you, Inspector Kershaw. As I see things, we're at last beginning to move forward into the light."

"Quite so," supplemented Anthony. "Now we're on to Elmer Oliver—and I'm convinced that news from the States will prove that my hunch is right—we shall soon find out what our next move's going to be. The 'motif' behind all our troubles is robbery—I'd stake anything on it! And Big Robbery at that. We shall hear in all probability what Master Oliver was interested in. And when we hear that, my professional colleagues, we shall be able to sort out a number of people in this little rustic retreat of St. Mead who interest me considerably. Miss Drusilla Ives, Aldermen Wall and Bumstead, the Stainsbys, the Tresillians and—"

"And who?" demanded Kershaw, noticing how abruptly Anthony had paused. Anthony smiled at the local Inspector's precipitousness. But MacMorran jumped into the breach to answer the question.

"Fred Lord," he volunteered the name. "I'm far from satisfied with that fellow's story. Too thin for words, in my opinion."

"I wasn't thinking of Lord," said Anthony, "although Inspector MacMorran has acted quite properly in bringing him back to my attention. His part in the affair has certainly got to be cleared up." He handed his cigarette-case to the two inspectors and then lit a cigarette for himself, as he rose to his feet. "Well," he said, "it's getting latish and I must get back to 'Palings'. I'll leave those two matters in your able hands, Andrew. Bring me the best news you can, as soon as you can. We've a long road to travel, as Inspector Kershaw indicated just now, but, taking it step by step, I rather fancy that we shall eventually come to something. Anyhow—we shall see. Good night, you chaps."

"See you later," called out MacMorran, to Anthony's retreating figure.

VII

It was three days before MacMorran brought Anthony any news. The latter was strolling in the garden at "Palings" when the Inspector was shown in to join him. The afternoon sun was hot for the time of the year, which was marching to its end in a blaze of autumnal glory.

"St. Luke at his best," sang out Anthony, "even though he may be a few days late. And I see from the gleam in the inspectorial eye that its owner has news. You shall tell me at once, Andrew."

"Give me time, now," said MacMorran; "give me time. Nothing was ever gained by impatience."

"Or by standing still and letting the grass grow under your feet," replied Anthony with a twinkling eye. "So out with it, Andrew, if you please."

"Well—I think you've scored on both counts. Elmer Oliver is not only well known to the American police, he left New York for this country in July last year. He was accompanied by his wife."

"So far so good, Andrew. Did you clinch it on our man?"

"How do you mean?" asked MacMorran quietly.

"Diabetes, Andrew! That disease which Dr. Pleydell noticed at his first encounter in Ebford's field. To say nothing of a left foot with a hammer-toe. You hadn't forgotten the points, surely?"

The Inspector replied in even tone. "As it happened, I hadn't, Mr. Bathurst. And you've clicked. Elmer Oliver was a diabetic. Been treated in two American hospitals. Looks good enough, doesn't it?"

"I should say so. As far as I personally am concerned, it leaves me without the shadow of a doubt. Now tell me this. In what particular direction had Elmer Oliver attracted the attention of the American police authorities?"

"I hate to tell you," replied the Inspector, "but the answer is 'burglary'. And I throw myself on your mercy. Please don't stoop to the obvious."

Anthony rubbed his hands. "I won't, Andrew! I'll be magnanimity itself. So our friend Elmer was a burglar, was he? Just a common 'tea-leaf'. What line did he go for, Andrew?"

"Anything and everything, so I'm told. He's served two stretches of imprisonment for burglary, the latter ending about three years ago. And in the opinion of the New York people, there was always a bigger figure than himself behind him."

"I see. Well—we're still progressing. Which is all to the good. Now tell me of the other count you say I scored on."

The Inspector continued in the same even tones he had used before. "Ada Oliver, née Steel, died of pneumonia on the twenty-fourth of September last. At a house in the Leytonstone district. She was only ill for a few days. Soon after the funeral, her husband left the district."

"Of course. To die in Ebford's field, himself. Equally suddenly, shall we say. Andrew, the general pattern is fitting into shape very nicely. We now have to discover what it was that Oliver stole, either in this country or in the States, which brought about his death. And I still incline to the opinion that it will eventually boil down to the old adage of 'thieves falling out'. Most probably in this case, with regard to the value of their individual 'cuts'. Ah—well, Andrew—not for the first time. It all runs true to form. There's no precedent established."

"No. Or for the last. But I'm still a little in the dark. Where do we go to from here?"

"One obvious place is that Leytonstone address you spoke of. We've got to link up with Oliver in every way possible. You must go through that place, Andrew, with a small-tooth comb. You may find anything there. Who knows?"

"Anything—or nothing—eh? In all probability, the latter."

MacMorran puffed at his pipe. "I'll tell you what does emerge from all this, Mr. Bathurst. Or at least, so it seems to me."

"What's that, Andrew, may I ask?"

"Stacey," replied MacMorran laconically. "How little Stacey, who claimed to know so much, knew about Steel or about Steel's connections."

Anthony looked at him curiously. "It's funny you should have said that, because the same thing has struck me. Still—there you are. In fairness to Stacey, you must realize and admit that he knew Steel only as a working mate. Colleague, if you prefer the word. Men at home and men at work are frequently entirely different propositions. The tyrant of the factory or the office may be a blue-eyed innocent on his own family hearth, and vice versa. And there's another point of view, too, Andrew. Steel may be completely guiltless in the matter. He may come out of the whole thing without a stain on his dead body. As I see it, that's more than likely."

The Inspector shook his head. "Don't think so, somehow. He must have had some very good reason to go post haste after Oliver down to St. Mead. And you can bet your boots that the incentive was cash. He didn't follow Oliver to Ebford's field because the chap had married his sister. Not on your life. That's the truest of all true sayings. 'Money's the root of all evil.'"

"On the contrary, Andrew, you err. It's the love thereof that finds its place in the proverb. Let us be accurate if we can't be intelligent."

MacMorran took the rebuff with the utmost composure. "Much the same thing, anyhow," he countered.

Anthony changed the subject. "I'll see Colonel Buxton in the morning. For one thing, I want to put him in possession of all the facts. Or, most of them. It's time he knew how far we've got."

"What's your own next move after that?"

Anthony pondered over the question. "I'll wait for you to take action on the Leytonstone end. If that yields nothing tangible, I must investigate as closely as possible one or two of those robberies we discussed a little time ago."

MacMorran raised his eyebrows. "Miss Ives?" he inquired with a wealth of meaning in his voice.

"That amongst others," returned Anthony.

"I guessed you were after that," went on the Inspector.

Anthony grinned. "Andrew," he said, "you can read me like a book. And even better than that. Between the lines as well."

But MacMorran remained grave under the banter and replied seriously, "I'll let you know about Oliver's Leytonstone address within forty-eight hours."

"Thank you," responded Anthony; "in that case, I'll make no further move until I hear from you."

VIII

MacMorran was as good as his word. He reported in the matter of Elmer Oliver and his address in the Leytonstone district in less than the time period which he had stipulated. Anthony sat down in the library at "Palings" (the same room as he had sat in and questioned Drusilla Ives) and listened eagerly. The "Yard" Inspector's first few words, however, condemned him to disappointment.

"Nothing, Mr. Bathurst," said MacMorran in his opening remarks; "not a sausage! When Elmer Oliver left Leytonstone after the death of his wife, he cleared himself out and all his belongings (such as they were) lock, stock and barrel."

"Sure of that, Andrew?"

"Sure as I am of anything on this earth."

"What did the Olivers have there? Furnished apartments?"

"Yes. That's just what they did have. When she died and he 'went', believe me, they left no trace. We were lucky with Steel, but it turned up the other way as regards the Olivers."

"H'm. Not so good! Very definitely not so good! Ah well, it means this. I must turn my concentrated attention on to those robberies, including"—and at this moment Anthony's eyes twinkled—"the particular robbery visited upon Miss Drusilla Ives at Bray. That's put in to please you, Andrew."

"I thought it might be," returned MacMorran, not turning a hair. "I indicated so the day before yesterday."

"I've also," said Anthony, "since I last saw you, had another interview with the Chief Constable. I've put him in touch with the position as we now have it."

"How did the Colonel take it?" asked MacMorran laconically. "So-so. I'm of the opinion that he's rather critical of our joint efforts, Andrew. You see, I started off on the wrong foot with him. I was introduced by my host here, with a positive fanfare of trumpets. That's always a mistake. Buxton, no doubt, looked for big results pronto. He didn't get 'em. He hasn't exactly got 'em yet, although we've made a move or two. Seeing, therefore, that this is thus, as Reggie Fortune would say, hence these tears."

"Don't know where he'd have been if he'd left the case in Kershaw's hands," put in MacMorran; "although, of course, I do if we come right down to earth and content ourselves with facts."

Anthony rose and stretched his shoulders. "Something more may turn up," he said, "even when we least expect it. We'll continue to exist, Andrew, in that lively hope."

MacMorran nodded his agreement. "I'll go further than you. Seems to me something's bound to turn up. But it may not be for some little time yet. And in the meantime—?" He paused on the question. Anthony answered it for him.

"In the meantime, I'll do a little canoe-paddling on my lonesome. I have strong hopes that Drusilla Ives may turn the scales in our favour."

"Hope you're right," replied the Inspector, "in case not."

CHAPTER V

I

ANTHONY's expressed hope, with which MacMorran had found agreement, was closer on their heels than either of them had anticipated. But even then, recognition of it, in addition to its acceptance, was purely fortuitous. Actually, it was Anthony who picked it up originally. Before that week had run to its close, he tossed *The Times* over to MacMorran, and the action was accompanied by a trenchant remark.

"Third column, Andrew," he said quietly, "and about two-thirds of the way down. Anything about it strike you as interesting? Interesting—to us—especially?"

MacMorran ran his eyes down the column Anthony had indicated and read what he presumed to be the relevant paragraph. These were the words which Anthony had pointed out to him, under the heading of "Distinguished American in London". "Mr. Dwight Conway, the famous American millionaire, arrived in London yesterday afternoon from New York via Southampton. This is his first visit to England and somewhat surprising because a short time ago he publicly announced that he had no desire or intention of ever leaving the United States. Mr. Conway is a devotee of the arts and an enthusiastic collector of beautiful things, of both ancient and modern origin. It is not known at the moment how long his visit will last."

MacMorran returned the paper. "What about it?" he inquired a trifle acidly.

"I think it's interesting," said Anthony.

"From what particular point of view?" asked the Inspector.

"Our particular point of view at the moment."

"And what makes you think that?" persisted MacMorran. "I must confess that I see little to—"

Anthony waved away the objection. "It interests me for three reasons, Andrew. And those three reasons are as follows. Firstly, Mr. Dwight Conway's home is in New York, a place not unknown to Mr. Elmer Oliver. Secondly, he's a collector of beautiful things of both ancient and modern origin, and thirdly he's decided to come to England after having publicly proclaimed that he had neither the intention nor the desire of so doing. And he's come. Subsequently, mark you, to the published news concerning a certain Mr. Elmer Oliver. I take that last point to be highly significant. Well—now that I've thoroughly exposed my hand, what do you think of it?"

MacMorran shook his head. "Not a lot. I don't think you have too many trumps. The man may have changed his mind for any one of a dozen ordinary reasons."

"And on the other hand he may not. He may have changed his mind for one excellent but definitely unusual reason. Such as . . ."

Anthony hesitated and paused. MacMorran was quick to notice it. He broke in. "Well—such as what?"

The words of Anthony's answer came slowly. "Such as something having gone radically wrong with, shall we suggest, a recent purchasing venture? It's a long shot, I know. Nobody's more aware of the fact than I am myself. But where you get 'acute' collecting interests, which very often border on a mania, and 'valuables', you invariably run up against man's passions, with the inevitable sequence, sooner or later, of crime. I've expected this case to run that way right from the start. And what I've managed to pick up on it hasn't caused me to want to vary my opinion one iota. As I said to you the other day, Andrew, the pattern fits."

Some time elapsed before MacMorran made any reply. Anthony took advantage of the interval. "Get what you can, Andrew, from the States, in re Mr. Dwight Conway. To know his particular 'flair' wouldn't exactly annoy me. And for all we know it might *possibly*— note the word, Andrew, I say only 'possibly'—put us absolutely on the right track."

MacMorran shook his head. "It's all too shadowy for me. And it's so unlike you to start making bricks when you haven't any straw."

This time Anthony shook his head. "I have *some* straw, Andrew. I am not entirely without it."

"Well, even granting you that fact, I still think you're running on too far ahead. You're making the lock fit the key—instead of the other way round. At least, that's how it appears to me."

Anthony made no reply. He knew that there was a good deal in what the Inspector was saying. He walked to the window and looked out into the garden. He stayed in that position for some moments. Suddenly he turned and faced the Inspector again.

"You may be logical, Andrew, and I may be merely taking a chance. But look at it how I will, I can't help thinking that I'm on the right track."

"You can't call it the science of deduction," riposted MacMorran, "whatever else you like to say about it."

"Perhaps not in particular detail," countered Anthony, "but you can, nevertheless, as an underlying principle. You're not going to put me off like that, Andrew," he added with a shake of the head.

"I'm not trying to," retorted MacMorran.

"Anyhow," said Anthony, "I'll sleep on it tonight. And in the morning I'll set about making plans. In the meantime, you get busy on Dwight Conway. I have an idea you'll run across something decidedly interesting."

II

On the Saturday of that week, Anthony put a copy of *The Times* in front of MacMorran and Inspector Kershaw. He put it in front of them with something of the air and action of a card-player who aces his opponent's king.

"Well, Andrew," he asked, "and what comment, pertinent or otherwise, have you to make on that?"

Anthony's forefinger picked out the part of the paper he desired the two professionals to read. The item was in the Personal column on the front page. It ran as follows—

"CONWAY. ARE YOU STILL INTERESTED IN CARTOONS? IF SO, PLEASE COMMUNICATE WITHIN A WEEK FROM NOW WITH WORCESTER BOX 222B."

MacMorran whistled. "Conway—eh? And cartoons? What about Drusilla Ives now? And the reply's to a box office number. Well, well, who would have thought it? When we find out who Worcester is we ought to be a good deal 'forrader' towards solving our mystery. Don't you agree, Mr. Bathurst?"

Kershaw, who had had Anthony's theory formulated to him by MacMorran, expressed similar opinions. But Anthony negatived MacMorran's question with a shake of the head.

"I don't know that I altogether agree with you, Andrew."

"Why not? Seems sound common sense to me."

"I agree," added Kershaw.

"Well," went on Anthony, "I have a very good reason for saying what I did. I know who Worcester is!"

"Who is he?" demanded MacMorran.

"I happen to be the gentleman myself," answered Anthony.

"Why Worcester?" demanded Kershaw.

"Why Worcester? Oh, in answer to Conway, of course, couldn't think of anything more fitting."

"I see," replied the Kersbrook Inspector blankly, and Anthony knew perfectly well that he didn't.

"What's the idea?" asked MacMorran, "to draw their fire?"

"Exactly, Andrew. Conway's fire. I admit it's a shot in the dark, but I stand to lose nothing by it and it's on the cards I may gain a lot. I told you I was going to make certain plans. That's by way of being one of them—the first in execution. I have one or two others up my sleeve, if the first one proves fruitless."

"A week," repeated MacMorran reflectively, "within a week. You haven't rushed him—you've given him plenty of time."

"There was deliberate intention behind that," declared Anthony. "I've got to allow for him not seeing the announcement for perhaps a day or two. You'll agree with that position, I take it?"

"Yes. I'll concede that. You must give the man a certain amount of time, I agree. That's only reasonable."

"All right, then. What we have to do now is to possess our souls in patience. The trap is sprung. How soon it will be before our tiger leaps into it is a matter of conjecture."

MacMorran rubbed his chin at Anthony's last remark. "I've always been given to understand," he said, "that a kid was used to catch a tiger."

"In that case then," replied Anthony with smiling eyes, "this method couldn't possibly be more appropriate."

III

Ten days passed. They seemed long, they were uneventful, and they produced in both Anthony Bathurst and Inspector MacMorran a feeling of apprehensive disappointment. But on the Wednesday week following the previous conversation their ears caught the first tinkle of the bell. A reply was received, addressed to "Worcester", at the box office number as advertised. It came to Anthony at a moment when MacMorran happened to be in his company, and Anthony, naturally, opened it immediately.

"Well," said MacMorran, as he watched eagerly and expectantly, "what have you got? A fish—or an old tin can?"

"Shall we say, Andrew," replied Anthony, as he handed it over, "that we have a bite? But a bite doesn't always mean that the fish that's biting will be landed on the bank."

MacMorran read the reply. It ran as follows. *"Meet Conway tomorrow Thursday Waldorf Hotel London 12.30 p.m. Table reserved. Lunch. Please ask for 'Woore' on arrival."*

MacMorran handed it back. "He's going," he said laconically.

"He is," returned Anthony triumphantly. "What about my despised hunch now?"

The Inspector shrugged his shoulders. "You can't make the whole journey on hunches."

"It's not probable, I admit—but on occasions, you *might*. Anyhow, we've been able to progress considerably on this one."

"Who's to go to the 'Waldorf' tomorrow? You or I?"

Anthony rubbed his top lip with his finger. "On the whole, Andrew," he replied, "and bearing in mind all the issues, I think I had better go. After all, the official police aren't in on Conway, are they? That is to say, at the moment."

MacMorran considered all the implications of Anthony's answer. "No, I suppose they aren't."

Anthony said no more. He waited purposely for MacMorran to elaborate. "Yes," said the latter at length, "you had better dine at the 'Waldorf'. Or lunch there. It will be the better course from all points of view. The idea of contacting Conway emanated from you, you know all the various points you have that lie behind it, so that you had better see it through to its proper conclusion. In that respect, I have no desire or intention to poach on your preserves."

"All right, Andrew," replied Anthony imperturbably, "we'll consider that settled, then. And I'll say this. I think you've come to a right and proper decision. I'll run up to town tomorrow morning and have lunch at the 'Waldorf'."

MacMorran noticed the lightness in Anthony's tone. "Feeling pleased with yourself, aren't you?"

"Most assuredly, Andrew! We started absolutely at scratch but any moment now we may find ourselves in the straight."

"I'm not so sure," returned the cautious MacMorran. "I shouldn't be surprised if we've a rare long road to travel even yet."

IV

Anthony had a comfortable journey from St. Mead to town on the following morning and had ample time to get to the "Waldorf" by easy travelling. As he entered, he looked at his wrist-watch. It was barely twenty-five minutes past twelve but he estimated that his "Conway" contact would be early for the appointment rather than late. After he had passed through the vestibule, a waiter of some obvious standing and seniority came forward to meet him.

"Have you booked a table, sir?" was this waiter's inquiry.

"I am to meet a gentleman by the name of Woore," replied Anthony, "by appointment here at half-past twelve."

To Anthony's satisfaction, the statement seemed in order and entirely adequate. The waiter understood immediately.

"If you would care, sir, to dispose of your hat and coat—just along there, sir—and come back to me here, I will conduct you to your table, sir. Your friend is awaiting you."

Anthony intimated that the suggested arrangement found favour in his sight, left his hat and coat in the cloak-room, returned to his waiter, and was then led through two rooms to a farther room, and to a table for two situated in the far corner. A young man with fair bushy hair, and wearing heavy horn-rimmed glasses, was already seated there. As Anthony came to the table he noticed that this young man was looking at his watch. When he saw Anthony he rose rather awkwardly to his feet and thrust out his hand.

"Mr.—er—Worcester?"

"As you say, sir," returned Anthony. "And I presume I have the pleasure of addressing Mr. Woore?"

"You have for sure," came the reply in an American accent. "Sit down, will you? I've given an order for the lunches and I do hope they'll meet with your approval."

"I shall eat only one of them," grinned Anthony, "but I've no doubt that the selection has been in good hands."

"If you can put your tongue to Scotch salmon and a Surrey fowl, you won't suffer acute disappointment, Mr. Worcester. I tried to put myself in your place."

"Thank you, Mr. Woore. I'll put my best tongue foremost in sincere appreciation of your efforts."

The waiter arrived with *hors-d'oeuvres*. "Now what will you drink, Mr. Worcester?" said the fair young man.

"Might I," replied Anthony consideringly, "seeing that it's a Surrey fowl, suggest a Burgundy? Say a Musigny—would it be possible?"

The waiter bowed. "I'll see what I can do for you, sir." Anthony's selection was successful. The waiter returned with a bottle of the nominated Burgundy and the wine was poured out.

"You," said the Conway ambassador, "are not altogether what I should have expected. No, sir." He shook his head emphatically.

"Ah," thought Anthony to himself, feeling his way. "I'm sorry," he said, "if I fall short of your anticipations."

"It's not altogether that. I was alluding to *type*, rather than your own personality. Of course, as you are doubtless aware, I have the honour, sir, to represent Mr. Dwight Conway. *The* Mr. Dwight Conway of Noo York. And you can take it from me, Mr. Worcester, he's a swell guy."

"So I believe," returned Anthony.

"Now, sir," continued the fair young man, "I figure you aren't here to enjoy the passing scenery. Your little advert tells me that. The password between us is 'Cartoons'. What do you know, sir? And I'll thank you to spill a mouthful with as little delay as possible." Anthony raised his glass and sampled the Musigny. "I should have preferred, Mr. Woore," he said quietly, "to have had the opportunity of discussing this with Mr. Dwight Conway himself. After all—and please let there be no offence or misunderstanding—I have only your word—" He broke off deliberately, for his *vis-à-vis* to fill in the blanks.

The bushy-haired young man shrugged his shoulders, put down his knife and fork, and spread out his hands. "I'm takin' you on chance, ain't I?"

"You know I'm the advertiser. *And*, Mr. Woore, you *want* something. Which fact always rather makes a difference, don't you *know* Dwight Conway, Mr. Worcester? Have you ever *met* him? Ever done *business* with him? Because if you haven't, let me tell you, sir, that D.C. *gets his way*! He gets his way, he gets his woman and he gets his man! Yes, sir—he gets 'em—come hell and high water."

"Really," said Anthony. "Acquisitive, eh?"

"Come, sir," said the young man in a slightly mollified tone, "let's agree on terms. It will save you wasting your time. It will save me wasting mine."

"I shall be only too delighted. What are they, Mr. Woore?"

Woore leant over the table. "Dwight Conway won't ask any, shall we say, *awkward* questions. We'll assoom you were clever enough to slip in between them cartoons and—er—somebody else. Well, in a way that's all to your credit. I'm the last person on earth to try to down a guy just because he's been hell smarter than the next man. What's your figure?"

This direct question was the one which Anthony didn't want, although he had been prepared for its coming. To answer it would force him too far into the open. What troubled him was how he could avoid this. He thought quickly and came to a rapid decision. "Ten per cent increase on what Conway offered in the first place. You are aware, of course, to whom I mean."

Horn-rims whistled. But he adroitly avoided the trap set for him. "Bit steep, isn't it?"

"Not too steep, I hope. When you offered a price to the man we'll call your first agent . . ." Again Anthony hesitated purposely. He had hoped that the sudden and abrupt pause might betray Woore, watchful though he undoubtedly was, into saying something indiscreet, but instead he saw a flash of surprise come into the man's eyes. Woore, however, was still wary.

"Our offer was a top offer, Mr. Worcester. That was very definitely understood. All the way along the line. As far as I know, Conway's limit. He may not feel inclined to go beyond it. But that remains to be seen. Where are the cartoons?"

Anthony looked at his nails. He noticed that Woore was eating very slowly. There came a silence. Woore's forehead wrinkled and he looked across at Anthony with a painful frown. "Where are they?" he repeated.

"You haven't accepted my terms," prompted Anthony with a shake of the head.

"I can't," snapped back Woore. "I told you I couldn't. I thought I'd made that clear to you at the start of our conversation. Conway's the only guy that can do that. But does that signify?"

"I think so. Definitely. Don't you think you'd think so in similar circumstances?"

Woore pushed back his chair and regarded Anthony with mock admiration. "Say, you do run risks, don't you? Talk about the gypsies and the wood! You're actin' like a big cheese."

Anthony studied his plate. "Sorry we can't do better than this. We seem to be making no progress whatever. From what you've said you've got to take orders from your chief. Presumably, Dwight

Conway. Well, that's all right. You know what I want. I made myself perfectly clear. Ten per cent over and above—"

"Give me your address," snapped Woore again, "where you live, I mean. Not that box stunt you shoved in *The Times*. The place where I can come and see you."

Anthony considered the proposal. After all, why not? "Give me a piece of paper," he said.

Woore fumbled before producing. Anthony scribbled with his fountain pen, "'Palings', St. Mead, near Kersbrook, Fernshire."

The bushy-haired young man regarded it somewhat superciliously. "And where the heck's that?"

This particular remark came as a surprise to Anthony. And a surprise which was definitely unwelcome. No pattern fitting here! Had he been a B.F. after all? He looked across at Woore. The man had turned sulky without a doubt. Anthony gave him directions as to how to get to St. Mead. Woore weighed in with another grouse.

"Did you *have* to live there?"

Anthony placed his knife and fork neatly on the plate in front of him and smiled sweetly on his companion. "You know," he said, "anyone overhearing us would imagine that it was I who wanted something very badly. Whereas . . ."

Woore glared at him uncompromisingly. "I don't know that I can accept all that, either! Granted, I represent somebody who does want something, you've got something you want to sell, haven't you? I guess that puts us on more or less equal terms."

Anthony thought things over. Should he persist in his attitude? To an extent, he was forced to admit inwardly that Woore, fortified by natural obstinacy, had called his bluff. The cartoons weren't in his possession and, what was more, he didn't know in whose possession they actually were. On the other hand, he considered that if he came out into the open, Woore and his principal would take fright, fly to cover and remain there until the cows came home. On the whole he thought that his best plan would be to call it a day and talk things over with MacMorran in the hope that Conway, through Woore, would make another move. After a few seconds' thought he decided to accept this position. He put it to Woore in this manner.

"It seems to me that we shall make little or no headway today. We can't—for this reason. You have pointed out to me that you are not a free agent. That you must return to your principal for further instructions. Well, as far as I am concerned, that's understandable. You have my address. I shall hope to hear further from you within the next two or three days. I suggest that for the time being we leave it at that."

Woore frowned and pushed out his underlip after the manner of a pouting child. "If that's your attitude, there's nothing I can do to change it. It may be, of course, that Conway will wash his hands of the whole business. In fact, I reckon that's just about what he will do. And what he darned well ought to do. In that case, Mr. Worcester— well, I guess you'll be wishing you'd been a shade more reasonable."

"I'm willing to risk that, Mr. Woore. In the meantime, I must express my sincere appreciation of an excellent lunch and the hope that I shall be hearing from you again in the very near future. I don't think I need say any more than that."

"Glad you liked the lunch," returned Woore. "I should have hated to have handed you out anything in the nature of a disappointment. Guess it would have hurt me, good and proper."

Anthony raised his glass. "To our next meeting then—and may it be soon."

Woore made no reply. Anthony drained his glass and rose to make his departure. Woore disregarded the action. He sat, slumped in his chair, with his back half-turned to Anthony.

"I'm sorry," said Anthony, "that you're taking this so much to heart. But that won't prevent me from wishing you a very good afternoon. And I do hope you share my admiration for the Musigny."

V

Anthony told MacMorran the details of his luncheon at the "Waldorf", in the presence of Colonel Buxton. The latter, when Anthony had finished, was uncompromisingly critical.

"So in effect you accomplished nothing, Bathurst?"

"Perhaps it would be true to say that in a way."

"Well, don't let's boggle with words, did you?"

"I've established the certainty that Dwight Conway has a more than ordinary interest in a certain collection of stolen cartoons. Beyond that, his emissary, I admit, wouldn't budge."

"Very true," continued "Pusher" Buxton, "so you may have, but you haven't established any connection with Conway, the cartoons, and our two dead men in Ebford's field. That's the point I'm endeavouring to make." The Chief Constable straightened himself as he spoke, in an attempt to emphasize his point.

Anthony defended his plan of campaign. "Although I failed to establish that, sir, the idea I had was worth trying. I couldn't be *more* direct—as things are at present. I had to depend on bluff, but I could only travel a certain distance on that particular ticket. When this fellow, Woore, called my bluff—which in reality is what he did do—I had to retreat. I couldn't, as it were, allow myself to be taken into another province and not know where I was going. To have done that would have been to court disaster. As it is, although I failed to effect anything particularly positive, we're no worse off than we were, and in some directions I think that I can reasonably claim that we're better off."

Colonel Buxton sat back in his chair and folded his arms. "Granted that then, Bathurst," he said eventually, "what's our next step?"

Anthony took an appreciable time over his reply. "I think that Conway will attempt further contact."

"With you?"

"Yes. He asked for an address where he could find me and I gave him Mr. Kemble's at St. Mead."

The Chief Constable became disdainful. "Well then, my dear Bathurst, in that case I consider you've committed a grave tactical error! Neville Kemble's address, of all people! Neville Kemble, brother of the Commissioner of Police at New Scotland Yard! I should say you've as much chance of seeing your acquaintance Woore again as I have of selling refrigerators to the Esquimaux."

Buxton closed his jaws with a snap. Anthony, however, remained imperturbable, under the Chief Constable's withering satire. After all, Buxton had requested his help on the case, so that in any circumstances he had the whip-hand to a certain extent.

"I don't share your pessimism, sir," he stated. "I feel this. Conway wants something. He wants that something badly. He thinks (a) that it's in my possession or (b) alternatively, that I know where it is. Ergo, he'll come after me for it."

"Well," replied Buxton, "you may have your opinion, Bathurst—I'll stick to mine. Personally, I think you're hopelessly wrong. In my opinion you've seen the last of your friend Woore and because of that you'll never get even a smell of Conway. Candidly, I think you've made a mess of things. Conway'll know the surname of the Commissioner of Police all right, take it from me. He's an educated American, remember—not just a Bowery tough."

"He's not the latter," said Anthony, "and he may even not be the former. Although a millionaire and an art-collector, he may yet possess no high degree of education. Still, our opinions must differ. Time alone will show which of us is proved to be correct."

Buxton turned to MacMorran. "The inquests on Peter Steel and the man you assure me is Elmer Oliver are fixed for next Wednesday. I suppose you'll want an adjournment, eh?"

"I think so," returned MacMorran, "for a month, say. That will be best for all parties. In a month's time we may know a lot more about things."

"You may," replied Colonel Buxton drily, "and on the other hand you may not. I can't say I'm impressed by the progress shown so far." Anthony bore the storm uncomplainingly. He was quite prepared to make allowances for Buxton's criticism. The man was undoubtedly worried and anxious and he knew that these twin conditions were mainly responsible for his acerbity. Buxton fell to thought after a few moments. Suddenly he looked up and translated his thoughts into words.

"Look here, you fellows, I've a proposition to make to you. And to my mind it's a rather attractive one."

"I'd like to hear it," declared MacMorran.

"Well, it's this. Why shouldn't we turn the heat on to Dwight Conway? In other words, why shouldn't we *make* him come to heel and disgorge his knowledge? If I'm any judge, he'd fight very shy of being mixed up in a police case dealing with a couple of murders. If he's the man I take him to be."

MacMorran looked at Anthony with a question showing in his eyes. Anthony nodded. "All right, Andrew, I'll answer that for you, if you want me to. I'll give the Chief Constable my reasons. He may not think overmuch of them. But, as I see things, if we approach Conway, all he has to do is to keep his mouth shut. Just lie low and stay dumb. We can prove nothing against him whatever. You can lay your life he'll give nothing or nobody away. To whatever question we put to him, all that he need say is, 'I'm frightfully sorry but I haven't the slightest idea what you're talking about.' Then, where are we? I *suspect*—and I'm pretty well certain in my mind—that he's over here after certain cartoons, which I think have been stolen, but suspicion and proof are two vastly different quantities. I've given you my view, Colonel Buxton."

The lines round Buxton's mouth showed how harassed he was. It was some little time before he made any rejoinder to Anthony's statement of opinion. "Perhaps there's something in what you say," he conceded. "But I scarcely like the idea of having this fellow Dwight Conway in my grasp and then waking up in the morning to find that he's taken the law into his own hands and slipped through my fingers. I should very much resent that happening, I can tell you."

"I don't think you need harbour that idea, sir," contributed Anthony. "I don't think it's the least likely—Conway hasn't crossed the Atlantic for the benefit of his health or to invite me to lunch with his secretary at a London hotel. We'll be hearing from him again—never fear. And when that happens, the situation may change considerably."

"I regret that I don't share your optimism, Bathurst, but let that pass. We've discussed all that before and no good purpose would be served by going all over the ground again." He turned and spoke to the Inspector. "Keep me in touch all the time, Inspector, will you? Because although I'm prepared to surrender some of my opinions, I'm not prepared to hand all of them over—lock, stock and barrel. I'm not a man who does that sort of thing. Never have been! Emphatically not!"

As he spoke, Colonel Buxton rose and with a curt nod to Anthony and the Inspector, made his departure. The Inspector looked at Anthony.

"H'm," he said, "it would appear that our worthy Chief Constable has a 'peeve' on."

Anthony smiled. "No doubt about that. But it's *his* 'peeve' and he'll have to get over it."

VI

The morning after the conversation with the Chief Constable that has been recorded, Anthony's spirits rose with a bound. The envelope of the letter which he received and which caused this rise in his spirits was inscribed "—Worcester, Esq. 'Palings', St. Mead, Fernshire." Anthony knew, of course, directly he saw this inscription that the sender must be either Woore or Dwight Conway himself. He slit the flap of the envelope and read the letter enclosed within. It ran thus.

> *London.*
>
> *Dear Sir,*
>
> *Further to your conversation with me last week at the Waldorf Hotel, I have reported on the same to my principal, as I indicated I should, and have been instructed by him as follows. If you will kindly make arrangements to call at "The Limes", Clancarty Crescent, Blackheath, unaccompanied, I think that the subsequent interview should prove to be to our mutual advantage. I suggest Friday evening of this week at, say, seven o'clock. If the suggested appointment should be inconvenient to you, please advertise to that effect through the same agency as you employed before and I will do my best to arrange another. Your silence will be taken to signify your acceptance of the offer.*
>
> *Yours sincerely,*
>
> *W. H. Woore.*

Anthony replaced the letter in the envelope, pushed the envelope back into his pocket and thought things over. "I can see no real reason," he argued to himself, "why I shouldn't go. I may be able to prolong the original bluff and extract an admission of some kind that should put a vital clue in our hands. If I go, I can't be any worse off. I've nothing to lose by going, and it's on the cards that I *may* pick up something valuable. Yes," he said to himself finally, "I'll see Andrew MacMorran and tell him that I've made up my mind to go."

Then he remembered the stipulation in the letter laid down—that his attendance must be limited. He was to appear "unaccompanied". He carefully considered all the reasonable complications that this condition might possess. He couldn't see that he would be in any danger. The part that he had assigned to himself to play was certainly not one that called for any violent action against himself. At least, so Anthony argued to himself.

Later on that same day, when he encountered MacMorran, after a telephone appointment, he put the matter to him and asked for his advice. Somewhat to Anthony's surprise, MacMorran concurred with his opinions almost immediately.

"Mr. Bathurst," he said, after he had been acquainted with the latest development, "I see no reason in the world why you shouldn't go. I'm not fearing any danger with regard to it. It's panned out just as you expected it would and it bears out pretty thoroughly the points you made to the Chief Constable yesterday." The Inspector's eyes twinkled humorously as he added, "And you'll certainly be able to score off Colonel Buxton."

"You think, then, that they've moved because they want something—eh, Andrew? As I hinted they would?"

"I think that's just about the size of it."

"What do you make of the 'unaccompanied' emphasis?"

MacMorran frowned at the question. "Just this. They're not taking any risks at all. They're prepared to deal with you and with you only. They don't intend having any truck with a third party. They think you've double-crossed their own particular agent and thereby placed yourself in a strong position. So strong that you're able to make 'em come to heel a bit. And they don't want anybody else to become heir to that position. Or even have a share in it. That's how I work it out, Mr. Bathurst."

Anthony nodded when MacMorran had delivered himself of his explanation. "Very much as I do myself, Andrew. Righto, then, I'll pop up to Blackheath on Friday evening and clutch whatever the gods chuck at me. There's one thing, you'll know where I've gone and if anything should go wrong—and I regard the chance as most remote—you'll know quite well where to pick up the trail."

"What new bluff are you going to put up?" asked the Inspector. "You won't be able to stall indefinitely."

"I know I shan't. And you've put your finger, Andrew, on my worst headache. I shall have to put on my thinking-cap between now and Friday and conjure up something. Let's hope my imagination will see me through."

"I've no doubt it will do that," concluded MacMorran warmly. He turned away but a remark from his companion brought him back again.

"By the way, Andrew," said Anthony, "have you seen anything of Fred Lord these last few days? Or has he vanished from the scene?"

"No, Mr. Bathurst," answered the Inspector. "I'm afraid I've relaxed on that. Why do you ask? Are you uncertain about him?"

"No, Andrew," replied Anthony, with a shake of the head. "On the contrary, I'm very certain about him. And when I return from Blackheath I think I shall be able to regale you with a most interesting theory I've formed with regard to him. It's quite feasible that it will cause you some strong measure of surprise."

MacMorran opened his eyes at the statement. "Good! I shall look forward to hearing it. But as to being surprised"—and here the Inspector made an eloquent gesture—"this game of mine has taught me to be surprised at nothing. And when you've been at it as long as I have, you'll think the same."

"Perhaps I shan't have to wait till then, Andrew."

VII

Anthony walked up from Blackheath station in the direction of the heath itself and was enabled to find with no difficulty the road in which the house lay, to which he had been invited. The houses were all detached, large and old-fashioned of type. He located "The Limes" and, having done so, looked at his wrist-watch. The time was ten minutes to seven. He resolved to pass away the margin of time he had to spare by walking round generally, and taking good stock of "The Limes" and its immediate surroundings. As a house it was no exception to the general rule prevailing in the locality. But it gave an appearance, externally at least, that it had not been too well-cared for in the past and had been allowed to shed a generous proportion of its former glory. This fact rather puzzled Anthony, and he fell to wonderment as to the interest of Dwight Conway in the place.

There was a large garden at the back of the house with a wall round it, which he estimated to have a height of approximately eight feet. A small flight of stone steps showed the way to the front door and Anthony made his way up these steps and rang the bell. The time was now exactly seven o'clock. He was little prepared for the amazing events which were to follow. The door was opened to him by one of the most grotesque figures it had ever been his lot to see. A man stood in the doorway. A man who was not only a dwarf but a hunchback in addition. At the sight of him, Anthony was taken aback. His whole appearance was forbidding and the look on his face malevolent. Then Anthony's eyes caught sight of his feet. They were huge—out of all proportion to his size. They were long and thin and the toes of them seemed to taper off into a kind of a sinister point. Then again, Anthony spotted something else. The dwarf had been holding his right hand behind his back. When he moved his hand, Anthony realized almost incredulously that the dwarf had a great black goat behind him which he held by a studded collar round the goat's neck.

The dwarf spoke. In a deep sepulchral voice. "Yes? Who are you and what do you want?"

The eyes of him glared malignant hostility. Anthony made an effort to recover from his shock and to pull himself together.

"I have an appointment with Mr. Woore," he said.

The dwarf took a step forward, and to Anthony's disgust the point of one of his shoes almost touched Anthony on the shin. He wanted to recoil, but he fought the impulse down and stood his ground.

"Come up, Satan," growled the dwarf, and Anthony understood that the command had been addressed to the black goat. The animal jerked forward as the dwarf said again, this time to Anthony, "Come in, then. If it's Mr. Woore you want to see. Walk behind me, please— and be careful."

For the first time Anthony felt uneasy. He found himself regretting the fact that he came unarmed on the venture. The dwarf made his way down the hall of the house. He walked with a curious flapping tread and the sound of it sounded eerie and horrible. The lighting was subdued. To Anthony's surprise, what light there was came from candles. The candles were in large brass candlesticks judiciously placed in various parts of the hall, and their incessant bickerings added to the macabre nature of the premises.

When they came to a room on the right on the hall, the dwarf turned the handle of the door and flung the door open. "In here," he croaked. "Mr. Woore will send for you in a few minutes. The master himself may be a little late."

As Anthony entered the room, the thought came to him that despite the unpleasant surroundings, he was at least in the right house. He had made no mistake—Woore and his principal were expecting him and would be with him before long. But when he saw the condition of the room into which the dwarf had shown him, Anthony experienced yet another shattering shock. With the exception of three or four rugs scattered here and there, the floor was uncovered. The paper on the walls looked old and stained. To assert that it was merely discoloured would be an under-statement. As with the case of the hall, the lighting effect came from candles. There were two of them—one at each end of the mantelpiece—and in large brass candlesticks. There were no chairs or seating accommodation of any kind. Much mystified, Anthony took the only course open to him. He stood up by the mantelpiece. Had it been cleaner he would have rested his elbow on it. But a quick glance at it warned him that to do so would be both unpleasant and inadvisable.

Then, in the act of half-turning, he saw something that momentarily took away his breath. Motionless on the wall of the room opposite the mantelpiece, and apparently arrested in the process of crawling towards the ceiling, was a huge, hairy spider. Anthony immediately named it to himself as a tarantula. Uncertain of its habits, but knowing well the venomous nature of its bite, Anthony kept his eyes fixed on it, hoping to hear his summons to either Mr. Woore or another as speedily as possible. Then, as he stood there watching the tarantula, there came the sound of a piercing scream. It was plain to him that the voice was a woman's and that the scream had come from one of the upper rooms. Without any mental argument, Anthony knew what he must do. With an economy of stride, he was out of the room and dashing up the staircase. As he ran up, he registered the thought that the staircase, in keeping with the rest of the house as he had seen it, was devoid of stair-carpet. Indeed, as he ran, the bare boards resounded under his feet.

Before he had reached the top, there came a second scream, even more piercing than the first, and it was a comparatively simple matter for him to detect the room from which the screams were coming, namely, from what, in the ordinary course of events, would be the front bedroom. Anthony ran like lightning across the expansive landing, pushed the door from him in his impetus, and rushed into the room.

To receive yet another in his swift succession of shocks. An extraordinary sight met his eyes. On a trestle-table, cornered by what he had now come to regard as the inevitable candles in the inevitable sticks, lay a coffin, the brass plate of which glinted in the flickering glare of the candle-light. The coffin had been built up in some way to a height which Anthony estimated to be in the region of six feet. At the foot of the coffin a girl was kneeling. Her head was bowed and her face buried in her hands. Her whole attitude was one of prayer, yet to all appearances and according to all evidence that was positive she must have been the woman who had so recently screamed twice.

As Anthony rushed over the threshold, the girl rocked herself to her feet. To present Anthony with his fourth surprise since seven o'clock. Her costume, to say the least of it, was unexpected. She was clad in a long, white flowing robe, girdled with a light blue sash. In her right hand she held a chaplet of flowers. Her face was distorted—raddled almost with an emotion which seemed to him to border on insanity. Her hair hung in strands over her face.

"He is dead," she cried—and the cry was abnormally violent—"he is dead! My husband! The tarantula got him! And if I go downstairs it will get me too! And you."

Her index finger seemed to shoot out into space and point straight at Anthony. The astonishing state of affairs into which he had blundered nonplussed him. All that he could think of to say was, "Are you Mrs. Woore?"

Her reply came at once, strident and harsh. "I was. But I am no longer! He is gone. He has been taken from me. But I shall be, because I was."

She lurched towards him and started to scream again. Anthony deftly avoided any close engagement. The idea had now taken possession of him that he must get out of the house and that the sooner this took place the better. The girl turned from him, went back to the improvised catafalque, knelt down on the spot where she had been kneeling when Anthony entered, and began to sing in a strange, hoarse voice.

"There is a willow grows aslant a brook, That shows his hoar-leaves in the glassy stream; There with fantastic garlands did she come, Of crowflowers, nettles, daisies and long purples, That liberal shepherds give a grosser name, But our cold maids do dead men's fingers call them."

Anthony stopped in the doorway and looked at her curiously. The words she used were almost unintelligible but gradually Anthony's ear caught a phrase here and there which was familiar to him. Yes—he was able to place them now—they were from the Queen's speech on the death of Ophelia—and he tucked the fact away in his brain to be neatly docketed there for future reference. He stood and listened, still in the doorway, and the curious look that had been his gave way to a look of puzzlement. Some cadence or inflexion in the girl's voice had influenced his ear and set him vaguely wondering. But the solution which his mind sought remained fugitive and refused to come to him. His brain was forced to concentrate upon his more immediate and pressing personal problem. What to do for the best at the moment. Any opportunity of meeting Woore, assuming that his was the body which the coffin contained, would now inevitably be denied to him. And the members of Woore's entourage, as evidenced by the habitués of "The Limes", as he had so far encountered them, didn't seem altogether to belong to that class of individual with whom one would choose to conduct anything in the nature of a confidential interview no matter the standard by which you assessed such.

With this thought uppermost, Anthony decided to descend again and have a few additional words with the goat-leading dwarf. In this way he might be able to obtain some degree of enlightenment. He therefore closed the door quietly behind him, gave a last glance at the kneeling woman, and made his way down the staircase. No sound, in response to his exit, came from the room, so Anthony concluded that the woman in white had no objection to his making his departure. As he descended to the floor below, the candle-light seemed to make the house more bizarre and more ghostly than ever. Keeping his eyes well open for any signs of a nomadic tarantula, Anthony found himself in the hall again. He could hear no sound of the dwarf moving in any of the rooms. Certainly from what his eyes told him and to his utter relief, the room which had housed the tarantula, and by the open door of which he now stood, was now empty.

Should he explore some of the rooms which he had not yet seen? Judged by his recent experiences, the prospect was neither alluring nor attractive. As he stood there at the foot of the staircase with the wavering light of the many candles ensconced in various places, making grotesque shadows in strange nooks and crannies, Anthony made an honest endeavour to come to a decision on the matter which was vexing him. He was on the point of reaching it, when it was decided for him. At least, it came to that in its ultimate effect and result. The door of the room next to that which the dwarf had first shown him into began to open . . . slowly . . . inch by inch almost. Anthony braced himself to stand and watch it. In time, the door had opened to the margin of at least six inches. Anthony, silent and now entirely defensive, watched it with a strange fascination. Then he saw what was happening. A gaunt, incredibly bony hand was extended through the aperture and gesticulated towards him. The fingers on it were almost repulsive—so much so that they gave the impression of a devilish claw much more than that of a hand.

Anthony stepped a couple of paces back, prepared for almost anything to follow the extended hand. More and more of the hand and wrist appeared. Anthony's eyes never left it and the thought came to him for the first time that real danger to him was imminent, although he would have been unable to explain the real reason for this thought, had he been taxed. His body was balanced and poised ready to challenge and to oppose whatever fearsome thing might be hurled at him. Then, to his amazement, the door began to close again, and the hand recede, in exactly the same manner and condition as the door had opened and the gruesome hand appeared.

Anthony stood still, rooted to the spot. And herein, as he realized afterwards, he made his worst mistake. For recovering himself in the space of a few moments, he took three or four quick strides towards the door of this room and, grasping the handle, flung it open.

"Of course," he murmured to himself, "I might have known—empty."

The time he had lost when he had remained motionless in the hall had given whoever it had been behind the door the opportunity to make his escape. The way of exit was obvious. A french door was unfastened and Anthony darted across to it, but the night was dark now with but scant moonlight, and he realized that any pursuit he might make would most certainly be ill-judged and prove to be ineffective. This room was like its fellow at the front. The paper on the walls, if anything, was in an even worse condition, and of furniture it boasted nothing whatever. Once again Anthony stood and thought things over. He wasn't long in coming to a definite decision. More than once afterwards, when recalling the incident, he has confessed that he left "The Limes" for the simple reason that he found that action much more attractive than its counterpart of staying there. As he made his way out—not troubling to close the front door—the house exhibited no further sign of life, and Anthony put his best foot forward along Clancarty Crescent. His mind was a prey to a whirling conflict of thoughts and emotions. All of which he knew he would have to sort out later under conditions of quietude and complete mental concentration.

When he reached the station, after a walk of a few minutes, he found that there was a train which would get him to town at ten minutes to nine. When there, he would 'phone Emily his maid, and tell her that he would be coming on to the flat. And in that case, the evening would conclude more propitiously than it had begun.

CHAPTER VI

I

ANTHONY lay in bed at his flat—on his back. His hands were clasped behind his neck and he stared at the ceiling. He was endeavouring to perform the sorting-out process which he had promised himself ever since he had left "The Limes", some few hours before. His mind still held a mixture of emotions. Amongst these may be cited surprise, annoyance and satisfaction. It was the last of these which he was now contemplating and considering. For two matters had come home to him, after a supreme exercise in mental concentration, that afforded him a strong measure of personal satisfaction. They both concerned the girl who had knelt by the candled coffin in the bedroom at "The Limes".

He was certain now that the words which she had uttered belonged to the "Queen" in *Hamlet*, and equally sure that the tone which had seemed in some way familiar to him when he had heard it, resembled, at least, that of Drusilla Ives. Therein lay Anthony's main problem as he lay in bed and contemplated the ceiling. He unclasped his hands from the back of his neck and rubbed the ridge of his jaw. Then a half-smile came to his face as he thought he began to detect a glimmer of light. The dwarf, the black goat, the tarantula, the scene of the coffin in the bedroom, and the final claw-like hand that had protruded round the door could only, as he saw them now, mean one thing. Anthony's half-smile developed into a full one. Conway and Woore must have been radically sure of their ground when they invited him to the evening at "The Limes". And at Blackheath, too! The more he thought matters over, it became increasingly plain to Anthony that something vital must have occurred in the lives of Woore and Conway since he had lunched with the former at the "Waldorf". He put on his best thinking-cap in an effort to work out what that happening probably had been.

After a comparatively short interval of thought, he nodded to himself two or three times. For he thought he could see quite plainly what it was that had induced their second invitation to him. An occurrence which had completely and effectively transposed their respective positions—his and theirs. All this meant that he was now called upon to face an entirely new problem, the successful solution of which he knew full well demanded the promptest of action. He must get into touch with MacMorran as soon as possible. Whether the Inspector would act as he desired, on the information which he would lay before him, was, he considered, extremely doubtful. It would be up to him to convince MacMorran, and it wouldn't be the first time by a long way that he had been called upon to do that. If MacMorran refused to take the steps which he wanted taken, the position would become decidedly awkward.

As he composed himself for sleep, Anthony found himself wondering whether—in the light of what he knew now—it wouldn't be a brainy idea to visit Bray within the next twenty-four hours. As he actually *fell* asleep, his last conscious thought was that the idea was eminently sound.

II

The residence of Miss Drusilla Ives at Bray was delightfully charming. Its white chalet-like appearance, its generally elegant appeal, its beautifully tended garden with its trim green lawns running down to the river, pleased Anthony immensely. The white-aproned, "neat-handed Phyllis" who answered the door to his knock was well in keeping with the rest—she had something, too! She looked doubtfully at Anthony as he announced himself, but decided evidently that she would run the risk. She invited him in, told him that Miss Ives was in residence and that she, no doubt, would be along to see him in a few minutes.

Anthony awaited the lady's appearance in a most daintily decorated lounge, and the feeling gradually took possession of him that he was on top of the world. In due course, Drusilla materialized. She was beautifully turned out, round-eyed and demure.

"Mr. Bathurst," she said, "this is a most pleasant surprise. Do you know, you're the very *last* person I expected to see sitting in here."

"And yet," said he, "it isn't so very long since we were together—is it?"

He watched her carefully to see if the shaft went home. But Drusilla neither batted an eyelid nor turned a hair.

"Do you positively *warm* under the influence of a whisky-and-soda?" she asked invitingly.

"You'd be surprised," he said.

"I'll chance it." She poured out two fairly stiff shots. "Come and sit here." She indicated the settee. "With me." She seated herself at his side. "Now tell me what it is you've come about."

Anthony said: "You know what I was interested in, on the occasion that I last saw you."

She elevated her eyebrows. "Let me see now. Oh, yes, my burglary. That was it, wasn't it?"

Anthony drank some of his whisky-and-soda. "Well—I'm not so interested in that as I was. You weren't expecting to hear that were you?"

She tapped on the carpet with her foot—the tap sounded somewhat impatient. "I'm sorry," she said. "One rather likes to feel important."

He said, "Yes, I suppose so. It's like being cast to play a leading part in a show."

A tiny point of colour began to show on each of her cheeks. She said, "Yes, I suppose one could describe it like that. In a way, that is. But I'm curious. You've *made* me curious. I expect, no doubt, that you intended to—all along. What's happened since I last saw you to relegate my notorious burglary to second place in your estimation?"

"Nothing," said Anthony almost stolidly.

She said, "I don't think I understand. Please explain more fully." The hand that lifted the whisky glass to her lips shook a little.

"Well, it's just this. It hasn't happened since I last saw you." Anthony paused deliberately and drank. She took it well, however, so he replaced his glass on the little table beside him and went on. "And your burglary isn't even second in my estimation. Nothing like it. It's an also ran. Disappointing, isn't it? In fact I rather think that I shall be forced to dismiss the whole affair from my mind. Put it away in a metaphorical coffin and decently bury it. That's really what I came to tell you."

He paused again and drank again. "No," he continued at length. "What I'm chiefly concerned about now is—when the next luxury liner sails for America. I've made inquiries this morning, and they tell me that the first boat sails in three days' time. From Liverpool."

Drusilla shook a bewildered head. "I should have imagined," she said with a toss of it, "that in these days of air travel—"

Anthony imitated her. But his head was far from being bewildered. "It isn't everybody, Miss Ives, who cares for the air. There are still some people old-fashioned enough to prefer the herring-pond."

"Really, Mr. Bathurst," she protested petulantly, "if you *must* talk in riddles."

Anthony, however, continued in his vein, with the utmost composure. "I always think," he said with a reminiscent air, "that it's the first step in these affairs which counts. *Facilis descensus Averno*. The action forms the habit. The habit develops the character. And *voilà*—there's your road to hell with its crazy pavement of good intention! It was the first step which meant everything."

"What am I supposed to do?" demanded Miss Ives. "Assume the white sheet of penance? I would, if only I had the slightest idea of what you are talking about. And when I think that you've come all this way to see me, in order to reprimand me with bell, book and . . ." She paused this time.

"Candle," added Anthony almost wearily. "Or if you prefer it, in the plural—candles. Yes, and what after that?"

She said, "How do you mean, what after that?"

Anthony said, "I'm taking you at your own word. You were obviously going to say more than you did. You stopped abruptly and I supplied the finishing word to your sentence."

"You're very attractive," she said, "but I think it must be my whisky-and-soda. It's really astonishing how it affects some people. Although I shouldn't have thought it would have affected you. Anything like as much."

"You never know," said Anthony, "perhaps I'm still suffering from the effects of last night."

She said, "Oh, that's it, is it? And I've been downright worried over you. It's just a hangover—eh? How frightfully commonplace."

Anthony shook his head. "You're wrong again, Miss Ives. I assure you there's nothing like that about it.—No—I ran into a terrible tragedy last evening."

She said, "You don't say."

"Yes," he said. "A young girl widowed in the most distressing circumstances. A girl, too, of a most unusually devout turn of mind. Most unusual these days. One of the saddest experiences that has ever fallen to my lot. It gets one! Makes one feel so hopelessly helpless."

"You mean," said Drusilla demurely, "that you felt you would give anything to be able to help her—and yet, all the time you couldn't."

Anthony said, "Exactly. You've put it as I would put it myself. That's just how I did feel. And more than that—just as I still feel. She was in a jam and I could do nothing to extricate her."

"Did she ask you to help her?"

Anthony shook his head again. "No. I think she was too overcome with grief. Her husband, you see, died under the most unusual circumstances. At least, as far as this country is concerned."

Drusilla knitted her pretty brows. "Er—how do you mean, Mr. Bathurst?"

"I understand—and she herself was my informant—that he was bitten."

"Bitten? How extraordinary! By a—dog?"

"No. Nothing so commonplace, believe me. By a tarantula." Drusilla gasped. There was no doubt about this. Anthony heard the gasp distinctly. But she still played up hard, however.

"A tarantula! I had no idea that such creatures were ever found in England. Was there any evidence to support her story? I suppose that she must have been telling the truth?"

"My dear lady! Would any woman, any decent woman, joke under such conditions? The idea of such a thing is harrowing. The possibility is too remote. I think we can dismiss it. The lady was good enough to warn me against the tarantula."

Drusilla shuddered. The shudder was as real as the gasp. "What did you do when you received the warning?" The words were almost whispered.

"What did I do?" said Anthony. "I took heed of the warning and made myself scarce."

"Mr. Bathurst," she said in mock severity, "how dreadful of you! And I thought you were both gallant and gay. Are you telling me that you left this lovely creature to her fate?"

"A tarantula isn't lovely," replied Anthony, "far from it."

"No. Not the tarantula, you idiot, I mean the girl. Did you leave her to—"

"A fate worse than death? No. Not exactly. I left her mourning her lost love."

Drusilla sharply changed her tactics. "To me this all sounds like utter rubbish," she said angrily.

Anthony said, "I know. I quite agree with you. It did to me! It *does* to me."

Drusilla ignored his intervention with an air of superb disdain. "Burglars and boat-trains and desolate women! Talk and tarradiddle and tarantulas! It just doesn't add up, Mr. Bathurst."

"You wouldn't think so, would you?" agreed Anthony with disarming candour. "And yet, Miss Ives, and yet . . ."

He paused. The pause was both deliberate and subtle. Drusilla swallowed the bait. "And yet—what, Mr. Bathurst?"

"And yet I think it does. Or rather, shall we say, that it's going to."

Drusilla resorted to elementary weapons. "And there was a time, not so very long ago at that, when I thought I liked you. What strange illusions do come to one."

Anthony said, "I know! Calf-love. We all suffer from it sooner or later."

"Now," went on Drusilla calmly, "I can't make up my mind as to whether I loathe you, hate you, or merely dislike you."

Anthony said, "Loathe, I expect, in all probability. Everything about you is superlative or extreme. You could never be content with middle courses or half measures. I can even imagine—"

Drusilla interrupted him summarily. The time had passed for any obeisance from her to conventional courtesy. "You can even imagine what?" Her tone was acid.

"Why, your reaction, Miss Ives, to a tragedy such as the one I have just described. Had it come your way, I can picture the agony of your distress. I can visualize how it would almost tear your heart in two. I can see you throwing yourself on your knees in prayer—lost to everything but the bitter pain of your own personal sorrow. No, there could never be any half-way house with you." Anthony shook his head slowly.

Drusilla said: "Yes, you are right. I know now. Loathe *is* the word."

Anthony said, "I was afraid so, as I indicated. Do you know, Miss Ives," he proceeded imperturbably, "I wonder you never turned your attention to the 'legit.' You were a marvellous dancer, everybody is in agreement on that point. But I'm certain in my mind that you would have hit the high spots in absolutely serious drama. Yes, even in Shakespearean stuff. Who knows? Lady Macbeth, Desdemona,

Portia, Cordelia—even Ophelia—might all have been well within your compass. Perhaps too Gertrude—the mother of the Prince of Denmark. For all that you and I may know the boards may have lost a second Mrs. Siddons. I'd go even farther than that. You might even have challenged the 'Divine Sarah' herself."

Drusilla set her lips primly and firmly. "I rather think that this discussion has been unduly prolonged. I will wish you a very good morning, Mr. Bathurst, and as I don't suppose I shall ever set eyes on you again, that good morning may also be regarded as good-bye." She rose to give Anthony his dismissal. Anthony imitated her and bowed. "I was afraid that you would say something like that. But I am unable to bring myself to the point of an apology. It would be mere insincerity on my part. At the same time I feel bound to point out that this is far from being 'good-bye' between us. For you will most certainly see me again. And more than once, I'm afraid. When, relatively speaking, the conditions may not be even so happy as they are now. Good morning, Miss Ives."

Drusilla ignored his remarks. "Gladys," she called, "show this gentleman out, will you? And if he calls here again, he is not to be admitted under any circumstances." She turned her back upon Anthony and stood looking through the window on to the garden, one of her feet the while beating a nervous tattoo on the carpet.

"Yes, ma'am," said Gladys from the doorway.

The maid waited pointedly for Anthony to precede her. He walked in front of her to the front door. Gladys showed him out as she had been directed. Neither of them spoke a word.

"'Curiouser and curiouser,'" he quoted to himself as he walked away, "and although I harbour no real doubts in my mind, I am far from being satisfied as to the 'whys and wherefores'. In the meantime, though, I must consult Andrew MacMorran."

Thus decided, he walked rapidly to the station. Arrived there, he 'phoned through to MacMorran. When he was through, he spoke to the Inspector thus:

"I'm coming down to you immediately, Andrew. Expect me somewhere about ten o'clock tonight. There's a train gets into St. Mead just about that time. Also, Andrew, be prepared for a fairly long sitting."

"Oh," said the Inspector, "I like the sound of that. I take it your journey wasn't altogether wasted and was really necessary. What have you found out?"

"You'd be surprised," replied Anthony.

III

As Anthony entered the library at "Palings", the clock on the mantelpiece showed the time at exactly a quarter-past ten. MacMorran had a chair for him, a plate of tongue sandwiches and a quart bottle of ale.

"Good man, Andrew," said Anthony as he sat down. "I don't know what I should do without you."

He at once fell to work on his supper.

"I'll ask no questions, man, till you've fed," said the Inspector.

Anthony grinned. "You can," he said between sandwiches, "but that isn't to say I shall answer 'em."

MacMorran packed tobacco into the bowl of his pipe, pressed it down with his thumb and then lit up. Anthony pushed away his plate, drained his tumbler and proceeded to tell his story of the night at "The Limes", Blackheath. MacMorran's eyes opened wide at the recital. Anthony refrained, however, from mentioning his suspicion of Drusilla Ives, and made no reference to the fact that he had visited her house that morning. When he had finished, MacMorran shook his head in gloomy resignation.

"I can't make head or tail of it, and that's a fact! And in addition, I'm bound to say I'm wondering why you're so cock-a-hoop. For cock-a-hoop you are and it's not the slightest use your denying it. I know the signs too well not to recognize them."

Anthony knew that he was now about to tread on delicate territory. "Yes, Andrew, I'm not going to say that I'm not pleased. We've made very definite progress. In fact, I'm so thoroughly satisfied that I'm all set on our next step."

He paused for MacMorran's inevitable come-back. "And what may that be?"

Anthony lit a cigarette before he replied. "I want you to do something for me, Andrew. And it's something, I'm afraid, that you won't care about doing. In fact, I fancy you'll kick against it."

Anthony tossed away the dead match-end. MacMorran regarded him with a certain amount of suspicion.

"Well, what is it you want me to do? Out with it, it won't get any better through keeping it."

Anthony blew a smoke-ring from his cigarette. "I want you to arrest somebody."

"What for? On what charge?"

"Having stolen property in his possession, well knowing it to have been stolen." There was a silence.

MacMorran sought amplification.

"Who's the man? Or maybe woman? I should like to know that before I answer you."

"He's a visitor to our shores—a Mr. Dwight Conway."

MacMorran intervened with a derisive laugh, and was guilty of a cheap reply. "Oh—yeah!" he exclaimed.

"I mean it, Andrew," said Anthony. "In fact I was never more serious in my life."

The Inspector was silent. "You'll have to do a rare lot of convincing," he began to argue, "before you'll get me to move as you want. Dwight Conway! One of the richest men in the States, and a man, too, with an absolutely clean record."

"So had Marcus Brutus," returned Anthony grimly, "up to the fourteenth of March. But not after that."

MacMorran looked up. Anthony continued, "He lost it the day after."

MacMorran still looked up. He began to realize that Anthony was out to manoeuvre him into an unfavourable position. "Start convincing me, then," he said coolly.

"Good," said Anthony, "now you're being more reasonable. Which is all I ask you to be. I told you all along that the St. Mead murders had their genesis in robbery. Did I or did I not?"

"You did. Still, that's a long way from—"

Anthony waved a deprecating hand. "Wait, Andrew. And listen to me. I'm willing to concede the point that Conway may be innocent of the original moves. Personally I don't think he is, but I'm prepared to give him the benefit of the doubt as far as that goes. But I give you my solemn word that he's after the proceeds of a certain robbery which took place some months ago. You know the one I'm referring to all right."

MacMorran looked surprised and startled. He was about to interpose a remark but Anthony went on relentlessly, giving him no chance to formulate an argument.

"To further his ends, my dear Andrew, our friend Conway (who is an avid collector, by the way) as soon as he realized that something had gone amiss with the works, came across to this country. You will remember how, at that juncture, you and I took a hand in the game. With the pleasing sequel (from our point of view, because it was just what we wanted) that Conway partly emerged from his lair and made contact with us through his agent, Woore."

"Who you tell me is dead," jerked MacMorran.

"Pardon me, Andrew, if I amend that last statement of yours. Who I was told was dead! I would remind you that I have no proof of Mr. Woore's decease."

"You saw the coffin—and the widow mourning him."

"True, Andrew. But I wasn't allowed to see inside the coffin. Quite a point, I think, don't you?"

"O.K.," said the Inspector, "go on with your fairy tale—I mean story."

Anthony grinned. He knew his MacMorran in this mood. Obstinate, unyielding and totally disinclined to surrender one inch of his ground.

"Well, call my narrative what you will, Conway as a result of taking my bait, got me to the 'Waldorf' to lunch with 'the maybe defunct' Woore. You know what happened when we met there."

MacMorran nodded. "Deadlock."

Anthony agreed. "Yes. I think that, justifiably, we might call it that. At any rate, Woore and I made little or no progress. But, Andrew— and I am compelled to draw your attention to this fact—they were ready and waiting to treat with me. They very definitely wanted what they thought I had."

The Inspector raised his eyebrows. "Sure of that?"

Anthony hesitated. He knew very well that MacMorran had put his finger unerringly on the weakest line of his defences. "Not perhaps 'sure'," he answered eventually, "but fairly confident that I'm right in thinking as I do."

"All right," said MacMorran, "I'm nothing like as confident as you are. But go on."

"That," said Anthony, "brought us to the next and latest stage. My evening invitation to 'The Limes'. When our friends from the States decided to extract a certain amount of surplus liquid from the Bathurst constitution. I've thought over the entire performance very carefully and the conclusion I've come to is this. It was a deliberate attempt to horrify me. To supercharge me with an unusual amount of fear of the Almighty. I didn't like any of it—I'll be perfectly candid as to that—but they never got my feet stone cold, or my knees knocking."

Anthony paused. "Do you reckon they banked on your taking fright?" asked the Inspector.

"I wouldn't know, Andrew. But whether they did or whether they didn't, I can claim to have made a reasonably dignified exit from their house of horror." He paused again. When he resumed he spoke more slowly. "But what you and I have to decide, Andrew, is *why* all that thusness?"

MacMorran said, "Bit of a poser, I admit."

"At first blush, yes perhaps. But when you get right down to it and face up to it, as the worthy Alderman of Kersbrook might say, it doesn't look quite so awkward a proposition. And my answer to it is this, Andrew. They were ready to dispose of me, write me off, as it were, *because* I had ceased to be of any value to them. And that was their somewhat contemptuous method of disposal."

MacMorran grunted. Anthony followed up. "And do you see where that gets us to?"

"Well," said MacMorran, "you might argue that, granted your view is the correct—"

Anthony cut into his sentence. "No argument necessary, Andrew. The avenue that's opened to us is quite a simple one to recognize and traverse. I had ceased to be of value to Conway and Woore *because* they had become possessed of what I had been pretending to hold in my possession." Anthony stopped abruptly. "There you are, Andrew," he added, "full score up to the fall of the last wicket."

Somewhat to Anthony's surprise, MacMorran leant towards him over the table and said, "Mr. Bathurst, I think you're r-right."

The roll of the strong consonant was evidence that the Inspector was stirred from his normal sangfroid. As he leant forward, Anthony pushed back his chair and grinned.

"Chief Detective-Inspector MacMorran," he said, "I'm delighted to hear it."

MacMorran nodded, with a strange solemnity which struck Anthony as semi-humorous. "Yes, I agree with you," proceeded the Inspector, "I think you've put your finger on the right spot. Absolutely! Something happened between your luncheon at the 'Waldorf' and your evening at the Blackheath circus which put those people—Conway's crowd as you call them—in possession of what they were after. Hence the change in their methods and in their reception of you."

"Exactly, Andrew. And that's why I'm asking you to arrest the gentleman by the name of Dwight Conway."

But hereat, some at least of the Inspector's enthusiasm appeared to evaporate. "Eh," he said, "but just a minute. There's a wee bit difference here. My thinking as you're thinking doesn't mean that I'm ready to arrest anybody—yet awhile. Have a care, man, and let's look round at things before we commit ourselves."

"If you don't arrest Dwight Conway when I tell you to, Andrew, I'll make one prophecy. And that's this. You never will arrest him!"

"Eh—and why not?"

"Because, my dear Andrew, he will have gone. Your bonny will be over the ocean, and once he lands anywhere near the Statue of Liberty, you can whistle for your man. You can take that from me, Andrew, as a genuine cast-iron stone-bonker."

MacMorran was beginning to see where Anthony had led him. He temporized. He said, "I've only got your word for that."

Anthony said, "Yes, and you've only got my word for lots of other things, but you know all time how right they are." He poured himself out the remainder of the bottle of ale. "Now look here, Andrew," he said persuasively, "Conway and Woore will leave this country in three days' time. They'll travel by the *Cyclonic*. She leaves Liverpool at the end of the week. If you ring up the shipping company, I'm open to bet their passages will be booked."

MacMorran looked at him round-eyed. "Do you mean to tell me, at *this* juncture, that you haven't checked up on that?"

Anthony shook his head. "Word of honour, Andrew, I haven't. I'm so certain of my hunch that I've not even troubled to verify it."

He drained his last glass of beer. As he did so, an idea occurred to him. He thought he saw a chance of persuading MacMorran to do as he wanted him to do. He at once translated the idea into a cold proposal. "I'll tell you what I'll do, Andrew," he said. "You test it! *You* ring up the shipping company, and if you find I'm right, and that Conway and Woore *are* flitting from us, well then—go the whole hog and arrest Conway as I asked you to."

He leant back again, so as to give time for the proposition to sink into MacMorran's mind. At the same time, he thought he knew the line which MacMorran would adopt. Anthony proved to be right. MacMorran looked up and said.

"No, you don't. You're not wheedling any hard and fast promises out of me. Not if I know it."

He sat back prim and straight in his chair and endeavoured to look as hard and unyielding as he felt. Anthony knew that he must embrace subtlety if he were to achieve his desires.

"All right, Andrew. I see your point and I'm content to leave the decision entirely to your own judgment. Test my theory, as I said, by ringing up the offices of the *Cyclonic*. That's all I ask you to do. You can then base your future action on what they have to tell you. But I'll warn you, Andrew—I warned you before and I'll warn you again—if you once let them slip out of your hands, you won't get a second chance! That's as certain as tomorrow's sunrise."

Anthony replaced the stopper in the beer-bottle, screwed it appropriately and put the bottle back on the tray. MacMorran sat and drummed with his finger-tips on the table. Some seconds elapsed before he made any reply.

"I'll let you know," he said at length. "I'll let you know when I hear whether your *Cyclonic* theory's sound or not. When I'm certain about that, I'll make my mind up about the other matter. I'll make no other promises."

"That suits me, Andrew. I'll ask nothing more than that. Because I'm perfectly certain that by that time you'll realize that I'm right.

You'll act! And at once! Because you'll know then you can't afford to risk anything."

A slow smile spread over the professional's features. "You'll do," he muttered. "And if you think you're going to talk me into an action I'm not in agreement with, you're barking up the wrong tree. You need harbour no illusions about that."

He shut his mouth with something like a snap and folded his arms on the table. But before Anthony could answer, MacMorran spoke again.

"And there's something else, Mr. Bathurst. Something I can't quite fathom. Maybe you've not thought of it. But it's been on my mind for some little time."

"What's that, Andrew?"

"You say this fellow Dwight Conway, with his assistant Woore, is anxious to get out of the country. Right?"

"Yes, undoubtedly."

"And to get back to the States as quickly as he knows how. Right again, eh?"

"Yes. I agree entirely."

"Well then, admitting that, why the heck doesn't he go by air?" MacMorran leant back in his seat with the look of a man who has administered the *coup de grâce* to his opponent. "Had you thought of that?" he added.

Anthony took his time over his reply. "Yes, Andrew, I considered that when I first saw how the cards were being played. And do you know how I shall answer it? Because I'm ready to admit that it's quite a good point."

"How?" demanded MacMorran.

"In this way. Conway came to this country by boat. *And* he was in a devil of a hurry to get here! He wasn't sure what had happened—at least that's my opinion—his mind was bemused and he just *had* to know as soon as possible, but *despite* all that he made the journey by sea! Ergo—I deduce that for some personal reason of his own, he prefers the liner to the 'plane and that he will return the same way as he came."

Anthony rose and stretched his arms. "Well—I'm for the hay. Does my explanation find favour in your sight, Andrew?"

MacMorran growled an unintelligible reply. Anthony in an effort to hear inclined an ear towards him. He concluded that what MacMorran had said had been, "Maybe it does—and maybe it doesn't."

IV

MacMorran did not telephone the offices of the "White Stripe" Shipping Company, as he had half intimated to Anthony that he would. Actually, he took a stronger line that that. He called at the London office in person. A somewhat supercilious clerk was rendered ineffective upon MacMorran disclosing his identity and subsequently producing his credentials.

"I think," said the clerk dubiously, "that the best thing you can do is to have a word with the manager. Just wait here one minute, will you, please?"

"I think it is," replied the Inspector. He cooled his heels in the outer office for the matter of a couple of minutes, at the end of which period the clerk reappeared.

The latter appeared, by now, to be suitably impressed.

"Come this way, will you, please?"

MacMorran came as he was asked and was shown into the manager's office. The latter cast a sidelong eye on the Inspector's card and invited him to sit down. The manager was a stout, fleshy man whose glasses gave his face the look of a large bird. MacMorran noticed that his top lip came over and enfolded his lower.

"You were inquiring about . . .?" asked the manager.

MacMorran told him the details of the object of his visit. The manager's face brightened somewhat.

"Oh yes," he answered, "Mr. Dwight Conway. *The* Mr. Dwight Conway. Yes, I remember, of course. He crossed on our liner, the *Typhonic*, on its latest trip. Yes—that is so. Mr. Conway booked one of our luxury suites for his return journey. That is . . . er . . . the title they're advertised under. Er . . . not title . . . description. Yes, quite right, Mr. Dwight Conway."

"Yes," returned MacMorran. "But I'm concerned at the moment with Mr. Dwight Conway's departure—not so much his arrival. There was, if I may say so, a certain amount of Press publicity given to his journey here. There hasn't been *any* publicity *yet* with regard to his return to his native land. That's why I'm here talking things over with you today."

The manager of the London office of the "White Stripe" Shipping Company eyed the Inspector curiously. "The police and Mr. Dwight Conway? Am I to believe my ears?"

"You can believe what you like," countered MacMorran curtly, "but please answer my questions."

The manager fluttered weakly. "Certainly, Inspector! Er . . . certainly. Only too pleased. And what's the information exactly that you desire?"

"Merely this," said MacMorran, again curtly. "Has Conway booked a passage on the *Cyclonic*? She sails, I believe, at the end of this week."

The manager drew his finger across his loose top lip. For a moment or so MacMorran was uncertain as to whether he intended to be frank or otherwise. Good sense, however, prevailed, and the Scotland Yard Inspector got the answer he wanted.

"Er . . . yes, Inspector MacMorran . . . Mr. Dwight Conway has reserved a luxury suite on our liner, the *Cyclonic*, which sails, as you say, at the end of the week. You are quite correct as to detail. Your information is perfectly sound." He smiled fatuously at the Inspector.

When the answer came, MacMorran realized with some surprise that his own forehead was profuse in perspiration. Absurd, he thought, what on earth's the matter with me? He wiped his forehead with his handkerchief and sat back in his chair.

"Thank you," he said, "that's what I wanted to know. For certain! Naturally, I always like to feel absolutely sure of my ground, I came here to make sure, because I always believe in going straight to the fountain-head. Thank you again."

"Is that the—er—sum total of the information you desire from me, Inspector MacMorran?"

"Yes—that's all, thank you."

The manager inclined his head in courteous recognition of the statement and pressed a bell. The clerk who had ushered MacMorran in now appeared for the purpose of ushering him out. The Inspector accepted the situation and made his exit.

In the train, on his return journey to St. Mead, the realization came to him, almost as a shock, that he had still to make a decision on the matter of the implementation of Anthony Bathurst's direct wishes. He couldn't explain to himself why he hadn't thought of this directly after the "White Stripe" manager had confirmed Bathurst's theory in relation to Dwight Conway. So, up to now, Bathurst had been right! MacMorran shifted uneasily in his seat. How could he evade the final steps? He took a half-crown from his pocket furtively and spun it a short distance in the air. "Heads for Bathurst—tails against him," he murmured to himself. The coin came down "heads". MacMorran frowned heavily at Fate. His face brightened as a comforting thought came to him. "Best of three," he whispered to himself. The half-crown, spun again, showed "heads" as before. Another frown from MacMorran. "Best of five," he mumbled to himself. He started to spin the coin again. "Tails" descended twice in succession. "Better," said MacMorran, "the long test is the real test after all." But the fifth came "heads" again and MacMorran was back to the unpalatable position he had been in before. The coin had fallen for Bathurst on the three decisive occasions! He sat bolt upright, his back pressed hard against the upholstery of the compartment. More than once he shook his head. He would have another conference with Anthony before he reached his final decision. Yes—that was by far the best course he could take. He wasn't going to be rushed into an impulsive and impetuous action against his better judgment. More than that—and there *was* more in it than that—against his *professional* judgment. And after all, he'd had *years* of experience, whereas Bathurst . . .

MacMorran assumed a more comfortable posture. He felt much easier in his mind now that he had come to a decision. In a way, he felt that his mind was now made up, when before he had wavered and vacillated. Although he would give Anthony the benefit of a conference with him, he knew what his own final judgment was going to be. Everything he had done today had been for the best and it all seemed to him to be entirely satisfactory. Musing thus, MacMorran closed his eyes until the train ran into the little station at St. Mead.

V

Anthony was ready for him immediately he got back to "Palings". He watched the Inspector's face as he walked up the garden towards him. But MacMorran was a wily bird with the experience of many summers, and his face could wear the mask of impassivity as well as the next man's when he so desired. The present was an occasion which fell into that category.

"Hallo," said MacMorran. "Waiting for me—eh? Sweating on the top line, I suppose?"

Anthony said with a grin, "I'm certainly not going to admit that. But I'm prepared to hear all you have to tell me."

"Come inside, then, and sit down. And before we start discussing things and arguing over them, I tell you straight that my mind's made up." The Inspector closed his mouth with a snap and stuck out his lower jaw. Anthony knew very well what this portended. He still had the job of persuading the Inspector against his will.

"Good. I'm glad to hear that I've convinced you so thoroughly that my line of reasoning's the correct one. Still, I was confident all the time. I know you're a man who will always see reason."

MacMorran glared at him. Anthony found two chairs and they seated themselves. "Cigarette, Andrew?" he said as he proffered his case to the Inspector.

"Thanks." Anthony supplied the necessary light and lit a cigarette for himself. Then he settled down to wait.

MacMorran also waited until he realized that he would have to make a start eventually. So he cleared his throat and started the ball rolling. "Well, I called at the London offices of the 'White Stripe' Shipping Company as I promised you I would." He paused. Anthony remained silent. So MacMorran went on again. "I saw the manager. And I put certain questions to him."

Anthony nodded. He said, "Good. That's exactly what I wanted you to do."

"I asked him about your man Dwight Conway. He came over on the *Typhonic*. He returns at the end of this week by the *Cyclonic*. He's booked a luxury suite on that liner. I had no difficulty in getting hold of that."

MacMorran stopped again. Anthony intervened—gently but firmly. "As I told you, Andrew."

"Er—yes. You did indicate that, I admit."

"So you were thoroughly satisfied—eh?"

MacMorran said, "I wouldn't say that."

Anthony said, "Why wouldn't you? That was what you travelled up to find out, wasn't it? You went for a check-up on the value of my deductions."

"In a way I suppose I did. You could put it like that, I suppose." Anthony said, "Well then, what's the matter? Surely that clinches my point?"

MacMorran fidgeted in his chair. "That's only part of the truth. Because all I've been able to establish is that Dwight Conway's returning to the States on the *Cyclonic*. I've established nothing else, have I?"

Anthony said, "What else did you expect to establish? That Dwight Conway's special pedigree sow has farrowed a litter of seventeen pigs way back in Wyoming or somewhere?"

MacMorran looked at him with suspicion. "What's the point of that remark?"

"None," replied Anthony cheerfully. "It was as completely pointless as your last remark. That's why I thought of it."

"This isn't getting us anywhere," said MacMorran, with a hint of resignation in his voice.

"I beg to differ, Andrew. Although it may not be getting us anywhere, it's helping to get Conway and his associate back to America. *With* the spoils of Elmer Oliver's robbery. Still, that doesn't matter. Only two men have been murdered so far because of it. And what are two amongst so many?"

"Maybe you know more than I do," said the Inspector obstinately.

"I don't," answered Anthony with hard emphasis. "You know all that I know. I've told you all that matters. And because of what I've told you, there's only one intelligent course open to you. And you also know what that is. I'm sorry, Andrew—I'm not disposed to spare you."

"If you would only put yourself in my place," began MacMorran.

"I'm ready and willing to do so. I always have been and always shall be. And you know the truth of that, you old sinner. But"—and here Anthony paused with deliberate intent—"if you persist in your present attitude, I shouldn't care to be in your shoes in a week's time. For, Andrew, as I told you before, if you let Conway slip through your fingers this time, your chance of solving the St. Mead murders will speedily evaporate. I've noticed that the gods have no mercy on those unhappy wights who are foolish enough to miss open goals."

MacMorran sat in his chair glum, irritable and silent. Anthony rose and strolled to the window. At last the Inspector broke the silence.

"I shall look a first-class B.F. if I arrest Conway and then find there's nothing on him. Dwight Conway of all people, too! An American! An American millionaire at that! If it were Bill Smith of Bermondsey I shouldn't mind so much—it would be a horse of another colour. I wish I could get you to see that."

Anthony changed his tactics. "My dear Andrew," he said, "I do see it. And I do understand how you feel about things. But I've never let you down yet. You'd admit that, wouldn't you? And I tell you confidently I shan't let you down on this occasion. If you like, have it out with the Commissioner himself. Put all the facts as we know them in front of Sir Austin. In that way, to an extent at least, you may be able to cover yourself. Well, how does that appeal to you?"

"Not a lot. Don't fancy I shall increase my popularity with the old man. I shall stand on the contrary quite a good chance of going off with a flea in my ear. You know how impatient he is. Especially seeing the way the case has gone. Or hasn't gone—to be more precise."

MacMorran's gloom grew noticeably. Anthony sat opposite him and waited. "If you do as I'm asking you, Andrew, I'll promise you something else," he said at length.

"What's that?" asked MacMorran.

"You shall arrest the murderer of Steel and Elmer Oliver within a week. Or, at the latest, within a fortnight. Put the bracelets on him, Andrew. Or her, of course! You get the idea—'Chief-Inspector MacMorran solves yet another murder mystery.' *Yet another*, Andrew. Sounds good that, doesn't it?"

With a sudden impulse, the Inspector got up from his chair. "I'll sleep on it," he said tersely. Anthony nodded his acceptance of the offer. MacMorran walked to the door of the room before he turned. "It's not so red hot that it can't wait till the morning," he added.

"I agree. When will you let me know your decision?" asked Anthony.

"At breakfast tomorrow morning," replied the Inspector. "I'll come down definitely, one side or the other, before you and I have finished breakfast in the morning. That's a promise."

"O.K.," said Anthony, "till tomorrow morning, then. I'll wait in patience."

"You see—" commenced MacMorran.

"I know," said Anthony, interrupting him, "but you've said it all before, Andrew. It will be sheer waste of your time and mine to say it all over again. Let's leave it as it is—breakfast."

When MacMorran pushed back his chair on the following morning, after having eaten a breakfast in solemn silence, he turned to Anthony and said, "I'm going up to town to see Sir Austin."

"Good," said Anthony. "Remember me kindly to him, will you, Andrew?" He grinned as MacMorran made his way out. "Oh . . . and by the way," he called to the Inspector in the doorway. "Wish him from me many happy returns of next Tuesday."

VI

Once again, Anthony waited for MacMorran's return to St. Mead. To his surprise, somewhat, the Inspector was back at a comparatively early hour, and to his satisfaction and relief, he saw that MacMorran's face had cleared and that he had obviously ridded himself of doubt and personal anxiety. He smiled as he walked towards Anthony.

"You win," he said, "so far, that is. I've had it out with the old man, and he's agreed to go ahead on your lines. Satisfied?"

"You'll be the bloke that's satisfied," said Anthony.

"That," riposted MacMorran, "remains to be seen. Still your blood'll be on your own head now, and if anybody's head is screamed for, after the balloon's gone up, yours is the one that will be supplied. And on a charger."

"That's a bet, Andrew. My head may land up bloody, but I assure you it will be unbowed."

"Right," said MacMorran, "now let's get down to strict business, Because it's time we did."

"Nothing," said Anthony, "would suit me better. It's the most comforting remark I've heard from you for days."

MacMorran ignored the sally. Now that he had crossed the Rubicon, there was no looking back for him, and from now on, all his energies would be fully directed to the task ahead.

"I've made all inquiries and the *Cyclonic*," he announced dispassionately, "sails from Liverpool on Saturday afternoon. Approximately at half-past four. Do I hold my hand until Conway is on board her?"

Anthony thought over the question.

"I'm afraid you'll have to. The goods, you see, will be on board her as well. Passenger's luggage—'not wanted on the voyage'. You'll have a warrant with you for search. Conway will have stolen property in his possession well knowing it to have been stolen. That's your line of attack, Andrew."

MacMorran came in with a second question. "No more detailed description than that?"

Anthony furrowed his brow. "No, Andrew, I don't think so, at the moment. Better be general, I think, than too particular. Then there will be less chance of our slipping up on anything."

"I agree. I feel as you do there. Now as to our own plans. Yours and mine. You coming up north with me? Or do I do the job on my own?"

Anthony considered the point. "How do you feel yourself about it?" he asked the Inspector.

"Open mind. Absolutely! Don't think I care particularly one way or the other. It's just how it appeals to you. If you want to accompany me, do so by all means."

"In that case, Andrew, I think I'd better make the journey with you. In all these cases, I've generally found that two heads are better than one. You never know what may turn up. Not that there'll be any likelihood of a rough house. The *Cyclonic*'s much too respectable! To say nothing of the luxury suite."

MacMorran nodded. "Suits me. And as you say, you never know exactly what may turn up."

"I've another reason," said Anthony, "for wanting to come along with you. It's just suggested itself to me. It's difficult to describe. Sort of wanting to be in at the death. Although it's not *quite* on all fours with that. It's this. I want to see my friend Woore's face when he sees me arrive in person, as your bodyguard. To say nothing of what his face will look like when he realizes how much the tables have been turned."

"They're personal reasons," grumbled MacMorran, "they have nothing to do with the case on its merits. I don't know that I'm interested in them. I can almost say that they leave me stone cold."

"Very true, Andrew," said Anthony, "but you didn't spend a pleasant social evening at Blackheath as I did. If you'd been included in my invitation, you might feel rather differently on the matter. Between you and me, I take a very dim view of my entertainment at 'The Limes'."

MacMorran regarded him with some surprise. "It's not like you to get the 'jitters'. You've been in tougher spots than that, many times. So I don't see why—"

Anthony intervened. "It had to be seen and endured to be believed. The mere recital of it, in the cold light of day, is hopelessly inadequate. It leaves far too much to the imagination."

"I'll take your word for it," said MacMorran. He rose. "When shall we travel up? Friday afternoon?"

Anthony nodded his agreement. "The afternoon of Friday, Andrew, is most certainly indicated."

"Right," replied MacMorran, "then we'll leave it at that."

VII

Anthony and MacMorran left the Palatine Hotel in Lime Street, Liverpool, at two o'clock punctually in the afternoon of the following Saturday. They had agreed on the time after some mutual discussion.

"I don't want to put in an appearance too early," MacMorran had stated, "and similarly, I don't want to cut it too fine at the other end."

A taxi took them to the Caroline Dock. "Whom will you go to?" asked Anthony—"the skipper?"

MacMorran nodded. "Ay! The skipper'll be my man. None other." He chuckled to himself after he had spoken. "Reckon it'll come as a surprise to the skipper of so famous a ship as the *Cyclonic* to find 'Scotland Yard' in the ship. New experience for him. And the 'Yard' not on a pleasure cruise, either—in attendance strictly on business."

MacMorran chuckled again. Anthony could see that the Inspector was finding the situation attractive. He was about to reply to him, when the taxi began to slow down and the driver slewed his body round towards his passengers.

"*Cyclonic*'s lying alongside Number 4," he shouted. "I'll run you down as far as they'll let me."

He turned the cab down a squalid turning where different-hued children were attempting to make a pleasure ground out of the amenities of the kerbs and pavements. The cab travelled down to the dock entrance and Anthony and MacMorran alighted.

"Number 4," repeated the taxi-driver, "and thank you very much, sir."

"Here's for it," said the Inspector as he walked forward.

"Here's to it," said Anthony as he followed his companion.

A uniformed dock official came to meet them when they had gone but a few yards. MacMorran went straight up to him.

"I am Chief Detective-Inspector MacMorran of Scotland Yard. Is Inspector Sagar here yet?"

"No, sir," replied the man addressed, "but he 'phoned through about a quarter of an hour ago to say that he'd be here about a quarter to three. He asked me to apologize on his behalf for the brief delay."

"He was to have met me outside," said MacMorran.

"Yes, sir," came the reply, "so I understood from him." MacMorran turned to Anthony. "Sagar's the local Inspector of Police. I had to bring him in on the job."

"I understand," replied Anthony.

"Annoying he's late," muttered MacMorran. He looked at his watch. "The sooner I get this job done the better I'll be pleased."

"In the meantime, though," said Anthony, "we must wait in patience here until your Inspector Sagar puts in his belated appearance. In the circumstances, there seems to be nothing else for it."

"That's right," said MacMorran, "we've got to wait. Let's hope Sagar's two-forty-five will be two forty-five and not three o'clock." MacMorran and Anthony waited by the large shed placed just inside the entrance to the dock. On this second occasion, the Liverpool police-inspector did not let them down, for he proved to be as good as his word. At seventeen minutes to three he walked in and shook hands with MacMorran and Anthony.

"I'm ready, Chief," he said breezily, "so lead on."

He was a trim, compact, brisk-mannered man with a smartly-clipped dark moustache, and neatness written all over him. He struck Anthony as efficient and more than ordinarily businesslike.

"Perhaps," suggested MacMorran, "seeing that you're familiar with the docks here generally, and know your way about, it would be as well if you did the leading on. What do you say yourself, Inspector Sagar?"

"That's O.K. by me," answered Sagar genially. "If you fall in and follow me, I'll lead you straight away to where the *Cyclonic*'s berthed. She's expected to get away about half-past four, you said, didn't you?"

MacMorran nodded. "That's quite right. We're all serene as regards time. Nothing to worry about in that direction."

Sagar led them down the dock, past several landing-stages until they came to the huge liner with the "White Stripe" Line flag fluttering in the wind. It was a cold but sunny afternoon and the big ship was a sight for sore eyes. Bustle and activity were in unmistakable evidence. The gangways from the dockside to the liner were thronged with people going aboard the mighty liner, and articles of luggage were being hoisted aboard her from all directions. Sagar led the way up one of the less-populated gangways. Anthony and MacMorran followed in close proximity. As they made the deck, Sagar turned to a steward who stood near by. The steward listened to what Sagar had to say and then turned a curious glance towards Inspector MacMorran. Then he nodded and said:

"Captain Legard is on board. I'll see whether I can communicate with him for you."

Sagar motioned to the other two as the steward made off and the three of them stood aside to give the right of way to the oncoming flood of people. Within the space of a few minutes the steward returned with one of the junior officers. He addressed himself to MacMorran.

"If you come along with me," he said, "I'll see if I can get into touch with Captain Legard."

Sagar fell in with Anthony and MacMorran and they advanced in the rear of the junior officer conducting them. Anthony saw that they were bound for the captain's cabin. After much jostling and quick avoidance of various people who all seemed intent on getting in each other's way as much as possible, Anthony, who made up the rear of the conducted party, saw their guide stop a few paces ahead of him and tap respectfully on a beautifully decorated panelled door. Then he saw their junior officer turn and say a word or two rather hurriedly to MacMorran and then disappear behind the door on which he had just previously knocked. Anthony knew then that his own personal testing-time was close at hand. After a wait of a few minutes, the junior officer reappeared and beckoned to them. In response to the invitation, Anthony, MacMorran and Sagar filed into the presence of the captain of the "White Stripe" liner *Cyclonic*. Anthony saw a stout, ruddy-faced, blue-eyed man standing behind a table almost in the middle of the cabin.

"Good afternoon, gentlemen," he said brusquely. "And please remember I'm an exceedingly busy man, especially at the present moment."

MacMorran returned the greeting and handed over a letter and his personal card. The captain read the former, glanced at the latter and frowned. Then he turned to his own officer and said, "You may go, Mr. Fraser."

"Very good, sir." The junior officer promptly left the cabin. The captain waved the three visitors to various chairs.

"Now, Chief-Inspector MacMorran," he said, "I've read your letter of credit. Kindly supply me with a few more details."

"Certainly, Captain Legard," replied MacMorran. "We have reason to believe—" and then he remembered that he had left something undone. "I'm sorry. I was forgetting myself. This is Inspector Sagar of Liverpool, and Mr. Anthony Bathurst—Captain Legard."

Legard nodded curtly. "Pleased to meet you, gentlemen. Though I can't truthfully say that I find you welcome just at this moment. Quite frankly I could have done without you. Now, Inspector, your details, if you please."

MacMorran started again. "We have reason to believe, Captain Legard, that you have on board, as a passenger to New York, a certain Mr. Dwight Conway."

Legard said, "So I'm told. What about it?"

"I have a warrant to search his possessions."

Legard raised his eyebrows. "Dope?"

MacMorran shook his head. Anthony saw that he had come all over gloomy again. He was preparing to shy at the water-jump!

"No," went on MacMorran, "robbery."

"H'm," said Legard, "bit of a tall order, isn't it? Asking me to believe that? The man's reputed to be a millionaire many times over."

"Well," said MacMorran, "I called it robbery. That was near enough. More precisely, we suspect him of having certain highly valuable articles in his possession well knowing the same to have been stolen."

A cloud came over Legard's face. "H'm—like that, is it? Must say I find it difficult to swallow. Still, you're Scotland Yard—you say so." He paused, to go on again almost immediately. "Well, what do you want me to do about it? How do you suggest we act? To avoid—too much—er—you know what I mean—publicity—er . . . disturbance—inconvenience?"

"Well . . ." began MacMorran, but before he could develop his reply Captain Legard cut in again.

"I know what you chaps are from Dept. C.I. of New Scotland Yard. I haven't lived as long as I have without coming into contact with you fellows at some time or the other. No matter how innocent I may look."

"Well," started MacMorran again, "my suggestion's this. I've considered it thoroughly and I don't think we can do better. Send a private word to Conway that he's wanted in your cabin. Tell him you'd like a word with him before you sail. If I'm any judge of the man he'll be flattered. He'll probably attribute the incident to his own importance and your eagerness to make his acquaintance."

Captain Legard smiled a frosty smile. "I'll say," he muttered from the corner of his mouth. MacMorran waited for the captain's decision.

"All right," said Legard eventually, with a suspicion of a shrugged shoulder, "we'll adopt your plan as suggested. Anyhow, we'll see what comes of it. There's one thing," he added, "we're safe enough if it comes to a show-down or a shake-up. We're four to one. Good enough odds for anybody."

Captain Legard leant forward, put a hand under his table and touched a bell. A uniformed attendant answered the call almost immediately.

"Find out where Mr. Dwight Conway is, give him my compliments and will he do me the honour of coming to my cabin, will you? Understand?"

"Yes, sir. Mr. Dwight Conway, sir. Very good, sir."

Captain Legard sat in his chair and lolled back in it. But he was icy-eyed, tight-lipped and spoke no more. After a slight interval, Anthony looked at his wrist-watch. The time was passing and he saw the seconds chasing each other on the dial. Two minutes became five and five became ten. The only change in the situation came from the impatient tapping on the carpet of Captain Legard's left foot.

After an interval of twelve minutes, the captain's messenger returned.

"Sorry, sir," he said, "but Mr. Dwight Conway hasn't come aboard yet."

"Thank you," returned Captain Legard. The man went. Legard swung his chair round to his trio of visitors. "There you are, gentlemen. You heard!"

MacMorran looked across at Anthony. Anthony nodded and spoke more to Legard, perhaps, than to any of the others.

"He's probably cutting it pretty fine. After all—why should he hurry himself? You sail round about 4.30—isn't that so, Captain Legard?"

The captain of the *Cyclonic* nodded curtly. "That is my intention." Then he seemed to sense MacMorran's embarrassment. "I suppose you feel a little awkward, Inspector. A case of the early bird being a trifle too early. Can't be helped. Better that way than the other. You're welcome for the time being, to the seclusion that my cabin grants." His eye took in Sagar and Anthony Bathurst. "And, for that matter, so are your sisters and your cousins and your aunts."

"Thank you, Captain Legard," replied MacMorran.

"Thanks for me, too," said Anthony, "on behalf of the relatives as mentioned."

Captain Legard's eyes twinkled. "Very nice of you."

MacMorran still showed signs of being fidgety. "How shall I know when Conway does board the ship?" he asked.

"Of course! Thoughtless of me. I should have seen to that. I'll rectify that at once for you." Legard pressed the bell again and the same uniformed attendant answered the summons that had done so on the previous occasion. "Go to Mr. Dwight Conway's cabin," said Captain Legard, "and stooge round there until he arrives. When he does put in an appearance give him the message that I gave you just now. That I'd like a word with him in my cabin immediately. Don't miss him on any account. Understand?"

"Yes, sir. As you said, sir."

The attendant made himself scarce again. Legard sat easily and comfortably in his chair. "That suit you, Inspector? Shouldn't be any loophole there. My man'll pick him up for you all right."

"What I'm afraid of," said MacMorran diffidently, "is that Conway may come on board bang on time and my subsequent business with him will mean delay from your point of view."

Legard smiled. "Don't get dithered up on my account. *Cyclonic* isn't tied to a minute."

"Thank you," said MacMorran, "I'm glad to hear that."

It was in these moods that they waited in Captain Legard's cabin. Sagar had a conversation with MacMorran which they carried on in almost a low-toned whisper. Suddenly Legard looked up from some papers which he had been studying.

"What do you fellows say to a little—"

Before he could complete what he had been about to say, there came a tap on the door. At Legard's curt "Come in", there entered the uniformed attendant who had been detailed to wait for Dwight Conway.

"Mr. Conway has come aboard, sir. I've delivered your message as instructed. He will be with you, sir, in the matter of a few minutes."

"Thank you, Boyd," said Captain Legard. "You heard that, Inspector? Get ready to say your piece, then."

MacMorran nodded. The crucial moment had caught up with him at last. He was called upon to endure a further tension-period of six minutes. Anthony timed it with exactitude. A second tap on the door heralded the arrival of Dwight Conway. When he entered at Legard's brusque invitation, Anthony took a good look at him. Conway was a middle-aged man with very fair hair that was now turning to a sandy-coloured grey. He had a narrow forehead, watery blue eyes, a receding chin and a weak, dissipated face. He was dressed in a suit of expensive tweeds and entered the cabin with an air of adroit assurance which sat on him rather incongruously. His gait, Anthony thought, was a trifle unsteady, as though he had not fully recovered from a recent bout of hard and heavy drinking.

As he crossed the threshold of Captain Legard's cabin, he became instantly aware of the presence of the third parties, and he pulled himself up with a sudden jerk. A look of arrogance came into his eyes, arrogance that was soon companioned by suspicion. But beyond this, he gave no sign that he was either embarrassed or even mildly perturbed. With eyes only for Captain Legard and completely ignoring the presence of the others, he walked towards the captain and said in a voice that carried a pronounced American accent, "You sent for me, I think, Captain Legard. Waal, here I am."

Legard smiled and waved him to a seat. "Quite right, Mr. Conway—I did. There's a gentleman here who wants a word with you." Legard indicated Inspector MacMorran.

MacMorran rose and faced Dwight Conway. "Good afternoon, Mr. Conway," he said.

Conway stared at him rather superciliously. "I am Chief Detective-Inspector MacMorran of the Criminal Investigation Department—C.I.D.," went on MacMorran. "There's my authority—if you wish to satisfy yourself on the point."

MacMorran flicked a document in front of Conway, and Anthony, to his satisfaction, saw the latter whiten round the gills. Conway collected himself quickly.

He summoned a smile for MacMorran's benefit.

"That's O.K., I've no doubt," he said, "but in what way does it concern me? I don't recollect having called in the Police."

"I have a warrant for search, Mr. Conway," continued the Inspector, "for search of your personal effects. Information has been brought to me that you are in possession of certain stolen property, knowing it full well to have been stolen."

Conway laughed, but Anthony's ear told him that the laugh was forced and false. "That's a good one, I must say," exclaimed Conway.

"If it weren't a serious matter, I'd say the joke was on me. I don't know the source of your so-called information, officer, but I'm afraid somebody's played you for a sucker, and I should have guessed you to be too old a bird to fall for it."

Conway thrust his hands into his pockets with an affected nonchalance. MacMorran's reply was short and sharp.

"That remains to be proved." He turned to the skipper of the *Cyclonic*. "Will you arrange, Captain Legard, for this gentleman's luggage to be brought here and searched in your presence? Inspector Sagar will supervise the removal."

Legard nodded his agreement with the suggestion. "I'll ring for Boyd."

When Boyd came in, the Liverpool inspector went along with him as had been arranged. Conway crossed his legs with an air of infinite boredom.

"I'm sorry this has happened—darned sorry—because I shall seek redress in the proper quarter. I promise you that! And I wouldn't care to stand in your shoes then, Inspector MacMorran, by any means. Still, you're the guy who'll be mainly interested in the funeral party." MacMorran judged it prudent to remain silent. But it must be confessed, Conway's attitude generally was causing him a certain amount of inward misgiving. He glanced round at Anthony Bathurst. The latter's eye met MacMorran's and the Inspector saw the right lid drop unmistakably. At this somewhat unconventional procedure, MacMorran experienced a surge of relief. If Bathurst were feeling like that about things, well and good! Conway still sat imperturbable and after a time began to hum a tune. Suddenly he turned to Legard.

"I've knocked about a good deal, Captain Legard, in many corners of this old earth and I've seen many strange sights, but I can honestly say that I've never run into a reception party quite like this."

Legard smiled his wintry smile. "My ship," he said, "can claim to be unique in many respects. Maybe this reception party, as you're pleased to call it, is one of 'em."

"Maybe," rejoined Conway easily.

He examined his fingernails with studied care. Ten minutes or so passed before the return of Inspector Sagar. When he did eventually show up, three men came with him, Boyd and two others, and they each carried a cabin-trunk on their shoulders.

"One at a time, if you don't mind," declared Legard.

Sagar saw that Legard's direction was complied with. Conway viewed the proceedings with a disdain he took no pains to conceal.

Boyd dumped his trunk in the cabin. The two others lowered theirs and waited outside until further orders should be forthcoming. MacMorran superintended the opening of the first trunk and Anthony and Inspector Sagar stood by in close attendance. But when the contents of cabin trunk number one were disclosed, it was seen to contain clothes and personal belongings only. Conway still watched the proceedings contemptuously but offered no further remarks.

"Bring in the second trunk," ordered MacMorran curtly. The same procedure was gone through. With, however, an entirely similar result. Conway took an elaborately designed cigarette-case from his pocket and offered Legard a cigarette. Legard refused the courtesy with a shake of the head.

"Number three," ordered MacMorran.

The third trunk was brought into the cabin and again the contents were carefully examined. Anthony watched everything keenly. But the results were exactly as before. MacMorran looked at Anthony. There was dismay on his face.

Anthony shook his head and said, "It's all right, Inspector. You haven't missed anything. They're not in any of these cabin-trunks."

He turned to Dwight Conway, who had risen and sauntered over to the corner where the search had been conducted. "Mr. Conway," he said, "where are your other things?"

"Everything I carry is there," replied Conway, "with the exception, naturally, of the personal stuff I shall require on the voyage. That stuff is in my suite."

"Will you kindly conduct us there?" said Anthony. "I'd like you to accompany us, Captain Legard."

Conway shrugged his shoulders dramatically but he bowed to the inevitable. The five men made their way to Conway's suite. When they arrived there, MacMorran went through the various apartments.

"Open all the drawers," instructed Anthony, "test the bed and look behind all the articles of furniture."

Conway leant against the door of his bedroom with simulated laziness. Anthony himself took part in the comb-out. MacMorran and Sagar left no stone unturned. Every drawer, every cupboard and every possible hiding-place in each of Conway's rooms was searched systematically and methodically. And it was during this investigation that Anthony saw again his acquaintance of the "Waldorf" luncheon-room. Woore made a quick appearance just outside Conway's main cabin, and then paused in astonishment on the threshold. Conway took it upon himself to attempt to explain matters.

"The British Police," said Conway with heavy sarcasm, "or a day in the life of Scotland Yard. Incredible, isn't it?"

Woore stood there irresolutely. "By all means come in," added Conway. "It's an education in itself, take it from me."

Eventually the whole of Conway's belongings had been subjected to the search. Anthony went round the various heaps to see if any ray of light should come to him. Suddenly he spotted something and called to Inspector Sagar.

"What are they?" he asked the Liverpool officer.

"Maps," replied Sagar. "Large-scale maps of various European countries. I took a glance at them myself to make sure what they were when I laid hands on them."

"Where were they when you found them?" asked Anthony.

"They came from one of those large drawers." Sagar pointed across the cabin.

"Untie them," said Anthony, "and let me have another look at them—do you mind, Inspector?"

Sagar took the maps and untied them as Anthony had directed. "How many are there?" inquired Anthony, his heart beating a trifle faster than was normal.

Sagar counted the maps. "Seven," he answered. "No—eight."

Anthony rubbed his hands. MacMorran was quick to see the old sign of satisfaction and drew comfort therefrom. But Sagar was still talking.

"Yes—eight—that's right. France, Germany," he began to detail them, "Spain and Portugal, Italy, Turkey, Greece, the British Isles and Russia. Eight, as I said. Eight in all."

"And what's wrong with that?" demanded Conway. He had come to stand alongside Anthony and the two inspectors and Captain Legard had moved along to the group as well. Conway continued his protest. "What's wrong with maps? Can't an honest citizen, even though he be singularly blessed with this world's goods, purchase a few maps to take back with him to Noo York? Since when has map-buying been a crime?"

"Spread them out," said Anthony. "To me at the moment, eight is much more the divine number than its immediate predecessor."

Sagar found a convenient place and spread out upon it the map of the Iberian Peninsula. Anthony bent down and examined it carefully. Then he turned it over and looked at the back of it.

"Observe the thickness, gentlemen," he said. "A much greater dimension," he added, "than would be found under ordinary circumstances. See what I mean? And also look at the bottom of the map itself. There is clear evidence of it having been cut."

MacMorran was now watching both Conway and Woore like a hawk. Captain Legard and the two inspectors went up to Anthony to look at the map which he was describing. Legard agreed with Anthony at once with regard to the unusual thickness. Legard pointed to the part of Spain.

"It's fatter than even Franco himself would make it," grinned the captain of the *Cyclonic*.

MacMorran craned forward and nodded his agreement with the opinion. Anthony took a penknife and scraped away at the top left-hand edge of the Iberian Peninsula. After a few strokes of the knife, the edge of another substance could be plainly seen.

"There you are, gentlemen," he said, "this map has been in some way that I can't quite yet fathom superimposed upon another article. I rather fancy that most of the work's been done with a needle."

He closed his penknife and replaced it in his pocket before turning to Inspector MacMorran. "In those eight maps, Inspector, you have the eight Rafaelle cartoons. Stolen on September 29th last from a private museum at Hampton Court and once the undoubted property of Charles the First of England. He lost his cartoons before he lost his head."

Conway took a step forward towards MacMorran. He was bristling with indignation and anger. "On September 29th I was a few thousand miles—"

MacMorran cut him summarily. "We know," he announced laconically, "but Elmer Oliver wasn't."

Conway pulled himself up with a jerk. His face went pale at the name which MacMorran had mentioned and a hunted look took possession of his eyes. "I'm afraid," continued MacMorran, "that there's only one course open to me. You know what that is as well as I do. Do you mind, Mr. Conway?"

Conway gave one glance at Woore and followed MacMorran out of his cabin. Captain Legard, Inspector Sagar and Anthony followed them. Woore, dumbfounded, crestfallen and incredulous, was left behind. Legard looked at his watch. He turned to Anthony.

"Very satisfactory! From all points of view. I shall get away on time after all."

CHAPTER VII

I

TWENTY-four hours after the events related in the previous chapter, Anthony sat in MacMorran's room at the "Yard" and listened to an expert's dissertations on the Rafaelle cartoons. The Commissioner, Sir Austin Kemble, the Assistant-Commissioner, Major Farrell-Knox, and Colonel Buxton, the Chief Constable of Fernshire, were also among the company. The expert, Mr. Greville Twining, was describing "the eight Rafaelle cartoons".

"The maps," he stated, "had been very carefully stitched on to the respective pieces. Like certain very old Continental brochure work. And the details are as follows. I presume that you would like to hear them. France covered the 'Scourging of the Money-changers in the Temple', Germany 'Peter Striking Off Malchus's Ear', Italy 'The Miraculous Draught of Fishes', The British Isles 'Simon Carrying the Cross', Russia 'On the Road to Emmaus', Greece 'The Raising of the Daughter of Jairus', Turkey 'The Pool of Siloam', and Spain and Portugal 'The Burial at Nain of the Widow's Son'. They are all very beautiful pieces and indicative of Rafaelle at his best."

Mr. Twining pursed his lips with that particular touch of self-satisfaction which seems to belong almost exclusively to total abstainers, politicians and experts.

"What's the value of them?" asked the Commissioner.

"That's an extremely difficult question to answer," replied Mr. Greville Twining. "But I should say their value might be best expressed as that particular sum of money which any opulent collector might be prepared to pay for them."

Anthony nodded his approval of Twining's opinion. "I think that Mr. Twining has put the matter in a nutshell."

"Even now," said Sir Austin Kemble, "we're still looking for our murderer. Conway's statement, so MacMorran here tells me, is that he purchased the cartoons in a perfectly bona-fide manner. And beyond that he won't say a word. He refuses to implicate anybody else, and, as far as I can see, we shall have a job to bring very much home to him. What do you say, Farrell-Knox?"

"I'm inclined to agree with you, sir," answered the A.C.

"That won't wash," said Anthony. "My own relationships with Conway disprove all that. The evidence provided by those contacts is convincing. He was out to get those cartoons from me, when he thought I had them, by fair means or foul. That fact was evident in all that he did."

"All the same, Mr. Bathurst," interjected MacMorran, "if he holds his tongue, we've got a hard task in front of us to prove much—always allowing for the fact that we haven't clapped hands on the murderer."

"Just my point," said Sir Austin testily. "And I can see nothing else to it."

"The murderer," said Anthony in an even voice, "is in some way that we haven't yet discovered *connected* with St. Mead. And the arrest of Conway must make a vital difference to him or her. If it's handled properly, if we play our cards right, we shall compel that murderer to move. And before very long. The move that will be made may not be exactly into the open—but there will have to be a move of some kind. For instance, there's this Conway connection, which is as near a certainty as I've ever seen. Who in St. Mead can possibly have that? That's for us to find out, gentlemen. We mustn't act too precipitately, but as I interpret things, if we give the murderer a sufficient length of rope, the sequel will come both naturally and inevitably."

Farrell-Knox grinned. "How do we supply the good hempen, Bathurst? Any bright ideas on the subject?"

Anthony shook his head. "At the moment—no, Major. But I shall have to think of something within the next day or so. As a matter of fact what's troubling me at the moment is where Dwight Conway actually picked up the Rafaelle cartoons."

MacMorran cut in. "The person that was holding them obviously got in touch with him."

"I know," said Anthony, "but where did the transaction take place? That's what I'm puzzled about."

Sir Austin put a question. "Do you think, Bathurst, that Conway knows of the two murders?"

"It's strange that you should have asked that, sir," responded Anthony, "because frankly, I have my doubts. In the vicious circle we have—or, if you prefer it, *had*—Elmer Oliver, Conway himself and 'X'. 'X' is the guilty party. Steel merely strayed into the circle in all innocence for the very good reason that blood is thicker than water. And it's our problem now to find 'X'."

Sir Austin said, "That has been the problem since the start of the affair. The situation hasn't changed. The original problem remains the problem. And I'm damned if we get any forrarder."

Anthony spoke to MacMorran. "I rather fancy that when Conway learns of the happenings antecedent to the transfer of the cartoons, he's bound to open out. If only a little. If I'm right he's certain to protect himself as much as he possibly can, and that will be his one way of doing so. Don't you agree, Inspector?"

MacMorran said, "Maybe so. Time will tell. We shall have to wait and see. What's worrying me is our next step. For the life of me, I don't know what to say."

Colonel Buxton had been busy for some time discussing details with Sir Austin and Major Farrell-Knox. Eventually he turned to Anthony.

"I confess, Bathurst, that I'm extremely sceptical with regard to the immediate future. If Conway elects to hold his tongue, I must agree with the others that we're pretty effectively snookered. Unless you can assume the role of conjurer and produce something out of a hat—that particular something being a murderer. So it's definitely up to you, Bathurst."

Anthony looked round the room. "I must say," he said, "that I'm disappointed. Here we've made a colossal stride towards solving a problem that has worried us for some weeks, and instead of looking up with bright and happy faces you're all in the doldrums of despondency. 'Pon my soul, you'd put Alfred Lester to shame."

Buxton raised his eyebrows. "Colossal stride? Do you regard that phrase as a fair description of what's been accomplished?" Anthony said, "Certainly I do, sir. Look at it in this light. We've been able to establish the *fons et origo* of the entire affair. The Rafaelle cartoons! In other words, we have the genesis of the business in our hands. I don't think that my 'colossal stride' is in any way an exaggeration."

There was a silence after Anthony had said his say. It was broken eventually by the Assistant Commissioner. Farrell-Knox stroked the hair at the back of his head and said, "Do you know, I'm inclined to agree with Bathurst. Having got so far we should now be able to finish off the job quite easily. It will be our fault if we don't."

There ensued yet another period of silence. Nobody seemed disposed either to agree with Farrell-Knox or, on the other hand, to join issue with him. After a time, MacMorran said, "It all depends on this fellow Dwight Conway. Just as I said before, and just how far he talks."

"I agree with you only to a point," said Anthony. "Even if Conway becomes first cousin to a clam, I still don't give up hope of getting our murderer. Still, as Inspector MacMorran sagely indicated just now, time will tell."

He rose to make his departure. Farrell-Knox began to hum the opening bars of "The Toreador's Song" from *Carmen*. He stood up and then walked to the door.

"All right, Bathurst," he said, "you buzz off and think up something wizard. Go on—scram! I, for one, wouldn't put it beyond you. And what's more, I'll back you to pull it off."

II

MacMorran came to Anthony in a somewhat pessimistic frame of mind.

"How now, Andrew?" Anthony asked. "Sickled o'er with the pale cast of thought? Or merely a trifle under the weather?"

MacMorran shook his head. It was apparent that the Scotland Yard Inspector was in no mood for banter. "Re Conway," he said glumly. "His solicitors have been in touch with us. He's engaged Ball, Eck and Bridgewater. The Devonshire Place people. They're pretty reputable too. Not to say as 'fly' as they make 'em. I ran up against them about ten years ago. A society libel case. Mrs. Clarke-Higson—remember?"

Anthony nodded. "Yes. I recollect it. The West End beauty-parlour affair. Your Mrs. Clarke-Higson sued the proprietor, Signor Luigi Ginistrelli, over a letter he wrote to . . . now who was it . . .?" Anthony furrowed his brows as he attempted to recall the details. "I know—Lady Eleanor Cleghorn of Little Stanhope Street, Mayfair."

"Quite right," proclaimed MacMorran. "That was the case I referred to. And I had a good deal of trouble with that particular firm. Well, this is the Conway latest. That he bought the cartoons in full faith and belief that the sale was genuine in every way. And—what's more—he's produced an appropriate receipt. He paid £40,000 for them—£5000 apiece, that is."

Anthony nodded. "Boloney—all of it. Sheer, unadulterated boloney. Still, let that go by the board for the moment. From whom does he claim to have bought them?"

"He says that a woman made an appointment with him by telephone. He accepted the offer she made him and she handed over the Rafaelle cartoons."

Anthony smiled cynically. "Upon which he immediately superimposed the maps of various European countries. Hooey—Andrew! Still, as I said before, let all that slide by for the time being. What was this woman's name? From whom he purchased the cartoons?"

MacMorran smiled. And as he smiled, his tongue touched the corners of his lips, as though he were secretly enjoying the satisfaction of something that he felt certain was going to happen. His smile lasted an appreciable time before he replied.

"The receipt he obtained—I am given to understand this—is on an ordinary sheet of notepaper. There is no business billhead, as it were. The name of the firm is merely written across the top of the sheet of paper."

Anthony said, "What's the name of the firm?"

MacMorran answered, "Anne Teak. And it's spelt like this." The Inspector gave the letters as they have been written.

"H'm," said Anthony, "a neat touch, eh, Andrew? Somewhat suggestive of our little adventure at East Brutton when David Somerset was murdered. I see! And who, if you please, signed this receipt for the £40,000?"

MacMorran's face was impassive as he replied to the question. He didn't bat an eyelid. "The receipt, so I am informed, is signed by a person who calls herself Annette Gayne. And there's no business address shown at all." MacMorran spelt out the letters of the two names as he had done before.

This second touch caused Anthony to grin. "Neat and even neater," said he. "You have a foeman worthy of your steel, Andrew. When Greek joins Greek—then comes the tug-of-war. And all—highly interesting, I must say."

"Point is," said MacMorran, "how do we prove our case against Conway? That's what's worrying me."

Anthony sat and reflected. "Do you know, Andrew," he said, "I've been thinking over very carefully what Farrell-Knox said to me when I called at the 'Yard' the last time. If you remember—he told me to scram and think up something wizard. I rather fancy that was his picturesque way of putting it. Let's look at things from a different angle. Just you and I. At the moment we don't hold the murderer, but, on the contrary, we hold (a) Dwight Conway and (b) the eight Rafaelle tapestry-cartoons. Of those three which do you consider the most important, Andrew? Take your time to answer."

MacMorran answered with sturdy certainty. "The first. The one we don't hold—that is, the murderer."

Anthony nodded. "Good. I hoped and also thought that you would say that. What would happen, now, Andrew, if we took the cartoons from our friend Conway (as we shall, of course) and beyond that entered what would amount to a *nolle prosequi* and do nothing to him beyond the administering of a severe caution? What do you say would be his first reaction?"

"If we released him, do you mean?"

"Ah-ha! That's what I mean all right. How do you think he'd react?" ❧

"Well," replied MacMorran slowly, "to get the correct answer, you've got to look at it from Conway's own point of view. He cuts a sorry figure, on those lines, all the way through the piece. He's minus his £40,000, he's lost his coveted cartoons and he's had his journey from the States—there and back, remember—all for nothing. To say naught of the fact that the police authorities have collared him and placed him under arrest. A pretty sickening record, don't you think?"

Anthony nodded. "Agreed, Andrew. But you haven't *quite* answered my question, have you? You haven't told me what you think he would *do*?"

"Why, if you put it like that—go for his forty thousand quid back. At any rate, that's what I'd do—were I in his place."

"Right! Now let's examine that as a definite proposition. In the first place we'll assume that the yarn he's pitching now is a true statement of fact. That he *doesn't* know from whom he purchased the cartoons, and that when he purchased them he didn't know that they'd been pinched. Well—that's going to cramp his style pretty effectively from the standpoint of recovering his £40,000. Taking the proposition at its absolute face value, it means quite simply that his chance of getting his cash back is—to say the least of it—extremely slender. In other words, Andrew, it resolves itself into this. To recover his boodle he's got to give himself away, risk rearrest and consequent punishment—because you will have 'tabs' on him all the time—and in the ultimate issue lose entirely his personal reputation."

MacMorran nodded. "I see your point."

Anthony went on. "And take it from me, Andrew, he *won't* do it! He'll go quietly. Back to the land of Freedom and Independence. He's a millionaire, you know. Makes a hell of a difference. What's forty thousand Jimmy o' Goblins to a man of his wealth?"

"Well," said MacMorran, "admitting all that—and I'll say frankly I'm prepared to admit it, how much better off are we afterwards? When Conway, to use your idiom, has 'gone quietly'?"

Anthony drummed on the table with his finger-tips. "I've been wondering, Andrew," he said quietly. He leant over and almost whispered to the Inspector. "We still have the cartoons. I've been wondering whether they might be used, Andrew. As bait! For our criminal. If we can get into that criminal's mind (a) that the case against Conway has collapsed, (b) that it collapsed because we knew nothing or next to nothing against him and therefore could offer little or no evidence, and not only get it into his mind but get it fixed firmly there, the temptation to collar them again might prove irresistible! Especially if they were presented to him on a plate with parsley sauce on it." Anthony looked at the Inspector. "What do you say to the idea, Andrew? How does it strike you? As a 'possible'?"

"I think it has a distinct weakness," replied MacMorran.

Anthony said, "What's that?"

"Why this! The *first* thief, the thief who stole the cartoons from Hampton Court, wasn't a *collector*. Otherwise he wouldn't have disposed of them to Conway. By doing that, he obviously valued the cash receivable more than the intrinsic value of the article. Therefore he's not in true lineal descent of all proper collectors. Do you follow me as far as that?"

Anthony nodded. He smiled and said: "Yes, that's all right. Now go on from there."

"Well," concluded MacMorran, rather lamely, "I don't think there's anything more to be said, is there? The thief has touched Dwight Conway's forty thousand quid which is all very nice to be going on with. Why should he run the risk again—especially seeing that it's been proved, by his own actions, he doesn't covet the articles themselves?"

"All very sound, I admit," commented Anthony, "but how about the lure of another forty thousand for the self-same articles? Especially if our friend thought that the fruit would almost fall into his lap by no more than the shaking of the tree?" Anthony paused and then went on again. "The thief might even be *led* to believe that, if the seeds of the idea were judiciously planted and skilfully watered. *Now* what do you say, Andrew?"

"Putting it like that," replied MacMorran quietly, "and I suppose that it *might* come off. But how is it going to be worked? That's where the difficulty lies, as I see things. The trap won't be an easy one to spring by any manner of means."

Anthony said, "We shall need to have the full co-operation of Sir Austin Kemble. *Ça va sans dire.* In conjunction with his brother Neville, our worthy and respected host. But with tact, diplomacy and finesse I think it might be arranged. I'll go farther than that, Andrew, I think it *can* be managed! It will mean taking about a dozen people into our confidence. Yes, Andrew, I'm of the opinion that it can be made an effective piece of business. All it needs is care, forethought and sound staff work. And you and I can see to all those."

MacMorran said, "It'll be up to you to see the old man. You can leave me out of that. I'm not chancing my arm again. I've risked enough on this show already."

"I'll do that," answered Anthony. "I don't mind in the least. It may require all the fire of my eloquence, but I'll do it."

MacMorran rose, a gleam of satisfaction in his eye. "When you're through with it, let me know. In the meantime, I'll go in the garden and eat worms. Woolly ones."

MacMorran went!

III

Anthony's conference with the Commissioner proved harder going than he had anticipated when he first launched the idea to MacMorran. But after showing even unexpected resources of obstinacy and remaining obdurate for a much longer period of time than Anthony had originally reckoned would be the case, Sir Austin ultimately came down from his high horse and surrendered to the persevering and persistent Bathurst.

"I'm glad to hear that you agree, sir," said Anthony at last, "and I think I'm safe in promising that you won't suffer any disappointment or even disagreeable consequences. And, after all, by entering a *nolle prosequi* against Dwight Conway, we don't chuck the towel in. We can always have another cut at him later if we so desire. But if things go as I think they'll go, you'll find that a second crack at Conway won't be necessary."

Sir Austin emitted a grumbled something from under his breath. Anthony affected not to hear it. He said instead, "And you'll let Chief-Inspector MacMorran make all the necessary arrangements, then, with regard to the Rafaelle cartoons? Yes?"

The Commissioner of Police nodded. "Yes. I'll see him myself and issue the necessary orders. So you can go home satisfied for once. As usual, you've got your own way."

"That's an idea, certainly, sir," replied Anthony with a smile, "only it won't be home, I'm afraid, until this job's been cleared up. Till then, it's St. Mead for me. In the house of your revered and respected brother—'Palings', to wit." He grinned at Sir Austin as he spoke.

"Ah well," returned the Commissioner, "you might travel further and fare worse. There are more unpleasant places than Neville's. And he's got some quite decent port in his cellar. Too good, in fact, for him."

"I'll tell him so, if you like, Sir Austin," sallied back Anthony. "Brotherly advice is usually welcome."

"You keep your mouth shut," retorted the Commissioner, "and say nothing of the sort. And the next time I see you, come and tell me that you and MacMorran have got to the bottom of this wretched case. It's hung on far too long. I tell you I'm sick of it."

"Some cases, sir," replied Anthony, "require infinite patience—and this is one. Nevertheless, sir, I can assure you that we'll do our level best."

IV

Neville Kemble inspected the eight Rafaelle cartoons with an excess of admiration.

"My dear Drusilla," he said to the lady at his side, "there are no two opinions with regard to them. There can't be. They are unique specimens of their kind. As designs for tapestries there is small wonder that they excited the envy of the late lamented Charles the First. Don't you agree, my dear?"

"You know I do, Neville," said Drusilla with a toss of the head. "Originally, you know," she went on, "there were fifteen of them. The others, I believe, are now housed at South Kensington."

"Is that so?" said Neville Kemble curiously.

"Yes. I've seen them. My uncle took me to see them more years ago than I care to remember. I won't say I've coveted them—but almost. Let's see if I can remember the other titles." Drusilla Ives knitted her brows. "There's 'Christ Walks on the Water', 'Feed My Lambs', 'The Death of Ananias', 'Paul at Lystra', 'Paul on the Areopagus'—"

"Where?" said Neville Kemble.

Drusilla laughed. "Why, you know—Mars Hill. Seventeenth chapter of the Acts of the Apostles. 'Then Paul stood in the midst of

Mars Hill.' Don't you read your Bible, Neville—or have you become completely pagan since I've given up visiting you regularly? Let's see—how many have I remembered?"

"Five," replied Neville Kemble.

"Two more," said Drusilla. "I know—'Elymas the Sorcerer' and 'The Barren Fig Tree'."

Her host nodded. "That's the lot according to your reckoning—an additional seven." Looking at her whimsically he asked, "Which of the eight here do you rate the best? I'm interested. I've always been a whale for comparisons—odious though they may be."

Drusilla walked up the line slowly in an exercise of assessment. Then she returned the way she had gone and at the same pace. " The Widow's Son at Nain', I think. To me in that particular instance, the artist has been happiest in his Christus. It's more like Him as I've always imagined Him to be. Yes," she concluded, with emphasis, "that's the finest. And if Rafaelle's are the most beautiful ever worked, the 'Widow's Son' must be the most beautiful in all history." Neville Kemble wrinkled his forehead. "Why—exactly? I don't know that I—"

Drusilla laughed, and there were both merriment and provocation in the laugh. "Why—Themistocles, of course!"

Neville said, "Themistocles? I'm still—"

"Of course! You remember—the Sorites. Of Themistocles. How he proved that his little son commanded the entire world. He argued it in this way—'My infant son rules his mother. His mother rules me. I rule the Athenians. The Athenians rule the Greeks, The Greeks rule Europe. And Europe rules the world. Therefore', etc., etc."

Neville's brow cleared at the explanation. "Yes, of course. I should have known. It's just like proving that Farmer Daniels's Drumhead cabbages, as the best in St. Mead, which is in Fernshire, are the pick of the world's cabbage basket."

"That's it," said Drusilla, "you've got the idea exactly. And when I look at that cartoon there—'The Widow's Son at Nain'—I feel just as though . . ." She paused abruptly.

A tread sounded in the adjoining room. Drusilla looked towards the communicating door, expectantly. When she saw and recognized the figure that was entering the room in which she was, she stiffened and suddenly became silent.

"Ah, Bathurst," said Neville Kemble in cordial greeting. "I've been wondering how long we should have to wait for you. You've met Drusilla before, haven't you?"

Anthony laughed. "I should think I have. We're quite old friends. In fact I was with Miss Ives but a short time ago, and when we parted company—much too soon, of course—I prophesied that we should meet again ere long. But doubtless Miss Ives remembers the incident as accurately as I do."

"I can assure you that I don't," retorted the lady tartly. "In point of fact, I had dismissed it from my mind—as an incident of little or no importance. I make a point of remembering those things only which I regard as worthy of remembrance."

Anthony smiled. "Well, well, well! Do you know, I should never have thought it."

Neville Kemble said, "Drusilla's been admiring the cartoons. I wrote and told her that they'd be housed here until the end of the week. And do you know, Bathurst, she knows a damn' sight more about them than I do—or can even pretend that I do. During the last few moments I have found Drusilla to be distinctly erudite."

"Don't tell me that fact surprised you," said Anthony. "As an artist herself, I can understand completely how all expressions of the artistic faculty would appeal to her. When do they go back?"

"Next Sunday evening. They're being sent up by special messenger in a specially chartered car."

Drusilla stood prim-lipped, her features set and her eyes disdainful. She made no comment on Neville Kemble's statement.

Anthony turned to her with a smile. "I can well believe, Miss Ives," he said, "that these cartoons would have caught the imagination of your uncle. He was a collector of beautiful things, so I've been told."

"I haven't the slightest idea," replied Drusilla. "I've always felt myself that beauty lies in the eyes of the beholder. So it's quite likely that my uncle may have held entirely different ideas from me." She turned her eyes from Anthony to Neville Kemble and held out her hand.

"Well, Neville darling, I must be going. I've stopped too long as it is. But I felt that I simply had to see your treasures before they were sent away—and another thing, I wasn't aware that you were expecting company. Had I known that . . ."

Neville Kemble took her outstretched hand. "I'm sorry you feel you must go, Drusilla. And as for calling Bathurst here 'company'—now I ask you! To tell you the truth, I've come to look upon him now as one of the family. I tell you, I shall miss him when he goes."

"I know what you mean," said Drusilla, "I know exactly what you mean. It's like the gap in your mouth after you've had a bad tooth extracted. When your tongue finds it—as it's always doing—the cavity feels like the Mersey Tunnel. But everything soon gets normal again. So don't get too discouraged and depressed."

Anthony grinned at her but otherwise made no come-back. Neville shook her by the hand. "When shall I see you again, Drusilla? Soon, I hope?"

"I'm afraid not," she replied with a shake of the head. "I'm going back to the Thames Valley within the next day or so. I've come all over nostalgic. So that it's unlikely you'll see me again for some time. Not this side of Christmas, I should say."

"Bad luck," replied Neville Kemble. "I had strong hopes that you would be staying with us for quite a time."

"Then I'm afraid you'll be disappointed," she said with exaggerated sweetness. "And now I must really say good-bye."

"If you're coming back at Christmas," said Neville, "make it *au revoir*. I like the sound of that a great deal better."

"All right. If that suits you—it'll suit me too." She turned and walked to the door. "Good-bye, Mr. Bathurst," she called over her shoulder. "As you *won't* be here at Christmas, you'll understand why I said good-bye in your case."

She waved her hand lightly and was gone, Anthony making no reply. Neville Kemble looked at him.

"What have you been doing, Bathurst, to upset the lady? Can't understand it for the life of me! Always thought you were a ladies' man."

Anthony smiled. "That's another injustice to Ireland, if you did but know." Then he shook his head at his host. "No, if the truth be told, the lady is annoyed I've found her out. She's deceived many a person in her time, but she wasn't too successful in getting one past me. I saw through her little game and was able to cry checkmate. And—as you must very well know—you're never popular when you unmask a person."

Neville Kemble looked annoyed. "I don't like to hear you talk like that about Drusilla. I've an exceedingly soft spot in my heart for her. And I simply *can't* associate her with anything like wilful deception. Are you sure of your ground, Bathurst?"

"Quite sure, sir. But let it pass for the time being. All the same, you must prepare yourself for several surprises in the very near future. In the meantime, may I talk to you about Alderman Wall?"

Neville Kemble, although still frowning, nodded his head. "Come in the library," he said, "and we'll talk things over."

V

Anthony Bathurst followed his host into the library at "Palings".

"Sit down," said Neville Kemble in invitation. Anthony sat down. "Now what is it you want to know?" asked Kemble. "With regard to tomorrow's Bench of Justices?"

"Merely this, sir. Who'll be sitting with you tomorrow?"

Neville Kemble took a diary from his pocket. "Let me see, I'll turn it up for you. Tomorrow! The Stipendiary sat today. I can soon tell you from this. Just give me a minute or two and I'll work out the rota for you."

Anthony waited patiently for Neville Kemble's information. "Here we are," said the latter at last, "with me there'll be Stainsby, Alderman Wall, Gilbert Tresillian and—er—there should be one other. Now who's that? Oh, I know! Alderman Bumstead. He's just been made a J.P. In place of Mrs. Featherstone—a lady who's recently resigned."

"Are they all certain to be there, sir?"

Neville Kemble pushed his fingers through his hair. "Well, there you are. I can't promise that. I can't say so for certain. All I *can* say is that they *should* be there. After all, it's like everything else. You've got things to contend with. Illness, other engagements—but you know as well as I do what I mean."

Anthony nodded. "I see."

Kemble went on. "I'll say this, though. Usually, and by usually I mean nine times out of ten, the full complement *does* turn up."

"In that case, then?" asked Anthony.

"In that case then, I'll make the arrangements that you've outlined to me. When do you want me to 'phone you? Before the court sits?"

"As early as you can, sir. In other words, as soon as you're certain as to how you stand. When I know that definitely, I can fill in the omissions and repair the breaches. You've got the idea, of course?"

"Yes," said Neville Kemble, "I think I know exactly what you want. You can leave everything safely to me as regards all those that turn up."

Anthony said, "That's O.K., then. And I'm in your hands."

CHAPTER VIII

I

SOON after ten o'clock on the following morning, Anthony received the telephone message from Neville Kemble for which he was waiting. Kemble 'phoned to "Palings" from the Justice's Room in the Town Hall at Kersbrook before the Court went into sitting. He had told the Clerk to the Justices that he desired to use the 'phone before the magistrates went into court, and when the Clerk heard Kemble get through successfully to his house at St. Mead and speak to Anthony, he beamed his approval and muttered, "Got your number already? Bai goom—that's chumpion."

When he received Neville Kemble's message, Anthony suffered a slight pang of disappointment. "In reply to your inquiry," said Neville Kemble, J.P., "I'm sorry to say that we've two defections this morning. Alderman Bumstead's not here, and Gilbert Tresillian's written to say that he's had to go North on important business. And he's not expected back until tomorrow night. Against that, however, Humphrey Tresillian, the Town Clerk—Gilbert's half-brother—will be in court. That's a stroke of luck from the standpoint of the arrangements you wish to make, and I'll see him for you. As a matter of fact Humphrey Tresillian's only in court very occasionally. But today he's taking a case himself for the County Borough. It shouldn't take overlong to see it through. Only routine stuff—a disorderly house prosecution, as a matter of fact. So, in a way, Bathurst, we're two down but unexpectedly one up. Which, worked out, comes to only one down."

"Not so bad," replied Anthony. "When you first began to tell me, I was disappointed. But nevertheless, things might have been a good deal worse. They're certainly not as bad as they sounded when you started to tell me. Righto, then, I know where I am now, and I'll cover up where necessary. Thank you so much for 'phoning. I know exactly where I am."

Anthony replaced the receiver and assessed the position as Neville Kemble had outlined it to him. The incident of Gilbert Tresillian's absence was awkward, to say the least of it, but if he were back in St. Mead on the following evening as Kemble had stated he was expected to be, the awkwardness would not prove to be insurmountable. And Kemble, too, would deal with Gilbert's brother, Humphrey. That left Alderman Bumstead for him to arrange with personally. Anthony looked at the clock on the mantelpiece and decided to accomplish that task as soon as humanly possible. He would go into Kersbrook that morning and make contact with Bumstead at his business address. He knew that the Alderman's place of business was in South Street, Kersbrook. More than that, he had seen him at work in the shop. Bumstead had a florist's business in Kersbrook, which, from all ordinary appearances, looked to be flourishing and lucrative.

Anthony, therefore, walked down to St. Mead station, passing Ebford's field on his way. He was aware that there was a train just before eleven o'clock which would run into Kersbrook in the matter of a few minutes. He was able to catch this train with a comfortable number of minutes to spare and when he left the station at Kersbrook he at once started to make his way to South Street and the florist's shop of Alderman Bumstead. As he walked along, Anthony debated within himself as to the most diplomatic manner by which he might approach his quarry. On the whole, he considered, the best thing for him to do would be to regard the encounter as entirely casual and come to the crucial point by using the same technique. His main hope was that Bumstead would be on the premises and plainly visible from the pavement outside when Anthony went by.

He reached Bumstead's shop after a walk of eight minutes. For some reason best known to himself, Anthony timed it. And as he came abreast of the main window, he saw with strong gratification that the worthy Alderman was not only in residence but was plainly visible from the pavement. Actually, he was engaged in unpacking a box of large bronze chrysanthemums. As he passed the front of the shop, Anthony deliberately waved to the industrious florist. Bumstead looked up, smiled with his little eyes, and returned the salutation. This was the golden opportunity which Anthony had hoped would be forthcoming. Bumstead smiled at him again. This was a much more authentic Bumstead smile, based upon a maximum effort with his teeth. Anthony stopped in his tracks and deliberately walked up to the front of the shop. He saw Bumstead's little twinkling eyes regarding him intently.

"Good morning, Mr. Alderman," said Anthony. "You took me rather by surprise."

"How d'ye mean?" asked Bumstead, looking a little surprised himself at the remark.

"For the very good reason that I expected you to be somewhere else."

Bumstead's smile gave way to a pronounced frown. "I wasn't aware, sir, that my doings—or if you like, my comings and goings—were of such interest to you."

This time it was Anthony's turn to smile. "Yes, I asked for that, didn't I? Led with my chin. No, it doesn't happen to be as bad as all that. The explanation, as a matter of fact, is absurdly simple. Last evening, Mr. Neville Kemble, in whose company I was at the time, happened to remark that, in recognition of your newly acquired honour, you would be sitting on the Bench at Kersbrook this morning. And when I saw you I was instinctively, I suppose, reminded of that fragment of conversation."

For a moment or so the Kersbrook Alderman made no reply. Anthony, at length, prompted him. "Well, sir, am I forgiven?"

Bumstead broke into his high cackling laugh. Anthony was irresistibly reminded of a whinnying horse. He was not pleased at this reminder, because he was a great lover of horses.

"That's all right," returned Bumstead with much geniality, "explanation accepted. Passed to you! No," he went on, "I really couldn't manage to get down to the court this morning. My chief assistant's away ill with bronchitis, and in the circumstances I'm left to carry on. That's the worst of having a business. You're tied to it so. No rest! No respite! Your time's never your own."

Anthony nodded. He considered he was getting on famously. He jerked his head in the direction of the box of bronze chrysanthemums.

"Very lovely," he said, with a look of admiration in his eyes.

"Beautiful," said Bumstead, "really beautiful! For what they are, they'll take a rare lot of beating."

"I agree," said Anthony, "and if I may say so, it's refreshing to find a busy and distinguished man like yourself so appreciative of natural beauty."

"Sir," said Alderman Bumstead oracularly, "no matter how busy a man may be, or how keen a business-man he may be—I make the distinction deliberately—he can always find time for beautiful things if he wants to. Mind you"—and here he looked at Anthony straight in the eyes—"I said if he wants to. And I mean it. There's a rare lot in that last remark."

"How right you are," said Anthony contemplatively. And then, as though a new-born thought had just come to him, he added, "Now I wonder if you're equally interested in works of art? The works of man's creation?"

Bumstead looked at him suspiciously. "Now what may you be driving at?" he asked.

Anthony smiled. "How do you mean?" he countered.

"I'm afraid," said the Alderman slowly and weighing his words, "that you're by way of being a smart Alec."

Anthony shook his head and laughed. "You're getting me all wrong! You are—really. I meant every word that I said."

"That's as maybe," frowned Bumstead. "I'm not so sure."

"All the same," said Anthony, "I see no real reason why you shouldn't answer my question. Whether you were an admirer also of the art of the craftsman? Because I assure you I didn't ask the question idly, wantonly or even unadvisedly. And when you hear what I'm going to tell you, you'll know that I'm telling you the truth." Bumstead's eyes ceased to twinkle. "What's behind all this?" he demanded. "Out with it, man, and put an end to the riddles."

"Simply this," returned Anthony. "Your fellow J.P., Neville Kemble, has a collection over at his house of the famous Rafaelle cartoons. They used to belong to Charles the First of England. And as a lover of art, as you've told me you are of Nature, it occurred to me that they'd be of great interest to you. You should pop over and see them—I have his authority to say that you're very welcome. In fact, had you been on the Bench this morning, it was his intention to invite you himself. It's an opportunity that may only come once in a lifetime." Anthony paused to resume again almost at once. "So there you are, Mr. Alderman, there you have the whole matter in a nutshell."

But Bumstead looked puzzled. "Tell me," he said inquiringly, "what sort of cartoons are they? Anything like what Low draws in the *Evening Standard*?"

"No," replied Anthony. "I'll try to give you an idea of them." He embarked upon a somewhat lengthy explanation to which Bumstead listened with patience. At intervals Bumstead sought information, and at others he contributed comment.

"Interesting," he said eventually, "very interesting. Most unusual, too, I should say. And, according to you, these cartoons are to be seen at Kemble's place, eh? Till when? Is there a time limit?"

"They're being returned to the owners on Sunday. On Sunday evening, to be precise. They were stolen, I should tell you, from a collection at Hampton Court some months ago. The police authorities have only just recovered them."

"From where?" asked Bumstead.

Anthony repeated his previous statement. Bumstead nodded. "I wasn't quite sure what you said," he remarked, apparently in justification of his question. Then he seemed to come to a decision for he made an announcement.

"Well," he said, "it's very kind of you, Mr. Bathurst, to extend me this invitation on behalf of my colleague Kemble, but as far as I'm concerned I don't think I'll take advantage of it, thanking you all the same. No offence, I hope?"

"Not a bit of it," replied Anthony with cheerful unconcern.

"No," went on the Kersbrook Alderman, as he placed a bunch of bronze chrysanthemums in a vase of water, "I don't know that I should care a great deal for the sort of thing that you described to me just now. I suppose my tastes don't run that way, being a plain man, so to speak. And speaking quite frankly, as far as beauty's concerned" (Anthony winced at the well-remembered phrase), "I can say that I'm a plain man in every direction. For instance, I like plain cooking. Cut off the joint and two veg—that's me. I never want any highly coloured sauces swimming round my plateful. You don't find any melon-pip jelly near my roast sirloin, or whatever it is the fools like to serve up with it. No," and here Bumstead shook his head and cackled again, "when it comes to admiration of the beautiful, give me the 'orticultural every time. What's nicer, for example, than a lay on the grass at Kew Gardens? Of course, I mean at the right time of the year and in the best of company."

"Well," said Anthony, still smiling, "that's as good a direction for a man's appreciation to take as any. You have no need to reproach yourself in that respect, I'm sure. And by reason of all these things that you've just been telling me, you must enjoy your work. Therefore, I'm going to say that you're a very fortunate man."

"I suppose I am," said Bumstead sapiently. "The trivial round and common task certainly furnish all I need to ask."

"In that case, then," asked Anthony sweetly, "what induced you to enter public life?"

Bumstead regarded him with a look of contempt.

"Why ask that? Isn't the answer obvious? The desire for service, sir! Service to others! Service before self! If I can 'pass over', feeling that I've done something to improve the lot of my fellow men I shall die content, sir."

Anthony looked at him and saw the expression coming over the Alderman's face which it had worn when Bumstead stood in the Council Chamber at Kersbrook.

Anthony knew that it was time for him to go; he began to edge away from the transformed florist.

"I must be getting along," he said to Bumstead. "Nice to have had this little chat. I feel that I've got to know you better. Or should I say that we've got to know each other better?"

The look of suspicion returned to Bumstead's little eyes.

"It doesn't matter to me, Mr.—either way. Still, you've pretty well heard my views, and, speaking quite frankly, as far as knowing one another's concerned—"

But at this Anthony surrendered unconditionally, waved his hand from the doorway of the shop and fled incontinently from the scene.

As he made his way back to "Palings" he scratched his cheek and murmured to himself, "I wonder."

II

The Stainsbys and Alderman Wall came over to "Palings" in the same car. The car was Stainsby's. Wall stepped out of it with a melancholy smile on his face, and held out his hand to Neville Kemble and to Anthony Bathurst.

"So 'ere we are again, gentlemen! And this time, on an errand appertainin' to culture and the 'igh arts."

Stainsby's right eyelid drooped in Anthony's direction. "The Alderman, under a cloak of seeming indifference, is actually labouring under the stress of high excitement," he said. "The truth is, that under his phlegmatic exterior, he's actually keener on a close appreciation of beauty than he is on the pronouncements of Karl Marx. Despite the fact that he'll spend hours arguing with you that he's a politician, first, second—and all the time."

Elizabeth Stainsby laughed gaily. "And you're just as bad yourself, Kenneth. It's not the slightest use your denying the fact." Stainsby shrugged his shoulders under his daughter's indictment, but he smiled at the company good-naturedly and said simply, "I'm ready to admit it. But you see, my dear Elizabeth, I have never *pretended* to be interested in things political."

Neville Kemble began to fuss round his guests. "Now it's up to you," he said, "to choose your plan of campaign. I'm your host and you shall exercise your own choice in the matter. And it's by way of being a momentous decision you're called upon to make."

Wall and the two Stainsbys regarded him questioningly. He grinned at them when he saw how seriously they had taken his remark.

"The decision is this," he said. "Will you have tea before you look at the Rafaelle cartoons, or shall it be the cartoons first and buttered muffins second? As I said, you can please yourselves entirely."

Wall looked at Kenneth Stainsby and Kenneth Stainsby returned the compliment to Wall. Neither seemed desirous of expressing the choice. Anthony entered the arena.

"Why not leave the choice to the lady? *Place aux dames*—what do you say yourself, Miss Elizabeth?"

Elizabeth clapped her hands. "That's very gallant of you, Mr. Bathurst. The only point is now—do the other two gentlemen agree?"

Wall smiled his melancholy smile again and said, "For me I'll do more than merely agree—I shall be delighted. And I think it's really remarkable 'ow Mr. Bathurst manages to 'it upon the correct solution of any problem that presents itself. To tell the truth, I don't know if it's knack or a 'eaven-sent gift."

"That settles it then," said Neville Kemble. "Now, Elizabeth, which shall it be? Muffins or masterpieces? Always remembering the care you take to preserve that schoolgirl complexion. To say nothing of the willowy figure."

Elizabeth turned to her host and produced a *moue* for his especial benefit. "I'll pay you out for that," she said vivaciously. "I'll keep you waiting for your tea. We'll look at the cartoons first and let the buttered muffins wait. You weren't expecting that, were you?"

"Good for you, Elizabeth," said her father. "But I might have known that you wouldn't let the side down."

"Talkin' of muffins," said Alderman Wall, "I've noticed that a lot of people refer to muffins when they actually mean crumpets. In the same manner, mere mediocrities are often hailed as masterpieces." He bowed in the direction of Neville Kemble. "Usin' your word, Mr. Kemble."

Neville took him up on the opinion. "Well, my dear Wall, what you say may be very true. Frequently, there's no doubt that I should find myself in line with you. But you've got to remember this. The microbe of mediocrity gets around quite a lot. He's a persevering sort of little fellow and as a bacillus takes a lot of snubbing. The result is—and it's inevitable, so it seems to me—there are any amount of mediocrities in this world of error and failure. Many more than there are masterpieces. I don't see how any different condition of things can ever prevail. Still, today we're going to be concerned with masterpieces for once in a way. So if you will all be good enough to step this way, the show can start. All fit?"

There was a chorus of approval and the various members of the company proceeded to follow their host into the library. Anthony brought up the extreme of the procession. Neville Kemble had arranged the cartoons in the same manner as when he had exhibited them to Drusilla Ives. Wall went down the line first. Behind him walked Elizabeth Stainsby—a few paces in advance of her father. It soon became evident that Alderman Wall was determined to retain his mood of impish criticism. Anthony, as he watched him, and heard his semi-mischievous comments, felt that had destiny and environment been kinder to Wall, in his early days, he might well have been a likeable character.

"Yes," said Wall, with his head on one side, "there's certainly something beautiful abaht them. Even an uneducated feller like meself can readily see that. But I don't know that they reely cetch me. I wouldn't wave any flags for them. And whatever they're worth, or reputed to be worth, I'd much sooner 'ave me fingers rahnd the cash. Give me 'ouse property every time. Go on, Kemble, now say I'm a Goth or a Vandal. I'm never sure meself which of them's the right one to use."

"I won't call you anything, Wall," replied Kemble good-humouredly. "Every man to his taste."

From the Stainsbys, however, following Wall in his tour of assessment, there came nothing but the most spontaneous expressions of delight. Elizabeth unavowedly confessed that they were all supremely lovely.

"I've never seen anything quite like them before," she stated, "and they're quite different from what I expected them to be. I suppose the word 'cartoon' misled me a little and made me anticipate seeing something else."

Stainsby himself was warm in his appreciation and admiration.

"I think they're marvellous," he stated. "I only wish I could afford to buy them. And I can well understand any genuine patron of the arts being covetous for their possession."

Anthony essayed to make explanation to Elizabeth. "The word 'cartoon', Miss Stainsby," he said, "is derived from the Italian 'cartone'. The actual etymological meaning of it is 'pasteboard'."

Elizabeth exhibited keen interest in what he told her. "I didn't know that, Mr. Bathurst. Now that's most interesting—and illuminating."

She turned to her father with a touch of colour showing in her cheeks. "I'm afraid I must confess to attaching its commonplace meaning to the word. Isn't it awful? Am I terribly ignorant?"

Kenneth Stainsby shook his head. "No need to reproach yourself, my dear. We all of us have a tremendous lot to learn, and in many directions. I don't know that I knew a frightful lot about the point myself."

He stopped to admire the cartoon on his immediate right. Anthony saw the enthusiasm the man felt reflected in his eyes. "By Jove," he said, "but this certainly is a beautiful piece of work."

Anthony noticed that the cartoon in question was "The Widow's Son at Nain". He remembered how he had heard Drusilla's eulogy thereon. But Stainsby was continuing the expression of his admiration.

"I say, Neville, old man," he went on, "I know encomiums are of little value, but, by Jove, I'd like to be the possessor of these pasteboards, as Bathurst described them just now. I would that! I should say that, in their way, they're absolutely unique."

Neville Kemble was obviously delighted by Stainsby's praise.

"Yes, they are good, old man, aren't they? So glad you like them, and that you don't consider your journey wasted." He sighed comfortably. "There's always that risk, you know, when you invite people to look at something on 'spec', as it were."

Wall looked back over his shoulder and smiled. "He's a set-off against me, Kemble. You've got 'one for' and 'one against'."

But Stainsby shook his head with infinite good humour. "I must speak my mind, Alderman Wall. Even when I'm in disagreement with your good self. And these cartoons are vastly superior to anything of their kind that I had ever imagined."

Stainsby stopped again and suddenly in front of another of the cartoons. It was the one which bore the title "Elymas the Sorcerer".

"This is beautiful," he said. "Even more beautiful than the 'Widow's Son'. These two, to my mind, are certainly the pick of the basket. The gems of the collection. I don't know which of the two I admire the more."

Neville Kemble came over. "What's this other one?" he asked, "which excites Stainsby's admiration so much?" Stainsby told him. Kemble nodded. "I agree with you, my dear chap. Lovely! Undeniably lovely!"

He tried Elizabeth. "Well, my dear, do you ever escape from your father? Or do you invariably see eye to eye? What's your opinion of the 'Sorcerer'?"

Elizabeth Stainsby looked at the two cartoons and compared them. "I prefer the one I saw first. I like it much better than this 'Sorcerer' one. Perhaps the real reason behind that may be that the subject of the one appeals to me much more than the subject of the other."

"It may be so," said Kenneth Stainsby; "all the same, and speaking for myself, I think the one's every whit as beautiful as the other. Still, there's no accounting for taste. I know this: I'd like to think they were all mine."

"Don't be greedy, Kenneth," said Elizabeth.

"I'm not being greedy," replied her father tolerantly. "I'm merely giving expression to 'what I should like', not as to 'what I want'. Let me put it like this—if I'm being guilty of covetousness, the sin is much more benevolent than malevolent."

His keen eyes flashed as he turned towards Anthony. "I'm sure that Bathurst here understands me and, because of that, won't misjudge me." Anthony smiled. "I think so, sir. And I fancy I can cite comparable circumstances. For instance, I've often admired a beautiful woman, who, luckily for him, has been the wife of another man, but that hasn't meant to say that I coveted possession of her."

Elizabeth Stainsby pouted. It seemed an appropriate gesture for her age. "I don't like the sound of that," she said, "it seems almost barbaric."

Wall chuckled. "That's because you won't face up to things properly and get them into proper proportion. Physical possession is really a far less important matter than a first kiss or the initial caress. I'm a peculiar sort of feller, I suppose, but I don't like the modern fashion that talks so glibly about physical love. Any more than I care for the glib talk with regard to religion. There are certain things in life which are private and which should be allowed to remain as private. After all, a physical self is only the expression and the real realization of a person's inward self."

Anthony looked at Wall with an entirely new interest and thought again what a strange mixture the man was of partisan politics, philosophy and emotion. But Neville Kemble coughed discreetly and uttered an invitation that was intended to include everybody.

"Suppose, now, that we all go in the next room for tea."

Elizabeth Stainsby, who had reddened under Wall's fire, caught at the welcome suggestion with both hands.

"I'm certain," she said, "that we couldn't do anything better. From everybody's point of view."

"Right," said Wall, with that curious movement of the head to one side which was so physically characteristic of the man. "'Avin' put mind before matter, we'll proceed with very good sense to put muffins before both of 'em."

He waved his hand dramatically and declared in his harsh, strident voice, "Lead on, then, Mr. Kemble."

As they moved into the adjoining room, Anthony saw MacMorran standing in the doorway. "Well?" queried the latter, with a lift of the eyebrows as he came forward. "How are things going?"

"Not too badly, Andrew." Anthony stooped and almost whispered the next words to the Inspector. "Let them go in to tea, Andrew, and I'll have a private word with you. Then I can pop in later." MacMorran nodded his acceptance of the suggestion.

"The Tresillians," announced Anthony, "will be coming along here tomorrow evening. Humphrey—that's the one that's Town Clerk of Kersbrook—has arranged it with Kemble here."

"Good," said the Inspector.

"Now tell me something," returned Anthony. "Re the car on Sunday night. Who'll be driving?"

"Hemingway himself," replied MacMorran, "with Chatterton inside with the cartoons."

Anthony nodded his approval of the arrangements. "That's all right. Couldn't be better, all things considered."

MacMorran said, "Glad you approve. Was half afraid you might be inclined to criticize."

"No, Andrew. Those arrangements satisfy me. I'll have another word with you when tea's over. In the meantime I'll pop in there with the others, otherwise they'll all be wondering what's become of me." He turned away, but stopped abruptly to swing back towards MacMorran. "By the way, Andrew, were you able to check up on that Fred Lord matter I spoke to you about?"

MacMorran nodded. "That's one of the things I wanted to mention to you. Yes, I looked into it. You were quite right."

Anthony smiled as he turned away again. "Good, Andrew," he said, "that's news which suits me."

CHAPTER IX

I

THE Tresillian brothers arrived about half-past six on the evening of the following day. Gilbert suave and soft-spoken, Humphrey, the Town Clerk, dark-jowled, hard-featured and generally minatory. Neville Kemble had invited them to dinner, and neither of them needed any spurring to the acceptance of the invitation. Dinners at "Palings" had acquired an enviable reputation in St. Mead. Neville Kemble on this occasion gave his guests a delicious cream soup, sole, saddle of mutton and partridges.

Humphrey Tresillian was soon in excellent conversational form, thanks to the food mentioned, an excellent Oloroso and an equally fine Musigny. Anthony used each brother in turn. Words fell from Humphrey Tresillian's brain and tumbled untidily into their midst. His best sentences seemed to be collapsing in his mind as will fall hopelessly and helplessly a built edifice of flimsy cards. His brother Gilbert deftly steered the conversation into the channel of art. Humphrey began to traduce the film as an artistic vehicle.

"Films?" he said with an open sneer. "There aren't any films nowadays as such. They're all colossal, stupendous, super films! The whole industry is swamped by waves of the superlative degree. Tainted and putrid from the very start."

Gilbert joined issue with him and Anthony listened to the verbal duel between the brothers with strong interest.

"You say 'tainted'," said Gilbert, "tainted and putrid. That's all moonshine. You can carry that argument to altogether too great a length. You speak of a tainted source. A putrid origin. Well, many other things would have a difficult job to avoid being in that category. No, my dear Humphrey, the film is an entirely justified expression of modern civilization. A natural outcome of the general journey which our age has taken. It affords amusement to the many. It gives pleasure to men, women and children. You assert, when you choose to condemn it, that it's vulgar, that it's tawdry, that it's cheap. It may be. I won't deny that it very often is all of these things. But what's my reply to those charges? Why, this! So are we! We are cheap, vulgar and tawdry. And it's not the slightest use our sticking our heads in the sand and pretending that we're not. I don't mean you particularly, Humphrey, but the *hoi polloi* at large."

Gilbert smiled as he concluded his defensive effort, and lifted his glass of Burgundy to his lips.

"People!" retorted Humphrey. "People! Is everything to be judged by what the plebeian desire? Good Lord, Gilbert, have a heart! At that rate, you'll place Chaplin in front of Shakespeare and Ketelbey before Beethoven."

"Not at all. And that's a supremely ridiculous statement to make. Your trouble, Humphrey, is that you don't live in the ordinary world and make companionship with ordinary people. As a result of that social segregation, you don't ever realize or understand how drab and dull the majority of human lives are. They're grey, cheerless and sombre. And humdrum people need something to set against those deadening conditions. To balance the banality of their lives. They want thrills, colour, sensation and emotional heart-throbs. And the films give them those things. You can't possibly argue that they don't." Gilbert smiled as he had smiled before. "Sorry, Humphrey, and all that, but you've forced me to devastate you."

Humphrey Tresillian shrugged his shoulders and deliberately changed the subject. "I'm afraid, Kemble, it's a far cry from the cinema to the cartoons of the great Rafaelle. But to me the modern cinema is a shattering bore."

"So may the cartoons be! The cartoons that I'm going to show you," replied Neville Kemble. "I can quite believe that they won't be to everybody's taste."

He looked across at Gilbert Tresillian. "Try that champagne, Gilbert," he said. "It's a Felix Poubelle 1884. You wouldn't be lucky enough to get it at any London restaurant even if you'd given the *maître d'hôtel* a thirty-three to one shot for the Royal Hunt Cup and had promised him something good for the Stewards Cup a month later. No," concluded Kemble, "no, bar a possible occasional bottle tucked away in an obscure cellar, I should say that it's virtually unobtainable."

Gilbert sampled the wine which the butler poured out for him. He quickly became appreciative. "Delightful, Neville; your eulogy is merited."

Humphrey intervened cynically. "Beware, my dear Gilbert," he said with a twisted smile. "Remember Menecrates, the physician of Syracuse and the banquet of incense to which he was invited by Philip of Macedonia. For all you know, Neville may have similar designs on you and me."

Neville Kemble denied the suggestion with an easy and complacent kindliness. "Have no fear, either of you. I'm regaling you with that bottle of wine as a sheer treat. Put it down to my genuine kindness of heart."

All this time, Anthony sat at the table quietly and took good stock of the two Tresillians. Like most brothers they possessed undeniable likenesses and almost incredible differences. As the meal progressed to its close, Anthony's observation became keener and more acute. Humphrey Tresillian became a shade more contumelious. And as his superciliousness increased, his brother Gilbert seemed to develop his own benevolent austerity. Anthony felt certain that Humphrey was deliberately emphasizing the differences between himself and his brother, and insisting that the Sybarite stared across the dinner-table at the Rechabite.

Thus it still prevailed when the time came for the exhibition of the Rafaelle cartoons. Neville Kemble had them arranged as previously and invited the Tresillians to the library for the inspection.

"Well," said Neville, "there they are." He indicated the cartoons with a comprehensive sweep of the hand. "Have a good look at them and I'll nurse the pious hope that you'll regard your visit as well worth while. Any other condition would grievously disappoint me."

The Tresillian brothers walked down the line of cartoons. Anthony watched for their individual reactions. Humphrey, if anything, was the more outspoken in comment. His cavalier manner to a degree had passed from him and he had become much quieter. Gilbert, on the other hand, seemed to have imbibed a new form of excitement. But this emotion showed on his face and in his eyes. It was not reflected by anything that he said. The two brothers came to the last of the cartoons. Nobody spoke. Anthony waited. But he knew the truth now. What he had previously only suspected had now become positive to him. He knew the murderer of Steel and of Oliver and the identity of the man who had passed on the cartoons to Dwight Conway. The only point that remained was whether the murderer would walk into the trap that had been sprung for him. But Neville Kemble was speaking.

"Well, gentlemen"—his tones were both quiet and easy—"what do you think of them? Do they make any sort of appeal to your artistic sensibilities?"

Gilbert Tresillian took it upon himself to answer first. His speech was not altogether devoid of hesitancy.

"Well," he said, and Anthony felt that he could detect almost reluctance in his voice, "they're unique in their way, I suppose—and, of course, singularly beautiful pieces of work, but all the same, Kemble—" He came to an abrupt stop.

"All the same—what?" Kemble took him up where he had paused. After a second or so, Gilbert Tresillian went on.

"Well, what I was attempting to say was this. I don't think they'd be everybody's money. I should say they'd be a rather 'acquired taste' sort of article. That's how they appeal to me. But, of course, against all that, I'm probably lacking in judgment. Nobody—even my firmest friends—would rate me as artistic. I haven't had an artistic education, so in all probability my opinion of them is worth little or next to nothing. Still, you asked me, Kemble, and you've had your answer."

Neville Kemble nodded smilingly and turned to Humphrey Tresillian. "And what does our Town Clerk say about them? I'm interested to know."

Humphrey's eyes flashed with more than a hint of mockery. Then he shrugged his shoulders. "After Gilbert's lukewarm effort? After that supreme example of damning with faint praise? Dear me! Who am I to succeed him and enter into judgment with him? A mere legal luminary of a somewhat obscure county borough! The thought almost unnerves me. Ah well, here goes! I enter into dispute with brother Gilbert directly the tapes go up. I think these cartoons of yours, my dear Kemble, are superlatively lovely. 'Acquired taste', says Gilbert?

Faugh! I can well understand anybody being covetous of their possession. And I shall go away from 'Palings' this evening with a far higher appreciation of the Royal Stuart than I ever had before."

He turned to them with a gesture of abandonment. "There you are, gentlemen, the poorest of oracles has delivered judgment. And now I wait for brother Gilbert to turn and rend me."

This time it was Gilbert's turn to shrug his shoulders. "Not at all, my dear Humphrey. *Quot homines tot sententiae*. I've never been, I hope, so essentially narrow-minded that I couldn't appreciate and respect another man's point of view. You like oysters, I don't. I like olives whereas you detest them. There you are. So what!"

Neville Kemble broke in. "This is all highly interesting to me. Because it brings me to another question I want to ask Humphrey. I might even ask Gilbert—but most certainly Humphrey." He addressed himself to Humphrey Tresillian. "Which of the eight cartoons do you admire most?"

Humphrey Tresillian looked at Kemble suspiciously, as though he was of the opinion that the remark held much more in it than appeared on the surface.

"Why?" he asked. "Does it matter?"

"Not really, I suppose," replied Neville Kemble, "but I'm interested, that's all. And I've asked that question of other people who've come here to look at the cartoons. It amuses me to contrast and compare their various opinions."

"I see," replied Humphrey. And then with a show of his white, even teeth, "And it would be churlish of me to deprive you of any legitimate amusement. Suppose I have another look at the works of the distinguished Rafaelle?"

He made his way to the cartoons again. Anthony watched him carefully. Humphrey Tresillian stopped in front of each one of the cartoons and gave it his closest scrutiny. The seconds ticked by. Eventually Humphrey came sauntering back to them.

"My vote goes to the 'Pool of Siloam'. The expressions on the faces of those poor wretches at the waterside are to my mind truly remarkable."

"Thank you, Humphrey," said Neville Kemble, "very nice of you! And in more than one respect I'm not averse from your opinion."

He turned to Gilbert Tresillian. "Now what about you, Gilbert? On which side are you coming down?"

Gilbert Tresillian rubbed his chin with his forefinger. "As I intimated to you before, I'm no judge. And I make no claims to judgeship. So whatever I may nominate means precious little, I'm afraid. Still, if you really want my seriously considered choice, I'll play the game and let you have it."

Like his brother before him he returned to the cartoons. Anthony watched him as carefully as he had watched Humphrey a few minutes previously. But it is doubtful if he gave the cartoons the same careful inspection that the Town Clerk of Kersbrook had. At length Gilbert was heard to declare his choice.

"My vote goes to 'Elymas the Sorcerer'," he said, "but for the love of Mike don't press me to give the inevitable reasons for my answer. Because for the life of me I couldn't! I just like that one the best—and that's all there is to it."

Gilbert gave a wry little smile and shrugged his shoulders. "And thank you, Gilbert," said Neville Kemble. "I'm glad that you didn't back out. It may seem a small thing to you—and no doubt it actually *is* a small matter—but it gives me an intense amount of pleasure to collect the different and varying opinions of my friends in all sorts of directions. And if I bear with them in relation to religion and politics, why shouldn't I enjoy the felicity of hearing them with regard to a little affair of the artistic?"

"How long are you keeping them here?" asked Gilbert Tresillian. "I suppose they've got to be sent back at some time or other?"

"Why do you ask?" inquired Neville Kemble. "Is there anybody else that you know whom you would like to have the opportunity of seeing them?"

"Oh no," said Gilbert, "I had nothing of that kind in my mind. My circle of acquaintances is by no means extensive—certainly I can't think of anybody else who would be interested. Especially in this district, and I should hardly suggest that anybody should make a special journey from town to see them."

Neville Kemble nodded. "I see. In that case, then, the arrangements I've made for their transit can still stand."

Humphrey Tresillian walked to the window and looked out. The moonlight was brilliant and he affected to shade his eyes with his left hand on his forehead. His thoughts appeared to be miles away from the room at "Palings" where they were standing. Neville Kemble went on with what he was saying.

"They're going to town on Sunday evening. Straight up there by a special car."

"Bit risky, isn't it?" remarked Gilbert.

Neville Kemble seemed to consider the question. "Oh, I don't know" he replied after a momentary pause; "don't think so. Why should it be? Nobody will know what the arrangements are. Bar people like yourself, who don't count in that way." Neville grinned as he concluded, "We shan't take the criminal classes into our confidence, you bet! Which is, I suppose, what you meant, when you alluded to the risk?"

Gilbert shook his head with misgiving. "You never know. Secret and confidential information has an unhappy knack of leaking out."

Humphrey Tresillian came back to them from the clouds. "Do you know what I think, Neville? That the conditions of the moment indicate an evening's Bridge. Bathurst and yourself—Gilbert and I. What could finish up the day better?"

"I shall be only too pleased to fall in with the suggestion, my dear Humphrey. I don't know, though, how Bathurst feels about it."

Anthony smiled. "That may depend, sir, on the run of the cards. I'm notoriously unlucky at the card table."

Humphrey Tresillian clapped him on the back. "I've a hunch, old chap, that this evening your luck will turn."

"Perhaps," returned Anthony. "But at any rate, I'll tell you this. Diamonds are my lucky suit."

Humphrey eyed him shrewdly. "Really? Spades are mine."

II

Superintendent Hemingway pulled the peaked cap of his chauffeur's uniform further over his forehead and roundly cursed the vagaries of the English climate. It was seven o'clock on Sunday evening and the November night had decided, in its perversity, to stage a really formidable fog. The first real fog of that winter. He had put his case to Chief-Inspector MacMorran and awaited new orders.

"Don't fancy driving in this, and no mistake. All I hope is that the Chief scrubs it out. Too risky, if you ask me—by a long chalk."

Chatterton nodded. "Too true, Super, too true. Proper dirty night this, and it don't look like getting any better. Where's the Chief gone now?"

"To have a chin-wag with Mr. Bathurst. If he'll agree to it, I'm pretty sure the Chief'll scrub it out. Which will suit yours truly down to the ground. I never was too keen on the night air. Unless you swallowed it on the way to the local."

Chatterton assented gloomily to his superior officer's point of view as expressed. "I gathered from you, Super, that tonight's do was going to be a piece of cake. Plain sailing, so to speak! I can tell you, I never bargained for a drop o' real London particular like what's rolling up now."

"You gathered," retorted Superintendent Hemingway contemptuously "you've no right to do any gathering at all or to expect pieces of cake, in the Force."

"Come to that," said Chatterton as gloomily as before, "I suppose I haven't. But there you are—every man lets his thoughts run away with him sometimes."

Chatterton fumbled in the pocket of his greatcoat for the packet of cigarettes he had placed in there about half an hour previously. For some reason he failed to find it, and Chatterton swore under his breath at the perversity of things in general.

"What perishin' luck," he cursed to himself. "A night like this bastard—and nothing to smoke!"

The fog was now getting appreciably worse. The air grew colder and the wind had dropped to nothingness. The headlights of the car as it stood outside "Palings" did little to diminish the obscurity of the night. The fog began to sting Hemingway's nostrils. By now he was almost as browned off as Chatterton.

"Wish they'd make up their ruddy minds," he commented audibly. "I'd like to know before very long where I shall be having my supper."

His throat now felt the acrid, pungent stinging of the fog as much as his nostrils, which fact made Hemingway thrust his hands deep into the pockets of his overcoat and pace backwards and forwards by the side of the waiting car. But gradually the fog seemed to close in on him and he had no doubt within his mind that it was getting thicker. His smarting eyes peered into the opaque distance as he did his best to pierce the grey, swirling murkiness. To test his latest impression, Hemingway extended his right hand in front of him and turned his hand—palm showing outwards. As he had thought, he couldn't see it. The Superintendent cursed again and muttered imprecations relative to the climate of our land.

As he did so, he heard the muffled sounds of footsteps behind him.

He retraced his steps, therefore, to hear the voices of MacMorran and Anthony Bathurst but a few feet away from him.

"Ah," said the former, emerging from the gloom, "I've seen the Chief Constable and he's content, so he says, to leave the decision in my hands. It's a nasty night, Super, but—"

"Nasty," broke in Hemingway with misplaced impetuosity, "it's a son of a bitch if ever there was one."

"Quite so," commented the Chief Inspector acidly, "but the job is on. Mr. Bathurst and I have decided that the possible disadvantages may, in the long run, help us rather than hinder us. So you'll get away, Super, at the time agreed."

"Very good, sir," said Hemingway, "ve-ry good, sir! I'm glad you know your own mind, sir. Mr. Bathurst likewise, sir."

Anthony's tall form came at him out of the grey wall of fog. Hemingway could see that his features wore a broad grin. "O.K., Super, and many thanks for the compliment."

"You know your instructions," added MacMorran. "Keep to them rigidly and leave the rest to us. Now get along back to Chatterton and get the car off at a quarter to the hour."

"Very good, sir." Hemingway touched the peak of his cap and went back to the car. MacMorran turned to Anthony.

"And we'll get to our car, Mr. Bathurst. From my point of view, the sooner the better."

Anthony stood and wiped the wet fog from his eyes and face. "Well," said the Inspector, "what's the trouble? Changed your mind with regard to anything? You seemed pretty confident just now."

"I've been thinking," replied Anthony slowly, "and don't bite my head off, Andrew—I'm inclined to suggest that in view of this nasty trick the weather has played on us, we make a slight revision of our previous arrangements."

MacMorran stared at him with unconcerned criticism. "Now, why?" he demanded.

"This fog," said Anthony.

"What about the fog? I thought we'd discussed all that with Colonel Buxton just now."

"I know. We did. We went into all of it pretty thoroughly. I'm well aware of all that. We considered the whole range of 'pros and cons'." Anthony paused again.

"Well," said MacMorran again a trifle sharply, "what's the point that you're leading up to?"

"Just this, Andrew. I think that I'll leave you to travel in the second car all on your own."

"And why that—in the name of goodness?"

"Because," said Anthony, with slow deliberation, "I think that this fog joke may cause the enemy to change his tactics, and I want us to be fully prepared to meet and deal with that possible change. If we split our reserve force into two halves—and you and I, Andrew, will each represent one half—I think we shall have a stronger disposition of that force. You go by yourself in the second car, ahead of Hemingway and Chatterton, take up the position we arranged and I'll work on my own."

"And where will that be?" demanded MacMorran.

"I think," responded Anthony, "that I'll work back to the house."

"In this fog?" challenged the Inspector critically.

"Um! I know the way all right. You need entertain no worries on that score."

"All right," agreed MacMorran after a brief spell of hesitation. "I don't say that I like it, but I suppose you know what you're doing."

"Thank you, Andrew," replied Anthony with a smile. "That's very sporting of you. But there's just this additional point I should make."

"What's that?"

"If nothing happens at your coign of vantage of the kind that we're anticipating, after say, half an hour, drive straight back to the house. You'll find me there, and I'm strongly of the opinion that I, in my turn, shall find your advent both welcome and propitious. Now then, I can't put it plainer than that, can I, Andrew?"

But MacMorran remained difficult. "That's all very well. From your standpoint. We can't shut our eyes, though, to the fact that this wretched fog may make all the difference in the world to our original plans. It's doubtful if I shall be able to see Hemingway and Chatterton go by. Assuming that they're untouched until then."

"That needn't worry you," returned Anthony. "They will still be able to give you the prearranged signal. If they do, you must follow at a discreet distance. And if you use the police-box on the corner, you can get the time of day the other end from Kershaw. You won't be any worse off without me than you would have been with me, whereas I shall be able to cover other, and possibly highly valuable, ground."

He looked up as he spoke. "'Pon my soul, Andrew, I believe the fog's lifting a little. I shan't grumble at that, and I know you won't."

"All right," conceded Inspector MacMorran. "I'll get along to Hemingway and check up with him on exact times."

"Good! You can't do better than that. There's one thing," added Anthony, as though by an afterthought, "the fog's beneficial in one direction. The attempt's bound to be made close home—near here, I mean. For them to let Hemingway get too far on the road's far too risky. Whereas before, had we had ordinary weather conditions, you know as well as I do that we couldn't gauge where the attack might take place. You remember how that possibility worried us. It might have happened a hundred miles from here. Whereas now . . ."

"That's true," admitted MacMorran—albeit a trifle grudgingly. "All right—I'll get along back to Hemingway and Chatterton."

"O.K.," said Anthony. "Cheero, Andrew, I'll be seeing you."

III

MacMorran made his way slowly back to the car outside "Palings". As he peered through the yellow gloom of the blanketing fog, he saw Hemingway trying to read the time by the clock on the dashboard.

"You've a couple of minutes yet, Super," he said.

"Just about, Chief. Not more."

"You won't want more. Enough's as good as a feast. Any word from Kershaw?"

"Nothing."

"Listen, Super. This is important. Mr. Bathurst and I have made a slight amendment of plan. I'll tell you what we've arranged to do."

MacMorran gave Hemingway the gist of the revised arrangements. "Don't know that I altogether agree," commenced Hemingway, but the Inspector quickly closured the criticism that the Superintendent had been about to make. "You needn't argue. Save your breath for the time when you'll want it. It's done now and what's done can't be undone. It's time for you to start. Get cracking!"

"Very good, Inspector." Hemingway turned to speak to Chatterton in the back of the car. "Fit?"

"O.K.," replied Chatterton, and the car moved slowly off, its lights blurred and strange-looking through the bank of malignant fog.

MacMorran listened to the car as it moved down the road at a crawl and heard Hemingway on the gears as it turned the corner. Just as he was turning away to go to the garage for what Anthony Bathurst had just described as the second car, his ears caught the sound of approaching footsteps. For a moment, as he stopped dead and listened to them he thought that they must be Anthony's, but he quickly realized that this was a mistaken idea. Even allowing for the presence of the fog, the footsteps lacked the decision and firmness that were characteristic of Anthony's. The "Yard" inspector listened and waited. He knew that if the person who was approaching kept a reasonably straight course, he or she must pass very close to where he himself was standing.

The footsteps came nearer. They were purposeless and shambling, and suddenly they touched, as it were, a familiar chord in MacMorran's brain. A lurching, shapeless figure appeared out of the fog. Breath steamed in a kind of wispy circle from its mouth, and MacMorran heard muttered words and incoherent mouthings. The figure came near enough to MacMorran for the Inspector to be able to detect the face. It was Fred Lord, the zany from the cottages on the hillside. Lord lurched away from MacMorran to avoid impact, and as he did so he seemed to slip on the edge of the kerb. Lord almost fell, but he righted himself by an effort and passed on into the fog and the night. MacMorran wiped his face with his handkerchief.

When he put his handkerchief back into his pocket he could still hear Lord mumbling away in the distance. The Inspector walked on to the garage. His hands and body generally were clammy and unpleasant. He shook his head as he opened the doors of the garage.

"Wish Bathurst had run into that," he said to himself. "If he had, his opinion might have been worth hearing."

IV

Hemingway, as may be well imagined, bearing in mind the climatic conditions, drove slowly and with an excess of care. Every now and then he would speak to Chatterton at the back.

"Can you see anything?" he asked, as they turned the corner and made the main Fernchester road.

"No," returned Chatterton, "not a thing. Only blasted fog. I can see that all right! And smell it! And feel it! And ruddy well taste it!"

Hemingway waxed cynical. "Pity you can't hear it! Then I'd think there was a fog knocking around somewhere. Some of you chaps don't know when you're well off."

"No," replied Chatterton. "Shouldn't think so! What I could do with now—if you really want to know—would be a nice glass of wallop with a head on it. I'd be feeling a lot better then."

"You don't say!" said Hemingway, with mock admiration in his voice.

The car continued at a crawl. "Thank God for these white lines down the middle of the road," he observed, "they're nothing less than a godsend on a night like this."

"Super," said Chatterton—he spoke very quietly—"when do you think it'll come off?"

"How the heck do I know? But before over-long, I should imagine, in conditions like this."

"Maybe it's clearer down the road. That'll make a difference."

"Should be," returned Hemingway, "when we begin to ascend. We're down in a bit of a valley here and the fog's at its thickest. We shall probably find it's in patches."

"Don't forget to give the signal when you pass the 'winker'," said Chatterton.

"Thanks for the reminder," answered Hemingway sarcastically. "Good thing they sent you along with me. I want somebody to hold my hand." He peered forward. "Hallo! It's better here! By a long chalk! I can step on it a bit."

The Superintendent accelerated. The conditions were as he had stated. The fog was lighter here altogether and, with an increase of wind on the higher ground, was contained more in a series of grey swirling patches than in the opaque, almost impenetrable, wall which it had presented before. The car gathered pace, and Chatterton even plucked up his spirits to whistle the chorus of "The Lambeth Walk".

"Should be close to the 'winker' now," he announced rather lugubriously, "judging by the time we've been on the road."

Again Hemingway peered forward over the wheel and into the windscreen. The "wiper" moved round with monotonous and seemingly impeccable regularity. Visibility was now much improved, and the Superintendent said laconically, as he settled back in his seat again, "You're quite right, Chatterton—we're almost on to it."

"Thought we must be." Chatterton rubbed at the glass with the tips of his fingers. "Blimey, it's clearer now, Super! Not near so much like the old pea-soup as it was down below there. Don't forget to sound your—"

"All right," retorted Hemingway savagely, "when I want your perishing advice I'll ask for it."

"Sorry, Super. Keep the party clean. It's only my zeal that makes me like I am."

"Sit back," said Hemingway, "and keep your mouth shut and your eyes open."

He gave the arranged signal as he piloted the car round the "winker". Chatterton nodded approvingly, although his superior officer didn't see the action. There was a silence of some minutes.

Hemingway said, "Stay put. I'm going to step it up a bit."

Chatterton said, "That's O.K. by me, Super. I'll keep my eyes skinned, don't you fear."

Hemingway increased speed. The car ran on for a distance of about five miles. As they ascended, visibility continued to improve.

At the Stoke Ferne cross-roads conditions were almost normal. A mile beyond, with Chatterton whistling the notes of "Through the Night of Doubt and Sorrow", a fast car came at them suddenly and without the slightest warning from what appeared to be no more than a side cart-track.

"S'truth!" yelled Chatterton. Hemingway braked fiercely and swung the wheel right over, but the ditch was too close. The other car drove straight at them and forced them down. A figure swung from the driving-seat holding a levelled revolver. The face was covered with a black mask.

"Crawl out and put your hands up." The voice was sharp and incisive. It went on to say, as Chatterton wiped the blood from a cut across his eye, "No nonsense, now! I'm in a hurry."

Chatterton looked round. He could see no sign of Hemingway, who appeared to be still in the ditch.

"You'll do as I say," said the voice, "or I'll break your wrist with a bullet. You'll find the metacarpals extremely painful when treated like that, believe me. Put the Rafaelle cartoons into my car. Pronto!"

Chatterton looked up at the masked figure. There was still no sign or sound from Hemingway.

"O.K., Claude Duval," he muttered. "I reckon you've got Dick Turpin and Robin 'Ood stone cold."

"Interesting," said the masked figure, "but, quite frankly, uncalled for. Make it snappy."

Chatterton bent solemnly and stolidly to his appointed task.

CHAPTER X

I

ANTHONY Lotherington Bathurst, after he left MacMorran on his way to the second car, made slow progress through the fog to the house which he had appointed for himself as his destination for that particular evening. He knew exactly where it lay, and he knew also the manner of his best approach to it from Neville Kemble's residence. But the circumstances of the fog imposed difficulties upon him which it took all his intelligence and acute sense of locality to circumvent.

Although his rate of progress was of necessity slow, it was nevertheless equally sure, and within the space of half an hour he knew that he had made no mistake in his bearings and that he had come to within a stone's throw of the house which was his primary objective.

Every now and then, Anthony would stop in his tracks and listen. Eventually he heard what his ears had been straining to hear—the sound of a powerful car travelling away from him. So far, so good, and Anthony plodded on his way, stealthily and purposefully. Two turns to the left and a turn to the right brought him to the house of his anticipated rendezvous. Anthony felt in his pocket to reassure himself that his revolver was handy and ready for any demanded occasion. The fog-wraith hid the shape of the house, but he passed through the gate and crept along the drive after having used his torch to satisfy himself that he had come to the right place.

An owl hooted somewhere away north-west as he walked slowly towards the house. Then he heard the infinitely faint throbbing and whirring of another car a good distance away.

"It's nothing, of course," he said to himself; "it's the fog which makes it all seem so eerie."

Shining his torch again, he saw that he was now but a few paces from the front door. Anthony stopped suddenly to think things out. Situated as he was now, he was compelled to consider who might be at home. There were long odds, he thought, against him finding the house absolutely empty. The gravel crunched under his feet as he took a few paces forward. Should he essay entrance at the front of the house or should he use the back? The question had scarcely crystallized in his brain when he discovered that he had come far enough and that the front door of the house was facing him. Then, again, there was the possibility that the hunch that he had discussed with MacMorran might prove unsound and let him down. Again he reviewed the chances in his mind and decided that his hunch would turn up trumps.

As he walked slowly up to the front door he came to a patch where the fog was not. He saw the house. It seemed to rise hollow in the ghostly light. It had an empty look, as though it were ownerless and knew it, and the look of it gave birth to feelings which Anthony found unwelcome and unpleasant. As he ranged himself alongside the front door, he heard footsteps on the stairs. They sounded ominous in a house so allied with the stains of crime. Anthony stood silent in the porch, but the footsteps had given him very seriously to think. Then he heard them again—this time making their way to the rear of the house. Anthony felt that the time for entry was now or never. He turned the handle of the big door. It yielded. The fanlight shone, and Anthony found himself standing in the hall.

II

Anthony closed the door. Draught and fog were unpleasant companions. The main rooms seemed to lie on his left. The first door was locked. The second was a lounge and was empty. A white sheepskin rug by the fireplace seemed rucked and rumpled as though somebody in a hurry had thrust it from its proper place. The drawer of a cabinet was open and gave the impression that somebody, searching there, had been abruptly turned from the task. Anthony wondered at these signs, for he had not been expecting them.

He tiptoed to the hall again, and had been there but a few seconds when he heard the sound of the footsteps returning. A door opened and shut—quietly. A second door was treated in the same manner. With even less noise. Anthony waited expectantly. His fingers were clasped round the butt of his revolver. He moved away from the circle of light that flooded the hall, but he had barely done this when a man's figure emerged from a side passage.

"Who's there?" a voice demanded imperiously.

"Good evening, Mr. Tresillian," said Anthony quietly.

Humphrey Tresillian moved towards him and stared at him with a mixture of amusement and amazement.

III

Anthony waited for Tresillian to speak. When this happened Tresillian was cool, calm and collected.

"I wasn't aware, my dear Bathurst," he said, "that I should have company this evening. I might have even gone farther than that, and said 'distinguished company'."

"You might," replied Anthony, "but you didn't."

Tresillian smiled. "No. Forgive the omission. It was an oversight on my part. Nice house, though, isn't it? And sumptuously furnished. I wonder where the cash comes from! You are here, I take it, in the matter of the cartoons?"

"I am," said Anthony. "I should hate to contradict you. And you?"

Tresillian shrugged his shoulders. "Put it down to a whim on my part. I followed an intuition and felt that I should like to be in at the death. You, I presume, felt much the same?"

"Hardly. Certainly not an intuition. Much more in my case, like backing a certainty. At the same time, though, permit me to extend to you my congratulations."

Tresillian grinned. "Oh, thanks! Permit me to return the compliment." He glanced at his watch. "Well, what are you going to do about it? That's what's beginning to bother me."

"As to that," returned Anthony, "I hope to arrest a thief and a double murderer I shall be most disappointed if I don't."

"How long do you propose to wait?" Tresillian eyed him warily as he spoke. There was a cold glint in his eye.

Anthony, in his turn, looked at his wrist-watch. "I should say, my dear Tresillian, the arrest may take place any minute now."

The words had scarcely left his lips when the front door opened again. A man entered. Anthony saw that it was MacMorran.

"Let me introduce you," said Anthony. "Chief-Inspector MacMorran of New Scotland Yard—Mr. Humphrey Tresillian, Town Clerk of Kersbrook."

Tresillian smiled. MacMorran seemed taken aback. "I wasn't—" He commenced to speak, when the wheels of a car were heard outside.

"Quick," said Anthony, "in here!"

The three men stepped into the lounge—the room where the rug had been disturbed.

IV

"Leave the door slightly ajar," said Anthony.

MacMorran nodded. Humphrey Tresillian smiled his most cynical of smiles. MacMorran whispered across to Anthony.

"I've just 'phoned Colonel Buxton. Told him where we were and what we were expecting."

Anthony held up his hand. "Coming in," he whispered curtly. "Hark!"

"I don't think we shall need 'em," said MacMorran in an undertone, "but I'm armed the same as you are. Just in case, like."

Tresillian made a pantomime of shrugging shoulders, but in the darkness of the room neither of the others saw him. The front door of the house opened and shut, not too quietly. Footsteps sounded down the hall. MacMorran caught Anthony by the shoulder.

"Coming in here!" he whispered. "Behind the door—all of us."

The Inspector and Anthony slid behind the door, and Tresillian followed their example. Scarcely had they taken this action when the door opened and they could hear a hand feeling for the electric-light switch. The hand found it, and the light flooded the room. A figure with a black-crêpe mask across the front of the face stood in the middle of the room directly below the large electric-bowl light suspended from the ceiling. Its back was turned to the men behind the door. Under the arms were carried the Rafaelle cartoons.

"Now, Andrew," whispered Anthony; "it's a sitting bird."

MacMorran stepped out noiselessly from behind the door. In two strides he was alongside and his hand went to the other's shoulder.

"Kenneth Stainsby—you are arrested for the murders of Elmer Oliver and—"

Stainsby swung round with an oath. His hand flew to his pocket. But before he could take effective action, Anthony's voice sounded incisively across the room.

"I shouldn't do that . . . I shouldn't really . . ."

Stainsby saw Anthony's revolver and realized that the game was up. His jaw set and he allowed MacMorran to handcuff him without resistance. Humphrey Tresillian's pose had vanished in the drama that had been played in front of him.

"Even more sensational than I had anticipated," he said, as Stainsby walked out, "and taken in the best possible manner—*in flagrante delicto*."

V

Anthony sat on the most comfortable settee in "Palings" and talked to Sir Austin Kemble, his brother, and Colonel Buxton. Tea and buttered muffins again took centre stage. Inspector MacMorran, Humphrey Tresillian and Drusilla Ives were also present.

"I shall always think of the case to myself," he said, "as 'The Case of Elymas the Sorcerer'."

"Pusher" Buxton came in immediately with an interruption. "Why? I don't get you."

"I'll explain that later, sir, if you don't mind. And as the Commissioner has asked me for a résumé of the case in accordance with his customary procedure, I'll do my best to provide it. Let me do the job properly and begin at the beginnings. We started off, if I may say so, with an almost clueless crime. Two nude bodies in a field—each poisoned by aconite. By reason of certain information we received from a man named Stacey hailing from an oil-cake factory in the East End of London, we were enabled to identify the second body as that of a man named Peter Steel. Steel led us to his brother-in-law Elmer Oliver, whom we then established as the first dead man. We had thus commenced to make headway.

"Actually the crimes were *not* absolutely clueless. For you will remember that we were fortunate enough to pick up in Ebford's field four tiny scraps of paper. If my memory serves me correctly, they bore these words or parts of words—'of Sil', 'Emma', 'Mai', and 'Temple'. They seemed, however, pretty thin and pretty hopeless when they first came into our hands."

The Chief Constable of Fernshire nodded his agreement. "I'll say they did."

"So you see," went on Anthony, "that for a time everything was all wet. But I had always felt that if I waited and generally bided my time, approach to, and contact with me would eventually be made. I was right, for up turned Peter Steel."

Anthony went on to describe his meeting with Steel.

"Just a minute," broke in the Commissioner. "How did Steel know that you were connected with his brother-in-law's case? I'm a bit puzzled at that."

"I've considered that myself," replied Anthony, "and I've reached the conclusion that he took the lie of the land and saw me in the company of Inspector Kershaw and of you, sir."

Anthony indicated Colonel Buxton. The latter nodded. "Yes, quite feasible."

Anthony went on. "After Steel saw me, he too was murdered, obviously on the lines that dead men tell no tales. But having seen him and talked with him, I was convinced that the genesis of our problem lay in robbery, and that Steel had merely been following up somebody or some interest that was concerned with this robbery. All the same, I had little or nothing on which to build. But I had St. Mead as a springboard, as it were. There must be somebody in St. Mead, I argued, connected with this robbery which I was certain had taken place. As MacMorran here knows, I waited for some appreciable time for another approach, but none came, so gradually I made the acquaintance of a number of local, shall I say, celebrities. And then I began to see with a certain sense of shock that the approach for which I was waiting need not take place *if* the person for whom I was waiting had already made my acquaintance! Note the significance of that, gentlemen—and lady.

"With that thought uppermost in my mind, I began, therefore, to keep a vigilant eye upon the various people to whom dear old Neville here had introduced me."

"Good point, Bathurst," intervened Humphrey Tresillian, "extraordinarily good point."

"Thank you, Tresillian. Which brought me"—Anthony turned and bowed to Drusilla—"to the acquaintanceship of Miss Ives." Drusilla grimaced at him. Anthony waved his hand in recognition. "And to the burglary at the Bray residence in May last. It was coincidental, I thought, and also extremely significant, that one of the residents in the St. Mead area should have suffered something of the kind for which I was looking. A burglary which she had discussed with me, and also with Mr. Humphrey Tresillian here."

"That's perfectly true," admitted that gentleman. "Drusilla had told me all about the heritage she had received from her uncle, Sir Herbert Ludford, and when the robbery took place she naturally told me the full facts as she knew them."

Anthony nodded. "And in the meantime, you had discussed Miss Ives's legacy with others—amongst them, Stainsby?"

Humphrey Tresillian nodded. "Yes, I don't doubt that for an instant. I was constantly in his company."

"Exactly," continued Anthony. "The result was that I went to the 'Yard' for help. To my old colleague here—and I'm proud to call him that—Chief Detective-Inspector Andrew MacMorran. After tackling him, I discovered that objects of a somewhat unusual nature had been stolen from a collection at Hampton Court on—I'm speaking from memory now—Michaelmas Day. And that the police authorities had not been successful in clearing the matter up. I gave this Hampton Court robbery some careful attention, and I noted the titles of the various cartoons which had been stolen. Gentlemen—and Drusilla—I was amply rewarded for that attention! For mark you, the fragment 'Emma' fitted 'The Road to Emmaus', the fragment 'of Sil' was appropriate to 'The Pool of Siloam', the word 'Temple' found its place in the cartoon of Christ scourging the money-changers and the 'Mai' had a relevancy with 'Peter Striking off the Ear of Malchus'."

Anthony rubbed his hands. "One of these might have been a coincidence, two might increase the weight of that coincidence, three would, I consider, have pointed unerringly—but four, I suggest, was such an appalling accumulation of probability that it almost made certainty more positive, and as such could not in any circumstances be ignored. I take it you all agree with me?"

There came a chorus of acceptance. Colonel Buxton said, "I take it—using your phrase, Bathurst—that those fragments we picked up in Ebford's field were part of a list?"

"I fancy so, sir. Which Oliver had put in front of Stainsby when he visited him here in St. Mead."

"I see. That's how it occurred to me. But go on, my boy."

Anthony took a cigarette from Neville Kemble. "Well, by now we were on to Oliver through Steel. And Oliver had recently come from America. He left the States in the July of last year. I felt that he must have crossed on his own account or been specially sent over with a definite burglary purpose. So I watched out for any development from the American side. It struck me that things from that angle must have gone all wrong and investigations and inquiries were almost sure to be started. Then I spotted that Dwight Conway, the famous American millionaire and collector, *who hated travel*, mind you, was coming across post-haste (from his own standards). I looked him up, and discovered that here was exactly the sort of man whom the Rafaelle cartoons would interest and attract. In other words, a man who filled the bill perfectly. When he arrived, I took a chance."

Anthony looked sideways at the Commissioner. "A chance from which, if it failed, I had nothing whatever to lose. I got in touch with Conway by public advertisement, offering him the cartoons, although, of course, they were very far from being in my possession."

"Reprehensible," muttered Sir Austin, "entirely reprehensible."

"Perhaps," replied Anthony; "but on any showing, my game was worth his candle. If he rose to the bait, it proved that I was on the right track, that something had gone wrong with the Conway-Oliver plans, that Conway would do almost anything to get hold of the cartoons, and that by association with him, I might link up with the murderer at this end." Anthony paused. "But I only partly succeeded. Conway came to the surface and swallowed the bait, but it was patent that he hadn't the cartoons and wasn't aware of the real reason for the hitch in his plans. But, as luck had it, while I was playing my Conway fish, Stainsby made the necessary contact and sold the cartoons to him. Which naturally effectively queered my pitch and made Conway mad with me—so mad that he decided to dish me out a fair portion of dirt. Harmless in its way—but decidedly unpleasant.

"Under the pretext of further negotiations, he invited me to an empty house in Blackheath having first obtained the key from an agent. In this house he went to the trouble of installing a theatrical setting with appropriately sinister properties. A dwarf, a black goat, an imitation tarantula, a coffin and other highly delectable effects were staged for my especial benefit and entertainment. In addition to a talented actress who regaled me with certain lines from Hamlet! Conway, evidently, had been put in touch with a theatrical agent who, I suggest, supplied the various articles of the outfit with the idea that he was contributing to a sensational practical joke. This idea, no doubt, was judiciously sown in his mind."

Anthony swung round suddenly to Drusilla Ives. "This actress, Miss Ives—have you any suggestion as to how Conway could have got hold of her?"

Drusilla was at her demurest. She folded her hands in her lap as she replied. "Well, it *might* have been that the lady was in town at the psychological moment that Conway desired the effects—she might even have been in the agent's company when the demand was made—and that she took the job on purely as a gigantic sort of leg-pull."

She shrugged her shapely shoulders. "That's all the light I can throw on it, and after all—to be perfectly fair—some people do go about literally screaming to have their legs pulled, don't they?"

Imps of mischief danced in her eyes. Anthony grinned. "Perhaps you're right, Miss Ives. Anyhow, we'll accept your solution for want of a better."

Sir Austin Kemble came in. "Then, I suppose, Conway tried to make his getaway with the cartoons, eh?"

"Exactly, Sir Austin. It was obvious to me that he'd catch the first boat back to America, and that he would conceal the cartoons, so MacMorran and I took the necessary steps to circumvent him. But you've already heard all about that."

Sir Austin nodded. "Yes. You called in the expert after that and took the Assistant-Commissioner's advice. I remember what he said to you." He looked across at MacMorran. "So you picked Conway up again, eh?"

"Yes, sir," replied the Inspector. "Yesterday morning. We never let him get out of our sight and there was no boat available for him till next Friday. He'll turn King's Evidence and be one of our chief witnesses against Stainsby—it'll lighten his own sentence."

"Tell me," said Humphrey Tresillian, "because it interests me most of all, how did you get on to Stainsby?"

"Well," said Anthony, "inasmuch as no approach was made to me in St. Mead by anybody with whom I was *unacquainted*, I felt pretty certain in my mind that the murderer was inside Neville's own personal circle. And it occurred to me that if I could parade the cartoons in front of him again, his fingers would itch to hold them again. Even though he knew that Conway had been apprehended. I arranged with Sir Austin for Neville to have them here at 'Palings' for exhibition purposes. Everybody in the circle of suspects was invited to see them and fed with all the dope as to the method of their return—transport, etc. But I laid a trap. A rather neat one, too.

I borrowed from the South Kensington collection the cartoon of 'Elymas the Sorcerer' and included it in the exhibition. I knew that Friend Murderer had never seen it and would be surprised when he clapped eyes on it. This done, I waited for reactions. I watched carefully when the various people inspected the cartoons. Stainsby's face, when he saw 'Elymas', gave him away completely. I knew then that I had my man. You're all aware as to how he acted subsequently, and how MacMorran and I trapped him, by my coming back to his house, although I admit that Mr. Tresillian here gave me something in the nature of a shock before the actual arrest was made. And, by the way, I'd like *his* explanation with regard to that."

Humphrey grinned his stock cynical grin. "I've been expecting that question for some time. If you want to know, I've suspected him ever since Drusilla's affair up the river. You see, I'd mentioned to Stainsby the fact that Drusilla had inherited a valuable collection of *objets d'art* and it occurred to me that he seemed extraordinarily interested. When the burglary came along a little later, I confess it set me wondering. Because, candidly, Stainsby always seemed singularly blessed with this world's goods, and yet you never heard him refer to anything financial. He never alluded to business or investments, and more than once I've exercised my mind and wondered what really was his source of income. Ostensibly he did no work at all. He was a gentleman 'fence', I suppose?"

Tresillian put the question generally, but MacMorran took it upon himself to answer it. "Ay! In a pretty big way, too. It's surprising the stuff that fellow's handled."

"How came the two murders, then?" demanded the Chief Constable.

MacMorran parried the question. "I think I'll let Mr. Bathurst answer that."

"Well," said Anthony, "I think what happened was this. Stainsby 'received' the proceeds of burglaries generally, but he made a special feature of what Tresillian described just now as *objets d'art*. Conway was a constant buyer from him—at darned good prices, too. Stainsby learnt that Conway was almost fanatically interested in the Rafaelle cartoons and negotiated thereon, promising delivery, I suggest, by a certain date. My opinion is that Stainsby's usual 'agent' either got 'jugged' or died, and Elmer Oliver, recently from America, took his place. Stainsby and he quarrelled over the 'cut' after Oliver had pulled off the job and handed over the cartoons. Oliver, in an ugly mood, came down to St. Mead to talk business, had a row with Stainsby, threatened to expose him, and Stainsby shut his lips for ever through the medium of a poisoned whisky-and-soda. But, for a time at least, he was forced to lie 'doggo' with them. Steel, knowing where Oliver had gone but not necessarily knowing 'why', followed up the visit. To meet the same fate! You know how Stainsby disposed of the bodies and the steps he took, particularly in the case of Oliver, to hide the identities."

"Tell me," said Tresillian, "why did you release Conway—if only temporarily?"

Anthony's smile embraced both the Commissioner and the Chief Constable. They nodded to him.

"Let's take Conway's frame of mind as a starting-point. He should have received the cartoons by a definite date. They weren't forthcoming. After the murders, Stainsby decided to hang on to them for a time for safety's sake. If Oliver were identified, the burglary traced to him, Stainsby wanted no cartoon contact with himself. He wanted the affair to blow over before he let them see the light of day again. Conway, suspicious, and almost fanatical for acquisition, decided to come over and take the time of day for himself. But Conway would not have squeaked on Stainsby under any circumstances. We soon knew that. He wasn't aware, for instance, how Stainsby worked. So we argued that, if we released him, the chances were *that he and Stainsby would contact each other*. They did! You know what happened after that. Conway had only to keep his mouth shut, you see, and we were at a dead end."

Buxton had another question. "Who was the woman that dealt with Conway when the cartoons were handed over?"

Anthony threw the ball back to MacMorran. "This time the Inspector can take over from me. Andrew—do you mind?"

"I'm sorry," said MacMorran, "but up to the moment we have not been successful in tracing her. It was definitely *not* Elizabeth, his daughter. But there's little doubt that this woman was in the habit of acting for Stainsby in negotiations of the kind from a London address. I hope, though, to be in a position to answer the Chief Constable's question within the next few days. The names 'Anne Teak' and 'Annette Gayne' obviously require no explanation. And, to revert to Elizabeth, I am convinced that she was oblivious of the whole business and of her father's career generally."

Sir Austin Kemble rose. "Well, Bathurst," he said genially, "you've pulled off another good job of work. A bit slow in your stride, perhaps, but satisfactory, all the same." He stooped and patted his brother on the shoulder. "Good show! I sent him down to you to recuperate. Nothing like being on the spot at the critical time! What do you say, Neville?"

Neville Kemble nodded. "I certainly agree with you, Austin. You must have had either second sight or been inspired. But there's one thing I'd like to ask Bathurst. I hope he won't mind answering it."

"Certainly," replied Bathurst. "What's the question?"

"In the early days I heard you express a certain amount of interest in a young fellow named Lord. He's by way of being some sort of village idiot, I believe? Were you able to satisfy yourself about him?" Anthony smiled. "Yes. Some time ago, sir. Lord's interest in Ebford's field and the gold in it had a natural and simple origin. A day or so before the first murder, we had a heavy shower here in St. Mead, relieved by strong sunshine. We were treated to a magnificent rainbow. Lord, in his childish way, and in deference to country lore and legend, imagined that the rainbow's end dipped into Ebford's field. Hence his aureate interest and excitement therein. I tumbled to that explanation quite early on."

"Curious," reflected Neville Kemble, "how a simple matter of that kind might have caused a complication. Thanks, Bathurst, and let me add my congratulations to those of my brother. You, too, MacMorran!"

He turned to Colonel Buxton. "Not forgetting you, 'Pusher'." Buxton acknowledged the compliment with his hand. Neville Kemble continued, "Well, what do we do now? Drinks all round?" Sir Austin beamed upon his brother. "My dear Neville," he said, "to repeat your words, that remark springs from either second sight or sheer inspiration."

THE END

KINDRED SPIRITS . . .

Why not join the

DEAN STREET PRESS FACEBOOK GROUP

for lively bookish chat and more

Scan the QR code below

Or follow this link
**www.facebook.com/groups/
deanstreetpress**

Printed in Great Britain
by Amazon

86791931R00132